Books in the COLONY Series

QUANT
ARCADIA
GALACTIC SURVEY
SILK ROAD
LOST COLONY
EARTH

Books in the EMPIRE Series

by Richard F. Weyand:

EMPIRE: Reformer
EMPIRE: Usurper
EMPIRE: Tyrant
EMPIRE: Commander
EMPIRE: Warlord
EMPIRE: Conqueror

by Stephanie Osborn:

EMPIRE: Imperial Police
EMPIRE: Imperial Detective
EMPIRE: Imperial Inspector
EMPIRE: Section Six

by Richard F. Weyand:

EMPIRE: Intervention
EMPIRE: Investigation
EMPIRE: Succession
EMPIRE: Renewal
EMPIRE: Resistance
EMPIRE: Resurgence

Books in the Childers Universe

by Richard F. Weyand:

Childers

Childers: Absurd Proposals

Galactic Mail: Revolution

A Charter For The Commonwealth

Campbell: The Problem With Bliss

by Stephanie Osborn:

Campbell: The Sigurdsen Incident

EARTH

A Colony Story

by

RICHARD F. WEYAND

RICHARD F. WEYAND

ISBN 978-1-954903-07-4
Printed in the United States of America

Cover Credits
Cover Art: Paola Giari and Luca Oleastri,
www.rotwangstudio.com
Back Cover Photo: Oleg Volk

Many thanks to
王睿
for verifying Chinese cultural accuracy.

Published by Weyand Associates, Inc.
Bloomington, Indiana, USA
January 2022

EARTH

CONTENTS

EARTH

The Road To Power

Jonathan David Wilson had not had a promising start in life, all the more surprising given where he ended up. Born Anup Patel, he had grown up on the streets, in the slums of Kolkata in the Bengal administrative region. His one overriding goal had been to get out of the slums and leave them behind forever.

The best way out of the slums started with schooling. The problem with that was that the best schooling was virtual, for which Patel needed a communicator with a heads-up display. Cheap communicators were available, but they were marginal at best for schooling, and even the price of the cheap ones was more than he had or could imagine having.

The easiest way to money for a youngster in Kolkata was theft. While most transactions – and all big transactions – were done virtually, cash was still used for small items. Patel became adept at picking pockets, snatching purses, and otherwise victimizing the unwary and unvigilant. The one thing he couldn't steal was a communicator itself. Once configured, they were unalterable, making a stolen one worthless.

Patel saved what he stole, concealing his growing stash. When he had enough money to buy a communicator with the features needed for the best education experience, he bought it.

When initially configuring the device, it asked him to enter his name. He had given a lot of thought to this step. Anup Patel was not a name that was going places. Light-complected because of his mixed ancestry, he chose a name that was not too pretentious, but was not an Indian name at all.

When it asked him to enter his age, Patel again lied, entering a value four years older than he actually was.

And so Anup Patel, age eight, became Jonathan David Wilson, age twelve, and plunged into his schooling.

The second item on Wilson's agenda was to get out of the Bengal administrative region. Too many people, and not enough to go around. Not enough for him, anyway. If you wanted to get out of the slums permanently, go to where there were no slums.

Affording passage was another matter entirely. At the age of twelve – but with a records age of sixteen – Wilson became a cook's boy on a small local freighter. The ship worked both sides of the Bay of Bengal, the west coast of the Indian peninsula and the east coast of Burma and Thailand in the Southeast Asia administrative region. The lie was believed because Wilson was big for his age, and had studied how the older boys carried themselves. Besides, age requirements in this part of the world were honored more in the breach than in fact.

When the ship once made port in Kuala Lumpur, three years into his employment, Wilson left the ship. With his earnings he upgraded his wardrobe, lied about his experience, and secured a berth as third officer of a larger freighter working the South China Sea, including Malaysia, Singapore, Cambodia, Vietnam, Indonesia, the Philippines, and China itself. This ship wasn't a tramp freighter, though, it was part of a larger company.

Throughout this period, in the long hours of boredom on ship, Wilson continued his education. Motivated and bright, he sailed through the K-12 curriculum – in English – and began his college work at the records age of eighteen, though he was in truth but fourteen years old.

Wilson began his degree in public administration, because he'd never seen anyone in government who was poor.

EARTH

Jonathan David Wilson his Vice Chairman and heir apparent.

World Authority Chairman was nominally an elected position, and always had been. But the limited terms of Bernd Decker's day were gone. Once elected, the World Authority Chairman was effectively dictator for life over all of Earth. He could be removed by a supermajority of the Council, but that had never happened.

At the age of eighty-six, after eleven years as chairman, Gunter Mannheim died. Jonathan David Wilson became Chairman of the World Authority – the outright dictator of Earth – at the recorded age of fifty-seven.

Wilson took office the same year that, three thousand light-years away on Arcadia, Chen JieMin and Chen ChaoLi became Chen Zufu and Chen Zumu of the Chen-Jasic family.

That was in 2391 on Arcadia, and 2397 on Earth, due to the longer day on Arcadia and both planets simply counting their unequal days along the same calendar.

It had been one hundred fifty-two Earth years since Janice Quant had transported two million four hundred thousand colonists from Earth to the twenty-four different colonies of the colony project.

Assessment

Jonathan David Wilson, nee Anup Patel, the new World Authority Chairman and dictator on Earth, did not take power ignorant of what Gunter Mannheim had been up to. As Vice Chairman the last eleven years, he had been closely involved with Mannheim's thought processes and decision making. As the former chairman aged, Wilson had become gradually more involved.

Even so, on taking power, with the decision-making authority now his, Wilson undertook a reassessment of activities and priorities within the planetary government.

One thing Wilson took another look at was the hyperspace project.

One thing the chairmen of the World Authority always took good care of was themselves. The World Authority Chairman's residence – more of a palace, really – was located on Chira Island in the Colorado Gulf of Costa Rica in the Central American administrative region. The World Authority had taken over the entire ten-square-mile island for the chairman's residence.

The site was selected because it had the world's best climate. Travel was possible from the island's airport/shuttleport, but the World Authority Chairman seldom if ever went anywhere. All meetings of the World Authority Council had been virtual, attended by avatar, for two centuries.

Medical care on the island was not an issue. Doctor visits were easy – they were brought to the island as required. There was an elaborate and well-stocked hospital ward in the residence. There were also guest houses on the island the visiting medical personnel could use during their stay.

Because it was an island, security was also not a difficult issue. The biggest security hole was the security people themselves. But Wilson had been in the World Authority Police himself, and personally knew people he could trust. There was no danger of a Praetorian Guard situation there.

Loneliness could be an issue, however. While the World Authority Chairman could contact just about anyone on Earth virtually, there was something about actual human contact that could not be simulated. There was plenty of household staff and security, of course, and that met some of the need for everyday human contact.

For more personal contact, there were beautiful young local women who enjoyed staying on the island in return for being accessible to the chairman. Never a family man, Wilson found them friendly and amenable enough to his needs.

When he had moved into the chairman's residence and things had settled down a bit from the initial transfer, Wilson brought up the hyperspace project with his chief of staff. It was a virtual meeting, of course, as the chairman's staff was not located on the island.

"Did you look into the current status of the hyperspace project as I asked, Tony?" Wilson asked.

"Yes, sir," Antonio Braida said. "The mathematicians have been hard at it the last ten years, and they're closing on a formalism that suggests how transition can be made between normal space and hyperspace."

"Do they think faster-than-light travel will be possible in hyperspace?"

"Yes, sir. The current thinking is they should be able to get something like twenty or thirty thousand times light speed."

"Put that in light-years for me, Tony," Wilson said.

"Between two and four light-years per hour, sir."

"So Alpha Centauri in a couple of hours."

"Yes, sir," Braida said.

"Perfect. And what kind of timeframe are we talking about?"

"Maybe two years to a working device, sir. Another two years before they have a design for a spaceship of some kind."

"Excellent."

Wilson thought about it a moment. He looked out his office window toward the pool. A couple of local women were tanning nude on the pool deck, while three others were in the water. But his thoughts were light-years away.

Wilson turned back to the three-dimensional display where Braida waited patiently.

"See if there's anything they need or could use to speed things up. I want to get this done."

"Yes, sir," Braida said. "My impression is that the prior chairman didn't see this as a hot issue."

"Yes, and I think that was a mistake. I want to go out there and see whatever happened to the colonies the World Authority sent out."

"That was a hundred and fifty years ago, sir."

"Yes, and one of three things has happened since," Wilson said. "First, they could be like Roanoke Colony. You go there a hundred and fifty years later and there's nothing left. There's nobody there. They're all dead of disease or famine or something.

"Second, they could be like the survivors of the crew of the HMS Bounty. You go find them, and they're scratching out a meager living without contact with the rest of humanity."

"We don't need more dependents, sir."

"Understood, Tony. That was Gunter's position. He focused on trying to better the situation of people here on Earth. 'We have enough problems here,' he said to me more than once.

"But there's another possibility, Tony. They could be like Massachusetts Bay Colony. You go there a hundred and fifty years later and they're a thriving, going concern, with access to resources and technology you don't have."

"Do you think that's likely, sir?" Braida asked.

"No, but it's not a remote possibility, either. They had some of the best people from Earth's population. They had fertile subtropical environments on planets with low axial tilt. They had millions of tons of supplies. They had advanced technology, including nuclear power and self-replicating metafactories. And they didn't have the burden of billions of people to support.

"In a hundred and fifty years, they could have tens of millions of people on each planet, and an advanced technology base. And with twenty-four chances, the odds are good that at least some of them do."

"But what good would that do us, sir?"

"The World Authority financed those colonies, Tony," Wilson said. "We spent an entire planetary annual product on them. We sent them out with all the advantages we could muster, advantages a lot of our own people don't have."

"What does that mean for us, sir?"

"We own them, Tony. They're ours. That was a World Authority project, and they're under World Authority jurisdiction. If they have that sort of technology, those sorts of resources, I want them. I need them."

"What if they won't give them up, sir?"

"Then, for the good of Earth's poor, I'll take them."

Three thousand light-years away, on the colony planet Arcadia, another new leadership team was also assessing their current status. Chen JieMin and Chen ChaoLi had just become *the* Chen, Chen Zufu and Chen Zumu, the ruling couple of the Chen-Jasic family. The family now had sixty thousand members, and were both wealthy and politically powerful.

The investiture ceremony had been the month before. As twenty years before, there had been a reception in the large upstairs banquet room of the Chen family restaurant on the southeast corner of Fifteenth and Market Streets, in the corner of the six-story Uptown Market that took up the entire frontage of Market Street between Fourteenth and Fifteenth Streets.

There had been five couples at the head table this time, including two retired Chen. Paul Chen-Jasic and Chen JuPing had been there. They were now a hundred and twenty years old, but looked like they were in their early nineties. Chen MinChao and Jessica Chen-Jasic were there. They were now a hundred years old, but looked like they were in their mid seventies.

David Bolton and Chen YongLin were the outgoing Chen Zufu and Chen Zumu. They were now eighty years old, but looked like they were in their early sixties. The incoming Chen, Chen JieMin and Chen ChaoLi, were sixty years old, but looked like they were in their mid forties.

New at the head table this time were the couple-in-waiting for being the Chen, Chen JuMing and Chen ChaoPing. They were in their mid forties, but, thanks to the Tahiti anti-aging treatments, they looked like they were in their mid thirties.

All the movers and shakers on Arcadia had been there to watch as David Bolton and Chen YongLin had stepped down and Chen JieMin and Chen ChaoLi took the dais.

Also as before, the prime minister of Arcadia had announced

he would not take another term as prime minister. In 2371, it had been Rob Milbank stepping down. Now, in 2391, it was Sasha Ivanov stepping down. He would support Luisa Bianchi, one of his long-time lieutenants in the Assembly, as prime minister.

Milbank, Ivanov, Bianchi, and their spouses were all there, at the table in front of the head table. Milbank and his wife, Julia Whitcomb, were now in their late eighties but looked like they were seventy. Milbank also stood up and supported Bianchi for prime minister, which made her a shoo-in.

Milbank was three times a hero in the Arcadia public's eyes, for the hyperspace project, the trade agreement, and his role in the epic journey of the *Wanderlust*, which had concluded six years before.

That was last month. This month JieMin and ChaoLi were settling into their roles as Chen Zufu and Chen Zumu. JieMin was now the senior, as Chen Zufu. He was the ultimate decision maker for the family. ChaoLi had outranked him for decades now, so this was a bit of a reversal.

As they had always consulted with each other, and had worked closely on the hyperspace project and its aftermath, such as the *Wanderlust* mission, it was not as big of a change as it might have been for another couple.

It was also not as hard as it might have been to take the lead role in the family. The Chen had always promoted competent people into secondary positions. The Chen made the big decisions, resolved the big issues, but they always had competent underlings. This meant only the difficult decisions came to them, and there were no difficult issues on the table at the moment.

That situation changed with the receipt of a single mail.

JieMin and ChaoLi were sitting on pillows in the doorway of her tearoom, looking out over the gardens south of the Chen-Jasic family headquarters. The iridium statue of Matthew Chen-Jasic, on its carved jade column set on a carved stone base, was directly in front of them. Youngsters worked in the gardens, tending the three and a quarter acres of heritage and hybrid plants that were the family's prized stock.

It was a beautiful day, even by Arcadia standards, and they took their mid-morning tea together as a break from their office duties. It was perhaps six weeks after their investiture as the Chen.

"It sure is strange to be sitting in these tea rooms as our own," JieMin said. "This was the room in which I met Chen JuPing forty-five years ago when my mother first brought me to the city."

ChaoLi nodded.

"And I became JuPing's tea girl fifty years ago, in this very room," ChaoLi said.

"That's comforting, in a way. The idea that the Chen is here, taking the long view, guiding things along, across the years."

"Yes, except now it's us. How did that ever happen?"

JieMin didn't answer, as they were both interrupted by a priority message.

"Oh, my," ChaoLi said.

"You, too?" JieMin asked.

"A mail from 'JQ' with a meeting request? Yes. You?"

"Yes. Same thing. I wonder what's happened."

"Well, let's go find out," ChaoLi said.

They both went into VR, accepting the meeting. Their avatars weren't much different than the reality this morning. ChaoLi sat in the center of her tea room doorway, and JieMin sat in the center of his. Janice Quant was in her office, decorated in the style of Earth almost two centuries ago, with books and papers piled about.

"Good morning, JieMin, ChaoLi. It's good to finally meet you both."

"Good morning, Madam Chairman," ChaoLi said.

"Now, you either have to call me Janice, or I shall have to call you Chen Zufu and Chen Zumu. Which is it to be?" Janice asked, smiling and raising an eyebrow.

ChaoLi laughed her little bells laugh, and JieMin smiled. He so loved her laugh, and was happy it had not changed with age.

"Very well, Janice. But you called us. What's going on?"

"There is a new World Authority Chairman on Earth, and he is changing things a bit. This will impact us. So I thought I would bring you up to date."

"Very well," ChaoLi said, and JieMin nodded.

"A bit of background first. When I was World Authority Chairman, the vice chairman and the chairman were both confirmed by the World Authority Council. Further, there were some policies and actions that had to be approved by the council. Budgets. Reorganizations. Major policies. The chairman served a finite term, and had to be reconfirmed by the council for an additional term.

"All that is gone now, and has been for some time. The chairman is effectively dictator for life. He selects his own successor, his vice chairman. Every level of the planetary government is under his direct control, and the council is advisory only. As their own budget and salaries are determined by the chairman, they do not buck him on any issue, large or small."

"So the council is a rubber stamp?" ChaoLi asked.

"Yes. Now, into that scenario we have a new chairman,

Jonathan David Wilson. He's a bit of a curious character. He's fifty-seven years old, but the records on him only go back forty-five years, to when he was twelve. He suddenly appears in the computer records and begins his schooling."

"At age twelve? There is no earlier schooling? No birth record, parents of record, or anything like that."

"No. Nothing. I've looked. Wilson simply appeared at age 12, in the slums of Kolkata, India. No record of parents. Nothing except name and age, and those have no provenance other than they are what he provided the communicator – a new one, purchased in Kolkata – when he configured it."

"So he could be anybody," ChaoLi said. "A street urchin."

"Correct. What Wilson did next is interesting. He excelled in his schoolwork, through a combination of being very bright and working long, hard hours at it. At the stated age of sixteen, he crewed on a tramp freighter in the Bay of Bengal. He became third mate for a ship operated by a freight line in the South China Sea, made it to second mate, then was promoted to a trans-Pacific ship.

"Having made it to North America, Wilson stepped ashore in Seattle, Washington, and signed up with the World Authority Police as an officer candidate."

"An officer?" ChaoLi asked.

"Yes. By this time, at a stated age of twenty-two, Wilson had completed a college degree in public administration. He was accepted to the police academy, scored very well, and was assigned to the security detail of Gunter Mannheim, a senior council member.

"He must have impressed Mannheim, because he was transferred to Mannheim's staff, becoming first an aide, then his chief of staff. During that period, he completed his doctorate in history, specializing in modern history, especially the history of the World Authority.

"Gunter Mannheim, meanwhile, was going places. He was made vice chairman and succeeded to the chairmanship eleven years ago. He made Jonathan David Wilson his vice chairman."

"And now Mannheim has died, and Wilson has become chairman," ChaoLi guessed, "with pretty much the same plenary powers the planetary chairmen of the colonies originally had."

"Correct. That happened four months ago. Since Earth's policy and governance is now totally under his control, I've made it a point to go back through everything known about Wilson. Everything he's written, all his mail, his whole history.

"I've also monitored his conversations, beginning about four years ago, when Mannheim's health started failing and it was clear he was going to retain Wilson as vice chairman."

"How can you monitor his conversations, Janice?" ChaoLi asked.

"All of the communications at the top levels of the World Authority are done remotely and have been for centuries. They don't have direct neural VR – all the best people in that area signed up as colonists and I put them all on Westernesse – but they do have three-dimensional displays and the same communicators the colonists initially had. It's pretty easy to listen in on that stuff, and I've had all of that on Wilson recorded for the last four years."

ChaoLi nodded. Quant couldn't record everything on everybody, but, if she had an interest in a specific person, she could record all of their communications. She had programmed hooks and back doors into all human technology while she had the chance as World Authority Chairman. All off the books, of course.

"What did you learn, Janice?" ChaoLi asked.

"One of the first things Wilson did is to increase the funding of the hyperspace project. He's pushing on it hard, and anything they want, they can have."

"Oh, that's not good. Do we know why?"

"Wilson wants to find the colonies. They may be dead or struggling, but, with twenty-four chances to win, he's betting some are thriving. He wants to harness them to the task of helping Earth's poor."

"Janice, the best way to help the poor is always going to be birth control and a decent education. He already has that capability."

"Of course, ChaoLi. And given the aggressive manner in which he pursued his own education, he knows that as well. But his empathy for the poor seems genuine. I think his original circumstances in Kolkata were far more dismal than he's let on since."

JieMin stirred and spoke for the first time.

"What is his basis for any authority over the colonies, Janice?" he asked.

"The World Authority funded the colonies in the first place. It was a World Authority project. So to him it's obvious that the World Authority has jurisdiction over the colonies."

"Interesting theory."

"And without basis, JieMin. The colonists all signed a contract when they signed onto the project. I wrote that contract. It includes a waiver by the World Authority of any authority or jurisdiction over the colonies in perpetuity. If there was a court of competent jurisdiction to consider the issue, he'd lose on summary dismissal.

"The problem is that there is no court on Earth willing to buck the chairman. They also get their funding from his budget, and they serve at his pleasure. A judge can be removed on his say-so alone. The World Authority courts are no recourse against him.

"Which means it will come down to force. Who is the stronger? He thinks he can't lose. We're going to have to convince him otherwise."

"Or convince him that trade is the better choice," ChaoLi said.

"The problem there is the numbers, ChaoLi. The colonies together have about a billion people. Earth has four billion."

"Janice, there is a solution to the riddle, How does a man eat a cow?"

"What's that, ChaoLi?"

"One bite at a time, Janice. One bite at a time."

"But trade will take time to work, ChaoLi. I think Wilson thinks he has a shortcut."

"What is your estimate of the timeline, Janice?" JieMin asked.

"I think Wilson will have hyperspace ships in the four to five year timeline. And with Earth's manufacturing capacity, and all of it under his control, he could field a navy very shortly after that."

"Then we must approach him soon, and present an alternative path to his legitimate goals."

"But what alternative, JieMin?" ChaoLi asked.

"Friendship. Trade. Mutual benefit."

"He won't take it," she said.

"He will if we work together to convince him he can't win," Quant said. "I have some thoughts on how to do that."

Mission Plan

When they dropped out of VR, JieMin and ChaoLi were still sitting in the doorway of her tearoom looking out on the gardens.

"Now we see how she was able to become World Authority Chairman," JieMin said.

"Yes. She's very charismatic. It's amazing what you can do with several hundred thousand multiprocessor blades."

"What Bernd Decker could do, anyway."

"Mmm."

ChaoLi sipped her tea.

"What about what she said, JieMin? Wilson really thinks the colonies belong to him?"

"Well, to the World Authority, at least, though I suppose it's the same thing now."

"For the benefit of the poor, of course," ChaoLi said, rolling her eyes.

"If he came out of the slums of Kolkata, that may very well be true, ChaoLi. People can have altruistic motives, even if they choose the wrong path."

"I suppose. It just galls me to think he considers the fruits of all our labors out here to be his for the taking."

"It's not like we didn't have a big boost getting started, though, ChaoLi. We just have to convince him there's a better way."

"And if we can't?"

"Then I think he's going to be in serious trouble with our friend."

"Fair enough. So what do we do first?" ChaoLi asked.

"Reconnoiter, I think. Then a diplomatic mission."

"How do you want to proceed?"

"Select a subordinate to do a mission plan, just as our predecessors did with us. Someone needs to go through all the details. Talk to all the players. Coordinate everything. Let them put the plan together."

ChaoLi nodded.

"Who did you have in mind?"

JuMing and ChaoPing were now forty-three years old, though they looked to be thirty-four, having received the Tahiti anti-aging treatments in the Arcadia Unified Clinic at age twenty-five.

Their youngest, the twins GangLi and GangJie, only two when they had set out on *Wanderlust's* four-year voyage ten years ago, were now twelve. LingTao, YanWei, and MinJing were all married, and ChaoMing, now fifteen, would likely be leaving the house soon. By this point, JuMing and ChaoPing had six grandchildren.

JieMin and ChaoLi's other children – LeiTao, the twins YanMing and YanJing, and JieJun – had been similarly busy, and the Chen's entire extended family now numbered almost fifty.

The whole family still got together at least once a month – as in the past, for Sunday dinner – though they now did so in one of the small banquet rooms in the family's restaurant across Market Street. JieMin and ChaoLi had always loved children, and, with dozens of grandchildren and great grandchildren in attendance, those family parties were always fun and happy gatherings.

As the heirs apparent to the Chen, JuMing and ChaoPing saw JieMin and ChaoLi pretty frequently on business as well.

While in private or family settings ChaoPing called her parents Fuqin and Muqin – Father and Mother – in their business meetings she called them Chen Zufu and Chen Zumu, the leaders of the family. Those meetings were a routine part of being the heirs apparent of the Chen.

This summons, however, was different.

As the heirs apparent to the Chen, ChaoPing and JuMing did not need a chaperone from the front desk to lead them to ChaoLi's tea room. They knew the way and had access to the secure doors along the way.

ChaoPing knocked on the doorframe, then slid the rice paper divider open. JieMin and ChaoLi sat on pillows on the other side of the tea table, with two pillows on the door side being empty. JieMin wore a simple lavalava. ChaoLi wore the patchwork embroidered silk robe decorated with flying dragons that she had worn to their investiture.

ChaoLi had protested when first presented with the robe, a work of art lovingly prepared for her alone by the best needlework artisans the family had. Each Chen Zumu received one and kept it after their term. The spectacular robe was such an ostentatious show of wealth and power it left her gasping. But JieMin had explained it was part of their position, a symbol of their authority and the regard in which they were held.

"ChaoPing and JuMing, Chen Zumu."

"Come in, ChaoPing, JuMing. Please be seated."

As ChaoPing was named first, she took the pillow to the left, the more honored position, on JieMin's right. They both sat, and ChaoLi's tea girl entered and poured tea for them all, first for ChaoPing, then JuMing, then JieMin, and ChaoLi, as host, last. They all sipped their tea in the same order, from ChaoPing to ChaoLi.

EARTH

"We have decided to initiate a new project, to contact and then negotiate a trade agreement with Earth," ChaoLi said. "You two will be in charge of this project."

"Yes, Chen Zumu," ChaoPing said.

"You should both delegate as many of your current responsibilities as you need to in order to give this project the attention that it deserves."

JieMin stirred then.

"This is the most important project the family has," he said. "May have ever had, in fact. Much depends on its successful completion."

"I understand, Chen Zufu."

"We expect there to be problems in carrying out this plan," ChaoLi said. "Bigger and more intractable problems than you faced on the *Wanderlust* mission. Earth is liable to see its much larger population and ancient status as giving it the right to a pre-eminent position with respect to the colonies. This is not the path we wish to take. We wish a more equal partnership, such as we have with the other colonies.

"The first part of this mission then must be to gather as much information as we can. About Earth. About its leadership. About its likely responses to our overtures.

"Once sufficient information is in hand, we will attempt a diplomatic mission to Earth. This has the potential to be dangerous, so it should be a small number of people and they must all be volunteers.

"We might also wish to look into hardware enhancements to the equipment used. In particular, having the ability to outrace Earth's own space vessels may be desirable."

"To escape them, Chen Zumu?"

"Yes, ChaoPing. As I say, we do not know how aggressive or belligerent they may be.

"When the sort of problems we anticipate arise, Chen Zufu and I will become directly involved. We would like to hold back our involvement, at least initially, so an escalation is available to the diplomatic mission."

"I understand, Chen Zumu."

"Your assignment for right now is to generate a mission plan. What equipment, what timeframe, what tactics, what strategy. We will review this plan with you before we commit significant resources to it."

"Yes, Chen Zumu."

"Know this," JieMin said. "This will be very difficult. There will be serious problems. I expect that we will need to become personally involved at some point to make this work. Your mission plan should have multiple alternatives at critical points. Decision paths that respond to Earth's actions, whatever they may be. You must plan for the unexpected. For flexibility."

"Yes, Chan Zufu. I understand."

ChaoPing and JuMing reviewed the meeting in the living room of their family apartment on the twelfth floor of the same building.

"Hoo, boy," ChaoPing said. "What a project."

"They said they knew it was going to be very hard," JuMing said. "How do they know that?"

"How did Jessica know we would find Avalon on that last leg of the *Wanderlust*? How did she know we would have to overthrow the Avalon government?"

"I don't know."

"I don't know, either," ChaoPing said. "But she was right. That's the point. Somehow they know Earth is going to be trouble."

JuMing nodded.

"OK, I get that. So, they anticipate the need to run away. Evade Earth's space-based resources, at least."

"And maybe weapons," ChaoPing said.

"Yikes. OK. Maybe even some counter-weapons thing, somehow. More velocity, both in the shuttle and in the ship. What else?"

"Well, if the diplomatic mission is already on the ground when things break, it could get dicey on the ground. So robots, I would think. Which probably means Rolf Dornier goes along."

"Or one of his kids, " JuMing said. "Klaus is what? Twenty-four by now?"

"Yes, but he and Diana have little ones at home. Anna, Rolf and Carla's youngest, is sixteen. She's engaged to be married before this mission ever lifts shuttle."

"Oh, that's right. And if it's that dicey, we want to avoid those kinds of losses. The ones where you have to tell children their father or mother's not coming home."

"That leaves us out as well, you know," ChaoLi said.

"GangLi and GangJie are twelve, and this mission won't lift shuttle for at least a year. I don't think that's the same kind of problem."

ChaoLi thought about it, then nodded.

"OK, that's fair," she said. "So, robots. More velocity, or, rather, more acceleration, on shuttle and ship. Some counter-weapons strategy. For missiles at least, I think. Anything else?"

"Not yet. Let me think about it."

Wayne Porter usually worked on-site downtown in Jixing Trading's design headquarters. Officially a separate company, and under separate management, they were located in Five Charter Square. Porter was now forty-four years old, but looked thirty-five.

Huenemann was there, too. The ebullient engineer was seventy-five years old, but looked like he was fifty-five. And he hadn't slowed down.

"Hey, Wayne," he called to Porter as Porter entered the conference room. "Now look what they got for ya. Hot rods."

Wayne took a seat and reviewed the preliminary design request. So no detailed design yet, but budgetary design. Can you do it, what will it cost, how long will it take sort of thing.

A shuttle that can outrun standard shuttles, by a lot. A hyperspace liner that could outrun 'other space assets (see details below)', again by a lot. And anti-missile defenses, type unspecified.

"What the hell?" Porter muttered.

"It's for a diplomatic mission, Wayne. And I think they expect that the natives aren't friendly."

"But we're in touch with all the other planets, Karl. And they're all friendly."

"Not all the planets, Wayne. There's one left."

Porter's eyes grew large and he turned to Huenemann. Before he could say anything, however, Huenemann held a shushing finger to his lips.

"Now they didn't say that, Wayne, and I didn't either. But I can read between the lines and so can you. But let's just keep that to ourselves."

Porter nodded, then turned back to the design request.

Making the shuttle much faster was easy. Double up on the engine nacelles first. Drop as much of the load as you could. Put JATO bottles on it, for that matter. It would go like stink. The issue there was not tearing the shuttle apart, and not having the thrust off center so it just flipped over and over.

The hyperspace liner was another matter. If the load was

way down, though, and you set off multiple sets of JATO bottles in the back, one after the other, that would make it scoot.

"How much payload in the liner, Karl?"

"Running light. Maybe a couple hundred containers."

Porter nodded. That was very light. So momentum wasn't a problem. The only question was whether the big ship would hold up to the stresses. A fully loaded ship had a lot more stress on it, but that stress was all from the centrifugal gravity of the cargo. That was a radial load, in a different direction than the fore-and-aft load of pushing the ship so hard from the rear.

"It doesn't look that hard to do, Karl, but we're going to have to run the numbers. There's going to be some pretty serious testing as well."

"How long you think, Wayne?"

"Six months from the spending authorization to full approval. I wouldn't want to push it any harder than that, Karl. Could take longer if we have to re-engineer something."

"OK, so six months minimum, and up from there depending on what we find out."

"Exactly."

Porter looked back at the requirements.

"So who's going on this little trip, I wonder."

The operations group, too, had a planning request. How would they propose surveying the planet?

"The goal is to capture a lot of radio data," John Gannet said. "The problem is that the target system – unspecified, by the way, so let's keep our guesses to ourselves – has a lot of space traffic. They're going to see a probe. Perhaps destroy it, perhaps intercept it."

"We're going to put a QE radio on it, right?" Chris Bellamy

27

asked.

"Could."

"Well, if we do that, and someone tries to intercept it, we can transition it to hyperspace, then turn off the field generator."

"Do that within the hyperspace limit and the probe comes apart on its own," Gannet said.

"Which also solves the problem."

Gannet nodded.

"Maybe the bigger question is how do we hide the probe as long as possible?'

Bellamy nodded absently as she re-read the request.

"Mmm. Maybe not. How does a magician do his trick right under your nose?"

"He gets you concentrating on something else."

"Exactly," Bellamy said. "Watch this shiny object over here."

"So what's going to be the shiny object?"

"The probe is. Or rather, one of them is."

"One of them?" Gannet asked.

"Sure. We transition two probes. One goes flying across the sky at a million miles an hour. The other one transitions with it but lies doggo."

"So we put one probe in and get everybody looking at it, but we really just wanted to cover up the insertion of the other probe, which is our real probe."

"Well, they're both probably real probes," Bellamy said. "But, yeah. The one we're relying on for some long-term data is the one we sneak in quietly along with the showy one."

"That's brilliant, Chris. Let's write that up and see what kind of reaction we get."

ChaoPing and JuMing were going over the initial reactions from the design and operations people.

"This all looks like pretty good stuff, actually." ChaoPing said.

"Yes, very good," JuMing said. "What the operations group suggests has me wondering, though. Can we extend that concept? The idea of hiding things?"

"How, JuMing?"

"Well, if Wayne puts JATO bottles on the shuttle, can we hide them? The nozzles, at least. Hide its capabilities. Same with the robots. Can we downplay them a bit more?"

"In what way?"

"You and I both know how fast and dexterous the robots are, ChaoPing. How fast they are, how good they are with weapons. They normally only move at human speed, though, so people are comfortable with them. Can we get them to move slower and more awkwardly than humans? If we need them to get us out of there, their capabilities would be a surprise."

"And surprise is good. Got it. I'll make a note of it, and we'll look into that further. But otherwise the plans look good?"

"Oh, yeah. This could be fun."

Mission Approval

Wayne Porter knew the basic rule of speed: If you want something to go faster, you need more thrust and less weight. He pulled up the current design of the hyperspace liners on the large three-dimensional display in his office. He could do this in VR, too, of course, but he liked the toolset in the display better.

As for lighter, for a small party on a single mission, Porter could do away with much of the cabin space. He also didn't need the large cargo hold. He cut the ship's length by two-thirds, so the front cargo space and the back cargo space were the same size.

Without the weight of cargo and the other two-thirds of the ship's structure, overall mass was down almost ninety percent. That meant it would be more than ten times the acceleration for the same thrust. Nice.

What did he do to achieve high thrust? JATO bottles were already in use on the hyperspace liners. But more JATO bottles meant you could keep up that high thrust longer. Just set them off in sequence, fifteen minutes apiece. How long would it be to the hyperspace limit?

If you fired off six sets of JATO bottles in turn, you could get to six times the velocity. So four hours instead of a day? Not quite, because the ship's thrusters, though much weaker, were also working in either scenario. Five hours maybe.

Wait. With the much smaller mass of the ship, you got ten times the acceleration for the same thrust. So half an hour to the hyperspace limit?

That couldn't be right either. You couldn't set off six sets of fifteen-minute JATO bottles in a half-hour. And in the current scenario, the velocity added by the JATO bottles was in the first fifteen minutes and lasted the entire twenty-four hours, it wasn't distributed across the run.

It seemed to Porter that it should be more like three hours, thrusting all the way. Something like that.

Where could he put all the JATO bottles? On the back wall of the rear cargo area was where they needed to go. Then where did the supplies for the mission go? The food, the fuel, the water.

Porter took the wall dividing the front and back cargo areas and flipped it around so back was front and front was back. All right, so now all the supplies were in front of that wall, where the cargo used to be. The back wall was completely open for JATO bottles and anti-weapon defenses, whatever those were. One problem at a time.

Porter ran the ship in simulation. Why was it so slow on the turn? Oh, because the much shorter ship put the side thrusters very close to the center of mass. What to do about that?

Porter put a trussed box member in the center of the ship, sticking out a hundred and fifty feet in front and another in the back sticking out a hundred and fifty feet behind. He mounted a single thruster on the end of each, and gimbaled them so they could point to a fixed side as the ship rotated.

OK, try that for the turn. Ah, much better. That did precession turns faster than a normal hyperspace liner, because it was continuous thrust exactly perpendicular to the rotation axis. The hyperspace liners had to sequence their maneuvering thrusters as they rotated through the correct position.

He rendered it, touched it up, and sent the renderings and simulations to Huenemann.

The operations group, too, was busy. They hadn't built any probes in a few years, but it was a simple process. They did not design a unit that had the properties they needed, they built them up from modules.

For the Earth mission, several modules would be bolted together. A hyperspace module, for the travel to Earth. A radio frequency scanning, recording, and forwarding unit. A QE radio unit, to send the results back to Earth and permit remote piloting of the craft.

Each of these was a single standard-size container. In addition, there was a standard control module – twelve feet by twelve feet by two feet thick – that could be bolted on the end of any standard-size container to provide the computerized control for the probe. It ran off power from the standalone QE radio's nuclear power unit and interfaced to the control runs into each of the other units.

Gannett's team put together a proposal for two such probes and sent it on up through management to the project leader, Chen ChaoPing.

Two weeks after getting the Earth assignment, ChaoPing requested a meeting with Chen Zufu and Chen Zumu. She found her parents, as before, awaiting her in ChaoLi's tearoom. After tea was served, ChaoPing jumped right in.

"Chen Zufu, Chen Zumu," she said, bowing to each in turn. "We have a preliminary plan together for the Earth mission, which I have sent you. I am here to answer any questions you may have."

"So soon, ChaoPing?" ChaoLi asked.

"Yes, Chen Zumu. This is not our first parade. The parameters of such a mission are, for the most part, well understood. Preparing the initial probes, in particular, is straightforward. But we can proceed no further in detailing the plan without the significant expenditure of funds and resources, for which I need your approval."

"I see. The first stage of the plan, then, is to build and deploy the probes, while building and testing the ship for the manned mission."

"Yes, Chen Zumu," ChaoPing said. "To gather the most information we can."

"And you will not use a normal hyperspace liner, ChaoPing? I thought you might use the *Wanderlust*."

"There is a nostalgic and public relations benefit to using the *Wanderlust*, Chen Zumu. But the *Wanderlust* is now in service on our busiest route, back and forth from Arcadia to Aruba. It is very popular, and people enjoy bragging they have traveled on the famed *Wanderlust*. More to the point, however, we anticipate using a new ship design for this trip."

"To increase the performance envelope," ChaoLi said.

"Yes, Chan Zumu. The performance differences are not small."

"I noted that. Mr. Porter has been busy, it seems."

"Yes, Chen Zumu," ChaoPing said with a smile. "Your initial briefing to me suggested the mission may have to make a run for it, and Wayne took that possibility to heart."

"But a new design, ChaoPing? Will there not be a great deal of testing required to ensure this new ship works as planned."

"We don't think so, Chen Zumu. Wayne rearranged the existing design elements of the hyperspace liners to create this new design. It was mostly a question of leaving some things off, flipping some others around. There is very little there that is new."

ChaoLi nodded and she turned to JieMin, who stirred.

"Thank you for coming to us today, ChaoPing. We must

consult others on this decision. We will contact you."

"Yes, Chen Zufu," ChaoPing said, bowing.

"No decision today, then?" JuMing asked.

"No. My father said they must consult others first."

"Who must Chen Zufu consult, I wonder. It is his decision."

"They did not say. But the authority to make a decision includes the responsibility to make it well."

JieMin and ChaoLi met with Jessica Chen-Jasic in VR. The avatar of each was seated in the doorway of their tearoom looking out over their gardens.

"Chen Zufu. Chen Zumu," Jessica said, bowing to each in turn.

She who had once been Chen Zumu knew how the system worked. Everyone in the family, herself included, paid respect to those who held the plenary authority to make decisions for the family. The position was a difficult one to do well, and anything to make it easier was of benefit to all.

Even over VR, as secure as it was, they spoke vaguely, the magnitude of the secret they shared being too great to treat flippantly.

"Jessica, we received a call request from that correspondent of yours, and met with her in VR," ChaoLi said. "Things are coming to a head. So we have sent you the preliminary plan for a diplomatic mission to Earth."

"I would appreciate your counsel on this matter," JieMin said.

"From whom else are you seeking input, Chen Zufu?"

"We plan to speak to Luisa Bianchi and your original correspondent as well before taking any action."

Jessica nodded. The prime minister of Arcadia and Quant.

"Very good. For my part I would add just one thing. I note the subterfuge of hiding the mission's capabilities. The speed of the ships. The capabilities of the robots. I think also that you should consider them hiding their VR capabilities. That would allow them to communicate among themselves, with the robots, and with you in VR through the radios in the shuttle, the Earth people remaining none the wiser."

"But without communicators, will that capability not be obvious, Jessica?"

Jessica shrugged.

"Have them take communicators, Chen Zumu. You should be able to dig them up somewhere. If the Earth people take them away, that tells you something as well."

JieMin nodded. That was a good idea.

"Excellent. Anything else for us, Jessica?" ChaoLi asked.

"No, Chen Zumu. The plan as it stands is well considered."

"Thank you, Jessica," JieMin said.

"Of course, Chen Zufu."

Luisa Bianchi was still in the first months of her prime ministership. Things were going well, because Sasha Ivanov had had things well in hand when he'd stepped down, he had kept her informed as the transition approached, and he had even been available to consult with her since the transition.

What she hadn't expected – so soon, anyway – was a call from the Chen requesting a meeting.

Bianchi knew the new Chen Zufu and Chen Zumu, of course. She and ChaoLi had worked closely together on various items affecting Jixing Trading Company in the Assembly. Not so much working for special treatment for the giant trading firm owned by the Chen-Jasic family, but fighting against special treatment against it.

When some people in government saw a large company, all they could think of was some way to tax it more highly than smaller firms. Bianchi and ChaoLi had fought to keep the tax treatment the same for large and small firms, keeping a level playing field.

ChaoLi had also been scrupulous in not seeking favored status from the government, which was the other side of the same coin: regulatory capture and special treatment. The temptation had to be large, and Bianchi respected her for that.

Unlike anyone in the Chen-Jasic family and most people outside of it, the Chen and the prime minister were on a first-name basis and had been for years. That didn't change with either of their promotions to the top leadership spots in their respective organizations.

Bianchi accepted the meeting request, choosing as her avatar the one of her sitting on a park bench outside in Charter Square. The Chen each appeared sitting on pillows in the doorways to their tearooms.

They looked absurdly young to be the Chen – in their mid-40s – but Bianchi knew they were, like her, actually in their early sixties. It was unusual to have Chen who were not already grey, but many such things had been changed by the Tahiti anti-aging therapies.

"Hello, ChaoLi, JieMin. How are you?"

"Very well, Luisa," ChaoLi said. "But we need to bring you into something we are considering, and we seek your counsel."

Bianchi nodded.

"Go ahead, ChaoLi. What's up?"

"We believe it's time for a diplomatic mission to Earth. To try to bring them into the trade agreement with the colonies."

"Why now, ChaoLi?"

"Two reasons, really. We are now well-established as a

united group of colonies. We have hyperspace ships plying back and forth among all twenty four. We're all prosperous and happy within this structure."

Bianchi nodded and ChaoLi continued.

"We also think the Earth is close to being able to field hyperspace ships of its own. We think it is better to establish contact now, there, than to wait until they show up out here."

How could they know that? Bianchi recalled something Rob Milbank had told her, years ago. The Chen had such good sources of information, they sometimes seemed almost prescient. He never questioned them about their sources, but he had never caught them being wrong on a major point, either.

"I see," Bianchi said, nodding. "Well, if they are on the verge of hyperspace, I agree with you, ChaoLi. Better to go there and say Hi than wait for them to show up out here, probably with a navy."

"Exactly. The question then is, What's the smartest way to go about it? ChaoPing has been putting a plan together. We'd like to send it to you for your thoughts."

"Of course, ChaoLi. I'll be happy to look at the plan."

JieMin stirred then, and made his only comment of the meeting.

"We would very much appreciate your feedback on this plan, Luisa."

"Of course, JieMin."

The prime minister had one piece of advice before she even looked at the plan: Be prepared for Earth to be belligerent. Bianchi was a student of history – Earth history in particular – and belligerence was a hallmark of Earth diplomacy and foreign policy and had been for millennia. It just seemed to be who they were.

The colonies had all that same heritage, of course. The combination of a self-selected population, the need to work together to get each colony going, and over a century of isolation from each other had, however, resulted in a different mindset. The colonies were biased toward cooperation.

When she had reviewed the plan, however, Bianchi saw she need not have worried. There were multiple contingencies built into the plan for dealing with varying levels of belligerence.

So Bianchi set herself to looking for holes. What could the Earth government do that they had not yet built in a countermeasure or contingency for?

Much as the Chen, the prime minister also had depth in retirees from her office she could consult. She sent the plan to Sasha Ivanov and Rob Milbank for review.

"What do you think?" Ivanov asked Milbank when they got together at Milbank's house for cigars and cognac the next evening.

"They've thought of a lot of different things. About the only thing I can think to add is to put fire extinguishers in the small passenger container," Milbank said.

"Fire extinguishers? But the small passenger container has a fire suppression system already."

"Yes, but fire extinguishers are almost invisible, and such containers can be used for many things other than being fire extinguishers."

Ivanov's eyes widened.

"I see," he said. "And what did you have in mind?"

When the ideas and suggestions from Jessica and Bianchi had been incorporated in an appendix to the original plan,

ChaoLi replied to the earlier message from JQ to request a meeting. She relied on whatever behind-the-scenes magic had gotten the first message to them despite the bogus From: address to work in reverse.

It must have worked, because they got a meeting acceptance back right away.

"Hello, Janice," ChaoLi said.

"Hello, ChaoLi. JieMin. How are you?" Quant asked around her charismatic smile.

"We're good, Janice. We have a preliminary plan for an Earth mission for you to look at."

"Excellent."

ChaoLi pushed the document to Quant, and Quant's avatar studied it briefly. The amount of processing power being expended not just for the avatar, but to read, analyze, and respond to the project plan took ChaoLi's breath away. This is how the colony project had been done, and it had still taken this computing behemoth twenty years to pull it off.

"This looks good to me, ChaoLi," Quant said after mere seconds. "I note they don't specify the location for the data capture probe. I would suggest L5, the trailing Lagrange point."

"Not L1, L2, or L4, Janice?"

"No. L1 and L2 are not stable. It would take a lot of orbital corrections over time. And they're only a million miles or so from the planet. The probe will be seen there when it makes orbit adjustments."

"And L4?"

"The leading Lagrange point sweeps the orbit in front of the Earth and is always full of debris. L5 is a little cleaner that way. And of course the advantage of one of the Lagrange points is that it moves with the Earth. L5 is always ninety-three million miles from the Earth, but it is always the same distance, and the sun is never in the way."

"I'll add that to the appendix, Janice. Anything else?"

"No, just to mention that I will be monitoring things, and will be able to step in if you need me. This needs to go well, in the end."

"I thank you for that, Janice Quant," JieMin said.

ChaoPing reported to Chen Zufu and Chen Zumu in response to their meeting request. When she got to Chen Zumu's tearoom, there was no other pillow present.

ChaoPing walked up to the tea table and, standing, bowed to them.

"You are authorized to proceed with the plan as proposed, ChaoPing, mindful of the ideas and suggestions in the appendix we added," JieMin said. "Even so, the final decisions are yours to make. You are authorized to prepare the data capture probes, as well as to design the ship for the diplomatic mission as outlined in this plan. You are not yet authorized to proceed with either deploying the probes or building the ship at this time. When the data capture probes are complete, we will want to see a further plan."

"I understand, Chen Zufu."

ChaoPing bowed to each of her parents in turn and left the room.

There was much to do.

The Plan Gets Under Way

"Some of these suggestions in the appendix are pretty wild," JuMing said when he reviewed the revised document.

ChaoPing nodded.

"The Lagrange point makes sense," she said. "That's a good idea."

"So is taking communicators."

"Yes. Keep them in the dark that we are in contact with VR. It also gives us a chance to see what they'll do about the communicators."

"I get all that. But what's with the seat backs and the fire extinguishers?"

"The assumption is the shuttle will be searched. So anything we want to have once we're there has to get past a search."

"But they'll find everything if they look hard enough."

"I think the thought is, if we appear innocuous enough, the search will be rudimentary. Or at least, superficial enough to miss those."

JuMing nodded.

"Do you think we'll need all that?"

"No way to know."

John Gannet, his project manager Chris Bellamy, and some of the senior operations people were meeting to hammer out details of their part of the mission. They had received authorization to build the probes and prepare them for deployment.

Unlike his counterpart in design, Karl Huenemann, Gannet

was quietly competent. Huenemann was competent, but one would never call him quietly anything.

"Well, I like the idea of using the Lagrange point," Frank Takahashi said. "Less station keeping means a less visible probe in terms of Earth seeing it there. We have to worry more about it colliding with debris, but the velocities will be small, so it's probably not a big deal. And once it's there, it will just stay there."

"I'm sorry," Bellamy said. "Why would the velocities be small?"

"Because if the velocities were large, the item wouldn't be trapped in the Lagrange point," Takahashi said.

"Ah. Got it."

"I'm more worried about appearance," Gannet said. "The probe is going to be three containers, right? QE radio, hyperspace generator, and multiband radio receiver. Call it twelve feet by thirty-six feet by eighty feet, and it's a rectangle. How is that not going to stand out like a sore thumb to a visual inspection? Or on radar, for that matter."

"I was thinking about that," Takahashi said. "One thing we can do is not jettison the JATO bottle once the probe is underway to the hyperspace limit. Just keep the assembly together. Then it's twenty-four feet square by eighty feet long."

"That's an off-center thrust, Frank," Mitch Fuller said.

"With the current bottles, yes, but does it have to be?" Takahashi asked. "Can we mount the nozzle in one corner, have it overhang the corner a bit, so it's in the center of a two-by-two stack?"

"That still doesn't solve the appearance problem," Gannet said. "It helps a bit by looking a little less unnatural, but it certainly doesn't solve it."

"No, but if we don't separate the JATO bottle, we can

disguise the whole stack," Takahashi said. "Coat the probe with a lumpy layer of spray foam."

"We can't do that before we get it into orbit," Fuller said. "Atmospheric drag would rip it all off. But we could get the robots to do it at the freight transfer station before we launched it."

"What about radar, Frank?" Gannet asked.

"Spray it with metallic paint," Takahashi said. "Something with a good radar reflectivity, to match a metal asteroid. We have to paint it anyway, just use the right paint."

Gannet looked to Fuller, who was thinking about it. After several seconds, Fuller nodded. Gannet turned to Bellamy.

"OK, Chris," he said. "Let's build that into the schedule. The mod to the JATO bottle design, some testing there, and the foaming and painting. We should probably send a probe to the Beacon shipyard and back to get good testing data. This is not a learn-on-the-job sort of situation. We have to get it right."

"Got it," Bellamy said.

Gannet turned back to Takahashi.

"Nice one, Frank."

"Thanks, John."

The design group had a much larger problem – two of them, actually – but it also had a much longer project schedule. The data capture probes would be on-site for months before the new-design ship and its hopped-up shuttles set out for Earth.

"Hey, Wayne," Huenemann called out as Wayne Porter entered the conference room. "We got authorization to do the new designs. And there's a slot at the Beacon shipyard coming up in a month that we can have. Can you be ready?"

Wayne sat heavily in a chair and thought about it. After a couple minutes, he stirred.

"Geez, Karl. A month is tight. I mean, we started the design two weeks ago, without any authorization. We do blue sky stuff like that all the time, playing with mods to hyperspace liner design and all, so we just jumped in. But a month is tight. We're still working with preliminary numbers."

Huenemann didn't say anything, just raised both eyebrows. Then he wiggled them, and Porter laughed.

"Yeah, we can probably do it. I'll tell you the trade-off, though. We test like crazy. Full-up tests. Out to Beacon and back. Maneuverability testing. The works. With a new design on a critical mission, I want to try to break it. Give me that, so we can make sure we didn't miss anything, and yeah, we can do a month. Not without, though, Karl. I won't sign off on it until I'm satisfied."

Huenemann nodded.

"That's fair. We were going to have to do extensive testing anyway, Wayne."

"Not like this. I'm going to instrument the hell out of it. Stress gauges. G-meters. We're going to really wring it out, Karl."

"You gonna do that with people on board, Wayne?"

"No. We'll have robots do the testing. But I want to make sure there isn't some fault, some mistake, that we don't find until it's on-mission. We'll find it here, and fix it, then it can go on the mission."

"OK, Wayne. That's a deal."

"I'll hold you to that, Karl."

"Oh, I know. I'm counting on it."

Porter gave him a quizzical look.

"I don't want to sign off on it prematurely, either, Wayne. You're my best excuse not to."

With the engineers hammering away at the plans for the Earth mission ship – they really needed a name for it! – Wayne Porter turned his attention to the shuttle design.

The basic concept was simple: double up on the engines and put JATO bottles on the shuttle. The implementation was anything but simple.

The engine pylons simply weren't designed to take the kind of loads two engines would produce, especially since the second one was further out on the pylon and had more leverage on the pylon mounting. The bearings, too, which allowed the engines to pivot, changing the thrust angle to the shuttle, couldn't handle the loads. Even the hard points the pylons mounted to on the airframe were too lightweight for the additional thrust.

It was a major re-design, with all that implied.

The JATO bottles presented their own problems. Once again, there were no hard points to take that kind of thrust load except the container latches at the bottom of the airframe. But putting JATO bottles under the airframe created an off-center thrust. It would be better if the thrust vector passed through the center of mass. Otherwise there was a pitch moment, lifting the nose of the shuttle and trying to flip it over.

The JATO bottles had to be arranged and fired in pairs, or there would also be a yaw moment, trying to rotate the ship to either side.

How to reconcile the various forces created by the huge thrust of the JATO bottles was the critical issue.

The breakthrough for Porter came when he considered using the shuttle's engines to compensate for the pitch moment. If the front engines were pointed up and the rear engines were pointed down, they created a counter-force to the JATO bottles' vertically off-center thrust.

Could the forces be matched sufficiently well? The engines needed time to spool up, but they also had thrust focusers and thrust spoilers. If the engines were spooled up before the JATO bottles were lit off, the thrust could be focused fast enough to compensate, Porter thought. Probably not by a human pilot, but a robot pilot could do it. It would still be a rough ride.

The JATO bottles would have to be smaller than the big ones on the hyperspace liners, so their thrust would be in the range that could be compensated by the engines, but he could mount more of them and fire them in sequence. That would also reduce the g-forces felt by the crew into an acceptable range. The big JATO bottles were just too big for something as light as a shuttle, even a heavy cargo shuttle.

Then he had to make the whole thing not fly like a brick.

Porter bent to his work.

Several days later, Porter had the shuttle design far enough along to turn it over to the engineers to work up the details. That would be in the future, however, as they were still pounding on the design of the main Earth mission ship.

The one remaining item for him now was anti-missile defenses of some kind. An extra wrench thrown into the works was the suggestion that the same or similar devices could be used as anti-ship weapons, to make sure the Earth mission ship could defend itself against other ships.

Back to first principles. The major characteristic of anything made to fly or space was how fragile it was. Acceleration, velocity, and lift were all functions of the amount of power and the amount of weight. More power and less weight gave greater performance, and made flight possible at all.

So anything that flew was made of the least amount of the lightest materials possible. To disable such a device, you just had to apply enough additional force somewhere to make it break. And it could be anywhere. Cockpit, engines, fuel tanks, airframe – all were near their limits when in operation. Exceed those limits, and you disabled the device.

The other important consideration was that targets were small and space was vast. How did one get the impact to the target?

One way was simply to blanket the volume of space the object would pass through. Use enough small pieces, and the target would hit one or more of them. If they were themselves moving in the opposite direction, the impact was greater. Make them both sharp and heavy, and they would have more effect from the same impact.

Porter started with a container. Add one of the small JATO bottles being proposed for the shuttle. A chemical explosive to distribute the contents into a volume of space. And the projectiles themselves. Platinum tetrahedrons had enough mass density, and the corners were sharper than those on a cube.

Such a device could be used defensively against missiles or offensively against other ships.

Porter started doing simulations. How big should the tetrahedrons be? How big should the explosive be? What sort of internal structure or reinforcing of the container would give the desired distribution of shrapnel? Could multiple explosives on the device give one choices of dispersion pattern? Or directions of the dispersal pattern?

As Porter refined his answers, he was surprised at how effective such a crude device could be.

There was also the question of missile defense for the shuttle. A whole container as a single-shot weapon was fine for the Earth mission ship, but for the shuttle something smaller was needed.

If Porter could devote just one container to weapons, how could he make that work? Assume the target was pursuing. Could he just eject bomblets behind the shuttle? How could he spread them out?

The same platinum tetrahedrons would work. If he arranged them around in clusters around central charges, he could put racks of those on a container. Maybe a small rocket engine, so that they wouldn't be just dropped behind the shuttle, but could be aimed, or at least scattered.

A couple of weeks in, Porter packaged up all his work and sent it to Karl Huenemann.

On Arcadia's interstellar freight transfer station, robots worked on the data capture probes. The two probes, now assembled from the four individual containers, were lashed to the station with ropes in eye bolts, not latched in the normal fashion. If they were latched down to a flat surface, they couldn't spray foam on the bottom side.

They were trying to avoid having even one geometrically flat side.

One robot did the spraying while the others wrestled the tanks and hoses around for him. It was difficult work, because they were not standing on the structure of the station. Instead, they clung to a spider's web of ropes crisscrossing the bay in which they worked.

The robot doing the foaming had mental images of several asteroids to work from, and was trying to emulate their irregular, pitted shape. Sometimes he let the spray foam up and bulge out, other places he placed a minimal coating. Gradually, the rectangular boxiness of the containers disappeared, first on one, then on the other.

The nozzle of the JATO bottle remained, in the middle of one end of the shape. The foaming robot worked the foam around the nozzle, leaving the nozzle itself to look like a small impact crater.

The foaming robot also had to work carefully around the antenna array on the radio data capture container and the navigation cameras and maneuvering thrusters of the hyperspace field generator container. These were much smaller artifacts, and did not detract from the disguise.

After the foaming, the robots sprayed metallic, radar-reflective paint over the foam. They wanted radar to bounce off the irregular exterior shape, not penetrate through the foam and bounce off the rectangular metal shape beneath.

When the painting was done, the web of work ropes was removed. Only the two fake asteroids remained, tied to the station.

Deployment

ChaoPing and JuMing had been refining and extending the mission plan, outlining branch points with options for action at each branch. They were aided by the list of enhancements to the ships currently in development, including the speed increase of the shuttle, the offensive and defensive weapons of the main ship, now called the *Endeavour*, the defensive weapons on the shuttle, and the seat-back caches and fire extinguishers in the small passenger container.

When they had the second round of the mission plan together, ChaoPing submitted it to the Chen and awaited the summons to a meeting.

ChaoLi and JieMin reviewed the plan before requesting a meeting. They discussed it in her tearoom during their morning tea.

"They have built in the ideas and suggestions from the appendix," ChaoLi said.

"And some things that were not in the appendix, like the disguises on the data capture drones."

"Have you seen the pictures? That was an inspired idea."

"Yes," JieMin said. "And ChaoPing has used the various ideas and suggestions to give her more options if things go poorly."

"You noticed that, too? The subtext?"

"That ChaoPing would lead the mission? Yes, of course. I expected it."

"I worry about her," ChaoLi said.

"I worry about anyone who goes on this mission."

"Yes, but she is my daughter."

"Everyone is someone's child," JieMin said. "Do you deny that she has the most relevant experience to give this mission the best chance of success, or at least survival?"

"No."

ChaoLi sighed.

"Who will she enlist as crew, do you think?" she asked.

"Oh, I think she has a crew already."

ChaoLi looked at him, eyes wide.

JieMin smiled and shrugged.

ChaoPing was summoned to attend the Chen at their afternoon tea that afternoon. A lobby clerk intercepted her, and led her out into the garden and around to Chen Zumu's tearoom, where the family's guiding couple – her parents – sat in the doorway facing out into the gardens.

"Chen Zufu. Chen Zumu," she said, bowing in turn to each.

She remained standing in front of them, two steps up from the ground level where she stood.

"Your mission plan is well considered, ChaoPing. You may proceed on to the next steps: constructing and testing the *Endeavour*, deploying the data capture drones, and assembling your crew."

"*My* crew, Chen Zufu?"

"Your mission plan signals your intention to go on this mission," ChaoLi said. "To head the mission. Did we misread that, ChaoPing?"

"No, Chen Zumu. But I did not know how to ask. I assumed you had seconds in line for the Chen if something happened to JuMing and me."

"Always," ChaoLi said. "The family must not be leaderless."

ChaoPing nodded.

"And so JuMing and I are free to go, Chen Zumu, even being in line to be Chen."

"Yes, ChaoPing," ChaoLi said. "And it is clear you are the best choice. When one wants something done correctly, call on one who has done it before."

"So assemble your crew, ChaoPing," JieMin said.

"Assemble my crew, Chen Zufu? I must recruit a crew first."

"I think you will find you already have a crew, ChaoPing," JieMin said. "If I am not mistaken, the adult crew of *Wanderlust* stands ready to space once again into the unknown."

ChaoPing's surprise must have shown, and JieMin continued.

"Like you and JuMing, they are unique people, ChaoPing. They have done great things. It is the standard of their own past accomplishments against which they measure themselves. This mission represents, once again, a great thing. Like you, they will not shy away from it. In fact, I think they will be aggrieved if you do not ask."

ChaoPing bowed to him.

"As you say, Chen Zufu."

JieMin nodded to her.

"That is all, ChaoPing."

"Yes, Chen Zufu. Chen Zumu."

ChaoPing bowed to each of them in turn and left.

"Can it be true?" ChaoPing asked JuMing that night. "Will they all just say, 'OK, here we are. Let's go?' Once more unto the breach, dear friends?"

"Sure. Why not? We did."

"Yes, but it seems such a huge request. To once again head out to a potentially hostile planet? To once again put everything on the line?"

"Of course, ChaoPing."

He looked her in the eye.

"It's who they are."

All of the children who had headed out on the *Wanderlust* ten years before were now fifteen years old or older – starting to work on their college educations, working, and either out of the house or the next thing to it – except three. Francoise Dufort was now thirteen, and Chen GangLi and Chen GangJie were twelve.

The twins understood their parents' need to go on the *Endeavour* mission.

"Of course," GangLi said. "When you become Chen Zufu and Chen Zumu, it must be obvious to everyone."

"Like Gramma and Grampa," his sister GangJie said, nodding. "Everyone said, 'Of course. Who else could it be?'"

"So we understand," GangLi said. "You must go."

"Of course, be careful," GangJie said. "Come back to us. But we understand that you must go despite the risks."

Francoise Dufort was even more insistent when Giscard Dufort and Marie Legrand at first hesitated, reluctant to go on a potentially dangerous mission and possibly leave her an orphan.

"No," she insisted. "You must go on the *Endeavour* mission. If this is a dangerous mission, if there are injuries and one of our friends dies, you will never forgive yourselves for not being there for them. Always wondering if, had you been there, you could have saved them. It will torture you forever."

"But we're worried about you, dear," Legrand said.

"I'll be fine, mother. All the *Wanderlust* kids are here, on

Arcadia. We're family. I'll have plenty of people to help me if it comes to that. But you *must* go. Our friends need you."

Julia Whitcomb had a different concern.

"Rob, what if we have to run for it? We're ninety years old."

"In a seventy-year-old's body, however," Milbank said.

"Even so, Rob. I worry we'll slow them down if they have to hightail it. That we'll endanger our friends."

Milbank was considering that when the robot in attendance in the living room spoke up.

"Excuse me, sir. If I might interject something."

"Yes, Tom. Go ahead."

"Thank you, sir. I understand there will be robots with the landing party."

"I believe so, yes," Milbank said.

"In that case, sir, none of the humans' ability to run will be put to the test. We can make twenty miles per hour on a solid surface while carrying an adult human, and I don't think any of the human crew can do a three-minute mile on their own."

"So if we ran for it, everybody in the landing party would be carried by one of the robots, Tom?"

"Of course, sir. We will get you all out of there if it comes to that."

Milbank turned back to Whitcomb and raised an eyebrow.

"All right, all right," she said, holding up her hands. "You want to go, and I do, too, if I force myself to admit it."

"So I should tell ChaoPing?"

"Yes. Tell ChaoPing we're in."

She sighed.

"Honestly, Rob. You'd think you would have grown out of this sort of nonsense."

Milbank gave her a wide-eyed look, and she laughed.

"That's it. The last one. I can't believe it," ChaoPing said to JuMing.

"How many of them did you get?"

"All of them. Every last one."

"That's pretty remarkable, actually," JuMing said. "I mean, I expected you to get most of them, but not all."

"I guess it's like you said. It's just who they are."

The shuttle drifted away on the slightest pulse of its maneuvering thrusters. The cables pulled straight and then taut, and the shuttle fired again, briefly. The fake asteroids began to move.

Faster now, the shuttle pulled away from the station, it's two auxiliaries in tow. The pilot gradually increased the thrust.

The goal was to get them far enough from the station to light off the JATO bottles without damaging anything else. So first, away from the station. Second, out of the local traffic. Third, pointed out into open space.

The cables were mounted to the outboard aft container latches on either side of the shuttle along the bottom. These were forty-eight feet apart, enough to keep the data capture probes separated.

The shuttle pulled the probes free of the inbound and outbound traffic lanes of the freight station and turned toward open space, accelerating gently all the way to keep the cables taut.

Once in the clear, the robot pilot of the shuttle pushed the remote cable release for both cables. He accelerated the shuttle up and away from the probes.

"Shuttle clear."

First one, then the other, the data capture probes lit off their JATO bottles and for fifteen minutes accelerated hard toward the hyperspace limit.

After twelve hours drifting at that velocity, they reached the hyperspace limit. They both initiated their hyperspace field generators and disappeared from normal space.

They both engaged ripple drive and made their turns, heading for a rendezvous point three light-months from Earth.

Compared to a six-hundred-foot long hyperspace liner, the *Endeavour* looked less than half finished when the Beacon shipyard factories pushed it clear of the asteroid they were working on. Five hundred feet in diameter, like the hyperspace liners, it was barely two hundred and fifty feet from bow to stern.

The only exceptions were the thruster towers that stuck out like an axle both front and rear, a hundred and fifty feet clear of the hull on each end. The thrusters needed the distance from the center of mass to turn the ship, and the ship just wasn't long enough to give them the leverage.

Endeavour looked very much like the wheel of a child's gyroscope, which in some sense it was.

Once pushed free, *Endeavour* used its maneuvering thrusters to slowly carry it clear of the asteroid. Once it had enough distance for safe transition, *Endeavour* powered up its hyperspace field generator and disappeared from normal space. It made its turn and headed for Arcadia.

Barely an hour later, *Endeavour* arrived at the Arcadia hyperspace limit and contacted Arcadia Orbital Traffic Control. A robot pilot remotely steered the new ship into a parking orbit several miles from the Arcadia freight transfer station.

Robots went aboard on shuttles loaded with construction materials, and began outfitting the ship.

"Well, the probes are gone and *Endeavour's* here," ChaoPing said to JuMing one evening.

"So we're making progress," he said.

"Yes, but it seems so slow."

"After the *Wanderlust* mission? With months at a time in hyperspace? You've sure gotten spoiled."

ChaoPing laughed.

"I suppose. We are moving along, though, as fast as we can, I guess."

"How long until we leave?" JuMing asked.

"Several months, anyway."

"Why so long?"

"We need to have enough data capture to get the best picture we can of what's really happening on Earth," ChaoPing said. "And the design people demanded an extra long testing period on the new ship design."

"That makes sense. They haven't fielded an entirely new ship design in twenty years. And they were pushed for time."

ChaoPing nodded.

"Yes, so I don't see pushing them on it," she said. "We need the data capture time anyway, so it's not like they're holding us up."

"When do they start testing?"

"Another couple of weeks. Once the outfitting is done. They want to test the ship in as close a configuration as they can get to its deployment condition."

"That's smart," JuMing said.

"In the meantime, I've been sending regular updates to the crew, so they have an idea of our timelines and all."

"When will you start briefing them on the mission?"

"Once we start getting some data analysis back from the probes' data captures," ChaoPing said.

"So a couple of months yet before that can even begin."

"Yes. I'd like to speed things up, but it's just going to take as long as it takes."

"Makes sense to me," JuMing said. "Don't try to rush things. We need to get this right."

EARTH

Disaster

When *Endeavour* appeared in Arcadia space, Justin Moore got in touch with ChaoPing with a request.

ChaoPing had been worried about Justin Moore and Gavin McKay. Everyone who had been aboard *Wanderlust* signed up for the *Endeavour* mission, but she knew piloting skills had to be kept in practice. She assumed captain's skills had to be kept in practice as well.

So ChaoPing had looked up what Justin Moore and Gavin McKay had been up to in the six years since the *Wanderlust*'s return. As it happened, they had been kept on the roster of reserve captains by Jixing Trading, available for assignment when illness or family problems kept someone from making a scheduled run.

A run out and back from Arcadia to another colony planet and back took between fourteen weeks and twenty-four weeks. Moore had made four such runs since *Wanderlust* returned, and McKay had made three, all as captains. Neither was more than a year out of the captain's chair.

But Moore's request surprised her.

"Hello, Justin. How're you doing?" ChaoPing asked.

"Good, ChaoPing. Good," Moore said. "Uh, ma'am, I have something of a request for you."

Moore's avatar looked sort of sheepish in VR, and ChaoPing wondered at that from the competent pilot and captain who had done so much in advancing hyperspace and interstellar trade.

59

"Sure, Justin. What do you need?"

"Well, it sounds kind of silly, ma'am, but I was wondering if we could have the same bridge crew on the *Endeavour* we had on the *Wanderlust*."

"It's you and Gavin, Justin. Just like before."

"No, ChaoPing. I meant the robots. Can we have the same robots we had on *Wanderlust*?"

"But they all run the same programming, Justin. It doesn't make any difference."

"That's what they say, ma'am. All the same, I've been out to Fiji and back any number of times on the *Space Merchant*, and we did that four-year trip together on *Wanderlust*. I've done several trips on various ships since then as well. And they're not the same. They're not different in any big way, but there's something...."

Moore ran his hand through his hair while he tried to come up with the words.

"I can't put my finger on it. Maybe it's me, ChaoPing, but I would feel a lot better with the bridge crew we had on *Wanderlust* for this trip, especially if it all falls into the pot."

Everyone said it didn't make any difference, all the robots were the same. But ChaoPing was not prepared to second-guess a ship's captain with the experience of Justin Moore. If he said it made a difference, that was good enough for her.

"I'll look into it, Justin. If we can do it, we'll do it."

"Thank you, ma'am. I think it's important. Or it may be, anyway."

ChaoPing checked the robots that had been assigned to *Wanderlust*. Playa kept track of them all by serial number, and she could filter and sort by assignment on the ship as well. As it turned out, the bridge crew of *Wanderlust* was still in place, and

EARTH

Wanderlust was eight weeks out of Aruba. She would arrive in Arcadia in two weeks.

Outfitting of *Endeavour* would take three to four weeks, so *Wanderlust* would be back in plenty of time to transfer the robot crew to *Endeavour*.

ChaoPing put the request in to Jixing Trading. With her project priority – and her status as heir apparent to Chen Zumu – it would certainly be granted.

If it was for the *Endeavour* mission, what Chen ChaoPing wanted, Chen ChaoPing got, whether it made any sense to anyone else or not.

When the fitting out of the *Endeavour* was completed, the stocking of the ship began. It would be fully stocked for its testing, except for the weapons systems.

While the stocking was going on, Moore and McKay went aboard to survey the vessel. The layout was different due to the foreshortened nature of the hull, but things were pretty much where they expected them to be, given the much shorter fore-and-aft corridors.

In particular, they found the bridge.

"Captain on the bridge," the robot second officer said as he got up and surrendered the captain's chair to Moore.

Moore didn't sit down, though.

"How are you all doing?" Moore asked the second officer, looking around the bridge.

"Very well, Captain. It is good to see you again. My associates and I wondered, when we were transferred from the *Wanderlust*, what was in store for us."

"Yes, I explicitly requested my *Wanderlust* crew back in place for this difficult mission."

"We are pleased that you place such confidence in us, Captain. We hope to live up to your expectations."

"I know you do, Number Two, and I'm counting on it. This will be a difficult mission, and the difficulty starts right here, with testing the ship. You will be in command during the testing. Mr. McKay and I are much more fragile than you all are, so we will be monitoring the testing remotely. You must not forget, though, that you are the commander on the scene. You have the conn. Do not wait for my orders."

"Aye, Captain."

"As for the testing, we need to make sure that, if anything is going to break, it breaks here, and not while we are on mission. Unlike Avalon, Quant, and Summer, the Earth has a large space-based presence in-system. We may need to fight our way out to the hyperspace limit. To be prepared for that, I need you to consult the term dogfight in your resources."

The robot second officer paused for several seconds as he accessed reference materials.

"I see, Captain. It is as much avoidance as it is offensive action."

"That's correct, Number Two. So you need to develop and practice avoidance maneuvers. Those are incredibly hard on a ship, so let's find out where the weaknesses are now, and not later."

"I understand, Captain. We won't let you down."

Endeavour headed for the hyperspace limit, not to get to a safe transition distance for hyperspace but to get out of the traffic lanes for in-system traffic. Beyond the hyperspace limit, local space was empty.

Without the weapons systems aboard, all of *Endeavour*'s aft cargo spaces were filled with JATO bottles. This was partially to make up the missing mass, and also to allow the robot crew to practice multiple maneuvers over a number of days under JATO-bottle accelerations.

Endeavour fired JATO bottles three times in succession to get up to speed leaving orbit. Normal departures from a system were a single use of JATO bottles, on a ship with ten times the mass. The normal twenty-four hours to reach the hyperspace limit was reduced to just over an hour for *Endeavour*.

Once at the hyperspace limit, the robot crew started putting *Endeavour* through her paces. Turns, flip-overs, skew turns, corkscrews, all under acceleration from the ship's normal engines. The gimbaled steering thrusters on the thruster towers fore and aft generated the torque required to carry out the precession turns of the big gyroscope of the ship.

The crew recorded all of their onboard conversations, carried out in radio, since there were no human officers aboard. They also recorded control settings, camera views, and stress readings from strain gauges located throughout the ship.

With maneuvers under normal ship's thrust completed and documented, the robot crew began the same series of tests while under the acceleration of the JATO bottles. They were generally aimed back toward Arcadia during these maneuvers, as their initial acceleration had left them with a velocity that was carrying them away from the planet.

Stress readings climbed as the *Endeavour* made all the same maneuvers under the thrust of the JATO bottles. The robot crew carried out their maneuvers first under half thrust from the steering thrusters, then the high-speed maneuvers under the full thrust of the steering thrusters.

When doing the corkscrew maneuver under JATO bottle acceleration, with full power to the steering thrusters, which were rotating around and around on their towers, the front tower twisted and bent where it met the hull. The thruster tower toppled, slamming into and penetrating the forward bulkhead of the hull.

The robot damage control parties of her crew worked on *Endeavour* for two days to get the ship capable of partial thrust for returning to Arcadia. When *Endeavour* had been made safe for such limited accelerations, the crippled ship headed back to the planet.

It had taken *Endeavour* just over an hour to get to the hyperspace limit. It took her almost two weeks to limp home.

She was not even air-tight.

The robot second officer had reported back to Moore once the emergency was under control.

"I'm sorry, Captain. We were carrying out dogfight maneuvers under JATO thrust, and the forward steering tower failed."

"Which is exactly what I wanted you to do, Number Two. You found a critical weakness, and exposed a few others. We need to fix all this before we go on the mission."

"You are not disappointed, Captain?"

"In you? No. In the ship? Yes, of course. But any new design is going to have its kinks. Your job was to find them, and a fine job you did."

"Thank you, Captain."

"You also saved the ship once the failure occurred. A fine job all around. Please pass my compliments on to the crew."

"I'll do that, Captain."

Justin Moore, Gavin McKay, and Wayne Porter were reviewing the recordings of the disaster on the big display in the conference room of the design group in Jixing Trading's headquarters at Five Charter Square in downtown Arcadia City. The *Endeavour* had just started her long walk home.

"I have the robot conversations in radio shown as speech there along the right-hand side," Porter said. "It's all digital, of course, so it's been translated into English equivalents. The various helm stations are on different frequencies, so many of the transmissions are simultaneous. The robots can sort them out where we couldn't."

The bridge view was shown, as was an exterior camera view of the thruster tower. Stress on the tower, acceleration readings, control settings, and other data were indicated along the bottom.

Porter walked the recording forward at much less than real-time speed.

"Here's where they start the corkscrew maneuver," he said. "You can see the thruster first fire, and then begin rotating."

The star view in the background of the camera view of the thruster tower wobbled up and down as it circled the spinning ship. The corkscrew turn kept wobbling the ship around in a circle, re-aiming the rear thrust so the ship actually followed a corkscrew path through space. It was a weapons-avoidance maneuver, trying not to be a stable target for a missile to lock onto and track.

"Hard to think of something that would put more stress on the ship," Moore said.

"Indeed," Porter said. "And not something we anticipated during the design."

"Hard as hell for a missile to hit her with her squirming around like that, though," McKay said. "I like the maneuver. I can see needing it."

"Agreed," Porter said. "We just didn't anticipate it."

Porter slowly walked the recording forward and stopped it again.

"Here you can see where the thruster tower begins to fail at the number three stanchion to the frame of the hull," he said. "The cyclical stress of the rotating thruster, with all that leverage out on the end of the tower, was too much for it."

"Cyclical stress?" McKay asked. "Like when you wiggle something to get it loose."

"Exactly, Gavin. The tower was built to take the continuous force of the thruster, but the continuous compression/tension cycle of the rotating thruster was too much for it."

Porter walked the recording forward just a bit.

"Here the tower member fails at the stanchion. The tower now hinges back and forth on the other two stanchions as the thruster rotates. Or it tries to. The failure of the tower member was reported in the data stream of the ship. The crew caught it very quickly, and the second officer shut down the thruster."

Moore and McKay looked at the bridge communication sequence in the right-hand column.

"Forward tower leg failure."
"Emergency shutdown all thrusters."
"All thrusters shut down."

"Of course, the JATO bottles are still thrusting," Porter said. "The JATO bottle puts a huge amount of thrust in a small package, but it does so at the expense of controls. In particular, there's no way to shut one off once it's ignited. With the lesser mass of the ship compared to a hyperspace liner, *Endeavour* here is accelerating at close to three gravities. The end result is the thruster tower topples onto and through the forward bulkhead of the ship."

Porter walked the recording forward, and the tower toppled in slow motion, hitting the forward bulkhead of the ship and penetrating it. When it did so, thruster fuel jetted from the end of the tower into the breach. The air escaping the breached hull blew most of the flames out into space.

"Oh, shit," McKay said.

"Yes," Porter said. "When the tower hit the bulkhead, the thruster fuel control valve at the thruster was broken off from the supply line, and thruster fuel started venting from the ruptured line. The thruster itself was still hot at this point, and ignited the self-oxidizing fuel. The resultant jet of fuel was mostly kept from entering the ship by air blowing out of the breach."

Moore looked over at the communications column.

"Loss of hull integrity. Air escaping."
"Thruster fuel leak in the forward tower."
"Close all thruster fuel supply lines."
"All thruster fuel supply lines closed."
"Fire in sector twenty, decks three through five."
"Fire-control parties to sector twenty."

"They shut off the supply lines at that point," Moore said.

"Yes," Porter said. "Those shutoffs are at the tanks, where the thruster controls are at the thrusters. The thruster fuel ran for a few seconds more, then stopped."

"And at this point they had active fires at the breach?" McKay asked with a shudder.

There was nothing worse, on a sea ship or a space ship, than a fire on board the vessel.

"Yes," Porter said. "The fires were started by the thruster fuel that wasn't blown out the hole by the air escaping. They would have been much worse if the thruster leak had lasted longer than the air escaping, but the crew shut off the thruster fuel very quickly. The air was still venting. Fire control parties arrived on the scene quickly and put out the fires."

"They saved the ship," Moore said.

"Yes, they absolutely did," Porter said. "And it was very quick action. Watch the whole sequence in real time."

Porter walked the recording back to the beginning of the failure of the thruster tower leg at the stanchion.

When he ran the whole sequence in real-time, it was less than three seconds.

"Shit," McKay said.

Porter nodded.

"It doesn't take something long to fall at three gravities," he said.

"All right," Moore said. "So with the thruster fuel shut off and the fire out, what did they do to get the ship back home?"

"They had to wait out the JATO bottles, which had another ten minutes of thrust. After that, the first thing they did was go out onto the hull and weld the fallen tower in place where it was so it couldn't flail about and do any more damage."

"They didn't cut it loose and jettison it?" McKay asked.

"No," Porter said. "They kept it for forensic analysis. We want to see why and how it failed, and I think they anticipated that."

Moore nodded. Smart.

"The second thing they did," Porter said, "was to go back to the thruster fuel manifold at the thruster fuel tank farm and disconnect the forward thruster fuel line and cap it off. That allowed them to restore the thruster fuel supply and bring the main engines, the maneuvering thrusters, and the rear steering thruster back on-line."

"That all took two days?" Moore asked.

"That location was not designed for maintenance access," Porter said. "An oversight. It is all hard-plumbed. They had to cut their way into it – making sure to do it in such a way as not to damage anything else – cut up the plumbing, and re-plumb it to their needs."

"And they didn't seal the hull breach?" McKay asked.

"No," Porter said. "They didn't need air on board to operate, and they preserved the breach so we could take a look at it back here and learn what we could from it."

"Are you anticipating hardening the hull at all?" Moore asked.

"No, Justin," Porter said. "Anything that flies or spaces is built no heavier than it needs to be. If we were to harden the whole hull for an impact like that, *Endeavour* would be a tank, not a space ship. Maneuverability and acceleration would go right out the window."

Moore nodded. That was his own take.

"What we are looking at, however, is the things we do need to change in the design, and that we can retrofit to *Endeavour* before the mission."

"What have you got so far?" Moore asked.

"First is to reinforce the thruster tower legs for the actual stresses seen, plus an engineering margin. That's obvious," Porter said. "Second is to put emergency shutoff valves at the thruster fuel manifold. That bulkhead is opened up now. There's no reason not to rework that while we have it open. We'll probably leave an access hatch there, because if you have remote-control valves, you have valve failures.

"Of course, we have to seal up the hull breach – replating that whole section, most likely – retest for hull integrity, and repair the damage from the fires."

"What about the human crew?" Moore asked.

"Yeah," McKay said. "No air is not good. It's unhealthy."

"Indeed," Porter said. "Don't forget I will be along on this little adventure."

Porter looked back and forth between them, and they nodded. He continued.

"We didn't put emergency bulkheads in the hyperspace liners because they are primarily freighters. The more aggressive safety measures used in seagoing ships during the height of sea travel in the nineteenth and twentieth centuries on Earth were not implemented on freighters, though most freighters had passenger cabins aboard and took some fare-paying passengers.

"We followed the same line there. Peace-time freighters, with passenger accommodations. I've now decided that is not appropriate here. Clearly the robots will get us home if they can. We just need to make sure we survive the trip.

"To that end, the passenger quarters we will actually be using on this trip will be sealed off from the rest of the ship, and we will have emergency bulkhead doors on each end of that aisleway. We will also have space suits for the passengers and an airlock."

"Space suits and an airlock?" McKay asked.

"Once they get us home, we still have to get off the ship."

"Oh, yeah," McKay said.

"We will also have an air recycler in the section big enough to last eighteen adults for three months. Food and water supplies to last three months. Everything we need to survive while the robots get us home."

"What about the bridge?" Moore asked. "Gavin and I have to be able to get back to where everyone else is if we're on the bridge when we lose hull integrity."

"Good point," Porter said. "So, seal the bridge, space suits,

EARTH

and an airlock. No long-term supplies, because you just need to get back to the rest of us so we can hole up for the trip home."

Moore nodded.

"The sick bay needs to be in that corridor as well," he said.

"Another good point," Porter said, making a note in VR. "Anything else?"

Porter looked back and forth between them.

"One more thing, I think," McKay said. "Make the sealed corridor with our cabins the central corridor on deck three."

Porter raised an eyebrow.

"It's the furthest from the exterior hull of the ship," McKay said. "Least likely place to get a hull breach."

"Of course," Porter said. "Excellent. This is why I wanted to get together today. If there's anything else you think of, either of you, let me know."

Moore got a call from ChaoPing a couple days later.

"I've read Wayne Porter's preliminary report, Justin. It looks like your request for the *Wanderlust* crew has paid dividends. They saved the *Endeavour*."

"We got lucky, ma'am," Moore said.

"In my experience, luck is something that happens to the prepared. It was a good call, getting your old crew aboard."

"Thank you, ma'am. It worked out."

"It certainly did."

71

RICHARD F. WEYAND

Data From Earth

While the *Endeavour* disaster unfolded, the two data capture probes continued to ripple their way through hyperspace to Earth, three thousand light-years and six weeks' travel away. *Endeavour* was still undergoing repairs and retrofitting when the two probes emerged from hyperspace three light-months from Earth.

They emerged within a few hours of each other. They were being remotely piloted from Arcadia via the QE radio each carried, so their locations were both determined by star parallax from camera views by their operators back in the operations center at Arcadia City Shuttleport.

"All right," John Gannet said in the operations center. "This is the tricky bit. Let's make sure we have all our i's crossed and our t's dotted, OK?"

There were a few chuckles at his deliberate mangling of the phrase. But they knew he was right. It was all on the line now.

New courses were plotted, carefully checked, and sent to the probes. Everything was set.

"We're good?" Gannet asked. "Everybody happy?"

He scanned the operations stations, collecting nods.

"OK. Let's do it."

The command was sent, and, three thousand light-years away, first one probe, then the other, powered up their hyperspace field generators and disappeared from normal space again.

72

EARTH

Lagrange 'point' is something of a misnomer. The Lagrange points L4 and L5 are regions of space both before and after the Earth in its orbit where the gravitational potential is a minimum.

At these locations, centrifugal force and the combined gravitation of the Earth and the Sun create something of a gravitational 'bowl' in which debris can be trapped. Debris can sit in the bottom of the bowl, and travel with the Earth in its orbit, or run around and around inside the bowl, which still travels with the Earth in its orbit. In the latter case, the debris circles around in the volume of space that makes up the moving Lagrange point.

The first data capture probe emerged from hyperspace at the edge of the Lagrange point volume of L5, moving at several hundred thousand miles per hour. Its path would have it cut across inside Earth's orbit and slightly out of the ecliptic, passing within twenty million miles or so of Earth on its way through.

The second data capture probe emerged from hyperspace within the volume of L5 at a low velocity, low enough to ensure it would be ensnared by the Lagrange point and follow Earth around in its orbit indefinitely. It remained ninety-three million miles from Earth, near the center of the Lagrange point volume.

The appearance of the fake asteroids disrupted the orbits of other debris within the Lagrange point.

"That's a new one," Conrad Berger said.
"A new what?" Lonny Winton asked.
"A new asteroid."
"Really. Let me see."

Winton looked into the display, the cleaned-up computer construction of the imagery.

"That's a pretty close one. How did we not see it before?" Winton asked.

"It came through L5. We can't see very well past all that crap floating around."

"Fair enough. What's L5 look like now?"

"Oh, it's all swirled up," Berger said. "All our former observations are out the window."

"Well, we better start remapping it, then."

And so they set about mapping the new orbits of all the objects caught in L5.

Including the second data capture probe.

"Astronomy picked up this new Earth-approaching asteroid. Can we get something out there to look at it?" Cal Vetter asked.

Fletcher Moran looked at the data on the new object.

"No. Did you take a look at these velocity numbers? Thing's going a quarter-million miles an hour. It'll be past us in two weeks. And it never gets closer than twenty million miles or so."

"Pity. Be interesting to see what it's made of."

"No doubt. But we'll be lucky to get some pictures of it as it goes past."

In the end, they did get some pictures from telescopes, but there was no new information in them. The new asteroid looked much like other asteroids they had seen over the years.

They could characterize it as a metal asteroid, though. Probably iron-nickel.

The radar imagery left little doubt of that.

EARTH

The data capture probes and their masters on Arcadia were unaware of any of this activity. The probes started monitoring radio data from Earth's networks and sending it back to Arcadia over their QE radio links.

There was a lot of data, but they did the best they could isolating the things they wanted to see. The operators on Arcadia could change the selection criteria remotely over the QE radio links.

They continued to tune what they were monitoring over the next several days as they looked at the data coming in. History, politics, government, military, and especially the new World Authority Chairman were their main interests.

Of course, they were also looking for news and status of the Earth's hyperspace project.

"So what do we have so far? Anything good?" ChaoPing asked John Gannet.

"We are getting data, and of the type we want," Gannet said. "Our selected topics. But there are a couple of limitations, right? We can only see something being transmitted. We don't have actual access to databases or references. We can see them when someone accesses them or sends them to someone else, but we can't initiate our own accesses."

"I understand."

"The other thing is that some of the data is encrypted. We expected that, and we've seen it before. Most of that is financial transactions or medical information – that sort of thing – which we have no interest in. But we've isolated the networks of people working on the hyperspace project, and a lot of their communications is encrypted as well."

"What about the military communications?" ChaoPing asked.

"Most of that is police traffic. They don't really have military per se. They have a police force which is militarized to the extent they can deal with an insurrection or something, but it's all under the police. And their crypto is laughable. The software we have from Hawaii shreds it.

"The hyperspace project crypto is something else again. We've not been able to break that."

"OK, John. I understand all that. Now, what are we getting?"

"First, the history," Gannet said. "We're getting quite a bit of the history of what's gone on in the last hundred and fifty years. We have more on the recent stuff, of course, but it's filling in further back.

"In a nutshell, the World Authority Chairmen have been consolidating power since Janice Quant died in the wreck of the interstellar transporter that placed all the colonies."

"Wait. Janice Quant died in the transporter?"

"Yes. We didn't know that before, but there's a pretty disturbing video from a drone the smaller transporter sent back to Earth. The big transporter they used to place the colonies broke up after the last colony was placed, and Janice Quant was aboard it. We found that right off."

"OK," ChaoPing said. "Go on."

"So the World Authority Chairmen since have been consolidating power. They nominally get appointed by the World Authority Council, but that's pretty much a rubber stamp. They can be removed by the World Authority Council, too, with a super-majority, but no Council has dared try it.

"As they've consolidated power, they've also been trending to a top-down, central-planning type of economy. Not completely. Not like Avalon. But regulations continue to increase, incentives and disincentives for specific economic behavior are stronger, and favored status for some players over others has become more common."

"Let me guess. The standard of living has gone down, and the birth rate has gone up."

"Got it in one," Gannet said. "The population is still pretty stable, because life expectancies have declined as well. They try to hide it or talk around it in the official publications, but we have too many sources buried in the data not to see it."

ChaoPing shook her head. So stupid. Humanity kept going down that path, with the same result every single time.

"What about the current chairman?" she asked.

"Jonathan David Wilson. He's kind of an unknown. Just came to power a year or so ago. Doesn't look like he's changing much, at least not yet.

"As far as his bio, we have a couple sources for that. He first appears on a merchant ship in the Bay of Bengal at the age of sixteen. By the age of twenty-two, he had his college degree and he enrolled in the World Police Academy. He was assigned to the protection detail of World Authority Councilman Gunter Mannheim.

"Mannheim ultimately made Wilson his chief of staff, then a member of the World Authority Council, then vice chairman. Mannheim was chairman for eleven years, but he passed away last year. Old age.

"Oh, and Wilson picked up a doctorate in history while working for Mannheim."

"OK, so he's not stupid. He's got to know where this is all headed."

Gannet shrugged.

"Just telling you what we know, ChaoPing."

"Understood, John. What else?"

"That's the big stuff. We're working up a preliminary report now, and will be updating it weekly as we learn more."

"Excellent," ChaoPing said. "Thanks, John."

ChaoLi read ChaoPing's and John Gannet's reports with interest. The encryption of most of the hyperspace project communications was troubling, however.

How close to hyperspace travel were they?

Then she had an idea.

"John Gannet here."

"Hello, Mr. Gannet. This is Chen ChaoLi."

Gannet knew ChaoLi very well, from the beginnings of the hyperspace project twenty years ago. She had risen far since then.

"Yes, Chen Zumu," Gannet said with a nod of the head, like a little bow. "It's good to see you again. How may I help you?"

"I understand you have the encrypted communications from the Earth's hyperspace project, Mr. Gannet."

"Yes, ma'am."

"Send me a pointer to those communications, if you would, Mr. Gannet."

"I can, Chen Zumu. But they have foiled our every attempt to decrypt them, even using the Hawaii software."

"Nevertheless, Mr. Gannet."

Gannet looked like he was going to make another attempt, but ChaoLi cut him off.

"I have access to computer resources you do not have, Mr. Gannet. Send me the pointer, please."

"Of course, Chen Zumu."

ChaoLi put the pointer to the encrypted communications into a mail and sent it to 'JQ.'

78

EARTH

Janice Quant followed the pointer to the cache of encrypted communications. This wouldn't be that hard.

Of course, Quant had the advantage of knowing what sort of software the hyperspace people were using, and having some of the communications in their unencrypted form. That wasn't that much of an advantage with modern crypto methods, however. It was still a nasty problem. A bunch of them, actually.

Quant assigned a hundred thousand of her radically advanced multiprocessor blades to the task.

It was three days later that ChaoLi called Gannet again.

"John Gannet here."

"Hello, Mr. Gannet. This is Chen ChaoLi."

"Yes, Chen Zumu," Gannet said with a nod of the head. "How may I help you today?"

"I have a pointer for you, Mr. Gannet."

ChaoLi pushed the pointer through VR.

"I'm sorry it took so long," she said.

When ChaoLi cut the call, Gannet followed the pointer and found a cache of messages internal to the Earth's hyperspace group.

How the hell had she done that?

Then again, Chen Zufu was a legendary mathematician. Gannet could think of a lot of reasons why, if Chen JieMin had broken modern encryption, the Chen-Jasic family would want to keep the secret to themselves.

Never one to look a gift horse in the mouth, Gannet sent the pointer on to his analysis crew. He then looked at the messages himself.

Gannet was no stranger to what it took to build a

hyperspace probe or field a hyperspace ship. He had been Karl Huenemann's number-two man in the early stages of the project, and had headed the operations group since Huenemann and the design group had moved downtown.

And now he had the engineering drawings of what they were up to on Earth.

What he saw did not amuse him.

Gannet reported his finds to ChaoPing.

"ChaoPing here."

"John Gannet, ma'am."

"Yes, John. What have you got?"

"We got those codes broken, ma'am. On the hyperspace project data. And I don't like what I'm seeing."

Gannet wasn't sure why he didn't mention Chen ChaoLi, but he didn't. Hell, ChaoPing was her daughter. If she wanted ChaoPing to know, ChaoLi could tell her.

"What are you seeing?"

"They have an initial design for a hyperspace field generator."

"Is it similar to ours?" ChaoPing asked. "Do you think it will work?"

"It's similar to our first hyperspace probe. It's laid out a little differently, but they have all the right pieces. And it's over-built, like our first one was. They clearly don't have any data to do optimization with yet. But yeah. I think it will work."

"Do they have the ripple drive or the screw drive yet, John?"

"I don't see any indication of that, ma'am," Gannet said. "But they are talking about the propulsion problem. I think they've concluded that hyperspace is an inimical environment."

"OK, so they're getting close. Anything else?"

"Yes, ChaoPing. They have some preliminary hyperspace ship designs. Very preliminary. Blue-sky stuff. But a lot of those designs have hard points for weapons racks, and very little cargo space. They look like warships, ma'am."

ChaoPing's eyes widened, then she nodded.

"I guess that's no more than we expected, but it's troubling to have it confirmed."

"And so soon," Gannet said. "They haven't even made first transition."

"All right, John. Thanks for the heads up."

"Of course, ma'am."

Second Testing

ChaoPing included John Gannet's new and troubling information in her next report. She and JuMing talked about it the evening of the day Gannet told her.

"So they're that close," JuMing said.

"Yes."

"We need to get moving. Is *Endeavour* completed yet? With the repairs and modifications?"

"Almost," ChaoPing said.

"Then we're good to go?"

"No. Design wants to run the testing again. Make sure the modifications hold up, and that we haven't broken anything else."

"Makes sense," JuMing said. "But can we afford the time?"

"We can't not afford it. The preliminary designs for warships makes it more likely we'll need those maneuvering capabilities."

"Because it casts light on their attitude."

"Yes," ChaoPing said.

"All right. I can see that. Do you have a schedule for departure yet?"

"Four weeks. I was just going to send notice to the crew."

"That is, assuming *Endeavour* passes this round of testing," JuMing said.

"Correct. Assuming that and the weapons testing go well, in four weeks, we're on our way."

ChaoLi and JieMin saw Gannet's information in ChaoPing's

report. They talked about it over tea that morning.

"Does this change our strategy at all?" ChaoLi asked.

"No, I don't think so. It emphasizes it, if anything."

"So try to be friends first..."

"And then, if that doesn't work, convince Mr. Wilson that he cannot win," JieMin said.

"But not by actually defeating him."

"No. No. That is to be avoided at all costs."

JieMin sighed.

"We cannot afford for Earth to become a conquered culture," he said. "Conquered culture syndrome is very real. We need Earth as a vibrant, thriving planet. A partner in building a better world for everyone. If a defeated Earth instead sinks into ennui and despair, we will end up supporting it for centuries. We cannot let four billion people starve, but such a burden will weight us all. Hold everyone back."

ChaoLi nodded.

"I see it now," she said. "Now that we're closer. You and our friend seem to have seen this all along."

ChaoLi lifted a hand toward the statue of Matthew Chen-Jasic that Janice Quant had given the Chen when Jessica Chen-Jasic was Chen Zumu.

"She saw the possibility long ago," JieMin said. "Before the colonies were transported. This is the final hurdle to achieving her long-term goals."

"Independent planets, at peace, prospering together."

"Yes. It was a tremendous vision."

JieMin looked out over the garden, but his eyes were unfocused, his attention thousands of light-years away. He spoke to the garden itself, it seemed, as he continued.

"We need now to see if we can get Mr. Wilson to see it as well."

Unlike Chen JieMin, Wayne Porter's attention was very much on the here and now. He and his team were going over all the little details for the umpteenth time, preparing for the second round of testing.

"You included the testing of the new valves on the thruster-fuel manifold as well?" Porter asked.

"Yes, of course. Here and here," Chet Voinovich said, pointing to portions of the test plan.

"OK, good."

Porter ran his hand through his hair.

"I'm fretting now, aren't I?"

"I wouldn't say that," Voinovich said. "But it is the third time you've asked me that question in as many days."

Porter chuckled.

"Well, I guess we must be ready to go then."

At the beginning of the trade agreement, nearly twenty years before, Westernesse and Playa had worked together to create a VR subsystem for the robots that allowed Playa's robots to communicate with humans over Westernesse's neural virtual reality links. Such communications were routine.

Justin Moore spoke to his 'Number Two,' the robot second officer, over VR before the *Endeavour* left for the second round of testing. The robot used an avatar of himself on the bridge.

"You pretty much ready for testing, Number Two?" Moore asked.

"Yes, Captain. We're doing subsystem tests now and ironing out whatever kinks we find."

"Anything serious?"

"No, Captain. We have things under control here."

"Good," Moore said. "Now, I wanted to talk to you before you left to emphasize one point. I don't want you shying away from any rigorous testing because the ship broke before. We need to be just as aggressive in testing *Endeavour* as the first time. Indications from the data we're receiving is that the Earth humans are, if anything, even more belligerent than we thought they might be.

"So don't let that first experience make you hold back in your testing."

"I understand, Captain. We will remain conscientious in proving out the ship."

"Excellent. That's exactly what I want. Carry on."

"Aye, Captain."

Endeavour maneuvered away from the Arcadia interstellar freight station where it had undergone its modifications and repairs. The ship used thrusters alone to gain distance from the station before engaging its main engines.

Once clear, *Endeavour* used its main engines to thrust in the orbital direction, spiraling higher in its orbit. Its maneuvering thrusters now went to full declination in the tangential direction and began spinning the ship, building up its internal apparent gravity. With a much lower moment of inertia than a hyperspace liner due to its much lower overall mass, the ship spun up to one gravity on its outermost deck in minutes instead of hours.

Endeavour then made a precession turn toward open space and ignited JATO bottles. With three sets of JATO bottles used in succession, the ship passed the hyperspace limit into space empty of local traffic in just over an hour.

The robot crew began working through the test plan as before.

When the robot crew got to the testing of the corkscrew turn, the robot second officer did not need to tell everyone to be ready for anything.

Endeavour initiated the corkscrew turn as before, slowly rotating the gimbaled steering thrusters on the towers. The precession turn wobbled the bows around, changing the direction of the JATO bottles' thrust. The ship corkscrewed through space.

A constant corkscrew is itself predictable though, and the testing had another wrinkle to it, one they had not gotten to before. Halfway through the first set of JATO bottles, the rotation of the thrusters was stopped for several seconds, and the ship heeled over harder.

On this new vector, the rotation of the thrusters was resumed, and the corkscrew continued. Once again the rotation of the thrusters was stopped for several seconds, and the ship heeled over hard in the other direction, then resumed corkscrewing.

This maneuver was continued through two sets of JATO bottles before the test plan was complete. *Endeavour* had passed all the maneuvering tests.

With a considerable current velocity toward Arcadia, the robot second officer ordered another set of JATO bottles fired to increase *Endeavour*'s velocity toward the planet even more. With clearance from Arcadia orbital control, the ship greatly exceeded normal approach velocity toward orbit.

The robot crew did a flip of the ship, aiming its stern, and the thrusters and JATO bottles, toward the planet. Full thruster burn and two successive rounds of JATO bottles slowed *Endeavour* to orbital insertion velocity. The ship made the run from the hyperspace limit back to the planet in less than two hours.

EARTH

One more round of testing was required. *Endeavour* would carry both offensive and defensive weapons on its mission to Earth. While the weapons were simple, that didn't mean deployment without testing was advisable.

At the same time, testing in Arcadia space – or in Beacon space, the neighboring star that held Arcadia's hyperspace shipyard – was clearly not suitable. The weapons testing would leave a lot of debris floating about, debris that had been designed to be most harmful to a ship impacting it.

Another red star, about ten light-years away, also had an asteroid belt, which would help with the testing of the offensive weapons by giving them targets to aim at. At ten light-years, it was just over three hours' hyperspace cruise away from Arcadia.

For the weapons testing, Moore and McKay would be aboard *Endeavour*.

It took several days to clear all the used JATO bottles from *Endeavour*, and then restock the ship with JATO bottles and weapons containers. Most of the weapons containers went into the aft cargo space of the ship, but some – the offensive weapons – went into the forward cargo space.

Also going into the forward cargo space for the testing were enough supplies for the two humans aboard. Not just for the several days of testing, but also survival rations waiting for rescue if something went wrong.

Finally, the spacesuits for Moore and McKay were put into a locker on the bridge, as well as a spare pair of spacesuits for them in the crew quarters space of the ship. If there was a hull breach on *Endeavour*, it could happen while they were on the bridge or in their quarters, so they had two spacesuits each, one in each location, unlike the rest of the crew.

The weapons systems for the ship were all exploding containers. The weapons systems for the shuttle were containers of exploding bomblets. *Endeavour* would test both during this test session.

Both weapons containers and bomblets contained platinum tetrahedrons, with one-inch sides. The explosion of a weapon would distribute a cloud of hundreds of thousands of pieces of this sharp-edged and sharp-cornered shrapnel in front of the target. Any ship or weapon hitting one of these pieces of shrapnel at typical space velocities was likely to be disabled.

The platinum itself was a waste product of the Beacon shipyards. Unlike the iron and nickel that made up most of metallic asteroids, platinum and the other soft heavy metals were unusable in construction of the hyperspace liners.

After twenty years of the construction of nearly a thousand hyperspace liners, the Beacon shipyard had tons of the stuff laying around, and platinum was both heavy and easy to cast, which made the shrapnel cheap and effective.

"Captain on the bridge."

Moore sat in the captain's chair and McKay took the secondary chair alongside.

"Status, Number Two?"

"We are coming up to one gravity now, Captain. On spiral departure course on main thrusters."

"When we're at one gravity, get clearance for our departure turn and take us to the limit, Number Two."

"Aye, Captain."

"I think we can use just two sets of JATO bottles for departure. What would be our time to the limit then?"

"Under three hours, Captain."

"Very well. Let's do that."

"Aye, Captain."

The robot second officer turned to face the forward viewscreen and relayed commands via radio.

"It seems strange to toss around JATO bottles like that, after skippering a hyperspace liner for so long," McKay said.

"Yes, but we have hundreds of them aboard. It's like it's part of our main propulsion system now."

"Oh, understood. It just feels strange. And hitting the hyperspace limit in a few hours instead of a day?"

"That could be a big issue if we have to make tracks at the other end," Moore said.

"How likely do you think that really is, though?"

"Given what I'm hearing through the grapevine, it's looking more likely by the day."

It was nearly six hours later that *Endeavour* emerged from hyperspace near the unnamed red dwarf star they had nicknamed Redeye for purposes of the testing. The ship emerged in open space in the system, having taken its bearings with a quick return to normal space a couple of light-months out.

"Deploy the reconnaissance drones."

"Aye, Captain."

"Time until optimum placement?"

"Fourteen hours, Captain."

"Very well. Number Two, you have the conn."

"Aye, Captain. I have the conn."

Moore and McKay walked back to their crew quarters for dinner and sleep. They reviewed on the way.

"So fourteen hours for the drones?" McKay asked.

"Yes. We want them far enough out to get good images of the dispersal patterns without getting hit themselves."

"Then we'll know what each explosive gives us in terms of coverage, so we know how to use them. That I get. But why not drop them ourselves, from hyperspace?"

"We also want each of them to have velocity to keep up with us, because we need to do each test where it won't overlap with the dispersal pattern of a previous test," Moore said. "We can do that dropping them ourselves, but velocity on exit from hyperspace is twitchy."

"OK. Got it. This way we get nice uniform velocities, and we can just move along with the reconnaissance cover for multiple tests."

"Right. Exactly."

"So tomorrow we get to blow stuff up?" McKay asked.

"Oh, yeah."

"Cool. That'll be fun."

"We're ready to begin testing, Number Two?" Moore asked.

"Yes, Captain. Reconnaissance is in place. Reconnaissance radar and cameras are also active on board, so we will get four views of every dispersal pattern."

Moore nodded.

"All right, Number Two. You may begin."

"Aye, Captain. Switching viewscreen to aft view. First container away."

Moore and McKay watched as a container was ejected from the aft storage area of *Endeavour*. A small thruster carried it away from the ship and then a small JATO bottle kicked in. The container streaked away from the ship.

"Coming up on detonation, Captain. Detonation, now."

The container, dozens of miles away from the ship, exploded in a spherical ball of debris. A cloud of what looked at this distance like tiny dust expanded from the explosion.

"Radar and visual imaging are tracking the shrapnel, Captain."

"What does the dispersal pattern look like, Number Two?" Moore asked.

"This was the explosive down the center of the container, Captain. The resultant shrapnel cloud is spreading as primarily a disk of material across the container's path."

"Let's go ahead with the directional explosives once we're far enough clear."

"Aye, Captain. Another fifteen minutes."

Endeavour expended a total of a eight container weapons and one container of bomblets for this part of the testing.

They could deploy containers with large, medium, or small dispersal patterns perpendicular to the container's path, or a directed cloud forward along the container's path, or even to one side or another, above or below, the container's path.

That last was so if a pursuer dodged the container to one side or another, the container could throw its payload in front them so they hit it as they went by. A little rotation on the front steering thrusters of the container could aim that cloud pretty precisely.

The spherical bomblets they dropped in groups, ten, twenty, or forty at a time. Once well clear of the ship, they ignited thrusters in whatever random direction they were aimed, spreading out behind the ship. When exploded, each bomblet produced a spherical cloud of shrapnel.

"Oh, I like those," McKay said. "Those will be on the shuttle?"

"Right. One or two containers' worth."

"And how many of them are in a container?"

"Fourteen hundred and forty," Moore said.

"Ten gross," McKay said. "Nice round number. Thirty-six drops of forty each."

"Right. Probably two drops on a pursuer, one after the other."

"Wow. I'd hate like hell to fly into a mess like that back there, much less one after the other. Talk about a bad day."

"That's the general idea," Moore said. "Give the other guy a really bad day."

Endeavour moved on to offensive weapons testing. The big difference here is that the containers were fired from the front of the ship, and steered to their target using their aiming thrusters. For targets, they used asteroids in the asteroid belt around Redeye.

For this testing, *Endeavour* did not enter the belt, but adjusted its velocity counter to the orbital velocity of the asteroids. This was the simulation of an approaching target. Asteroids were generally much bigger than a ship that posed a threat, so they could focus on the debris pattern on the asteroid's surface as it hit the cloud of shrapnel.

"Look at that," McKay said as they watched the telescopic imagery from one of the reconnaissance drones.

"Yeah, that looks pretty effective," Moore said drily.

"Gee, you think? That guy isn't going home."

"Hopefully the target isn't small enough to fit through a gap in that cloud."

"Watching that, I think we're good, Justin. That was obnoxious."

Moore nodded.

"All right, Number Two. Mission accomplished, I think. Let's go ahead and head on home."

"Aye, Captain."

EARTH

Endeavour was in free space, not within the gravity well of any major body, so it transitioned directly into hyperspace and made its turn for Arcadia.

"Estimating Arcadia arrival in three hours, twenty minutes, Captain."

"So what about all the junk we left floating around back there?" McKay asked. "All that shrapnel?"

"Empty system," Moore said. "Not a problem."

"And if we use them while we're at Earth?"

"If they force us to use them, then they can deal with the consequences."

"We dump a bunch of crap like that in their orbitals getting out, they're gonna lose some satellites and stuff. It's going to be a navigational hazard for years."

Moore shrugged.

"As may be," he said. "I won't feel sorry for them."

Departure

When *Endeavour* arrived back in Arcadia from the weapons testing, the serious preparations for the mission began. More weapons, swapping out used JATO bottles, stocking the gardens, supplying the ship for a crew of eighteen for a potential six-month journey, including time spent on Earth.

Assembly and briefing of the crew began as well. They were all put up in the big hotel in downtown Arcadia City, and began getting briefings on the mission. Those briefings included all the data gathered by the data capture probes.

ChaoPing and JuMing prepared the final version of their mission plan and submitted it to JieMin and ChaoLi – Chen Zufu and Chen Zumu – for approval.

ChaoLi and JieMin talked about the mission plan before giving ChaoPing approval to proceed.

"Do you think the diplomatic mission will succeed?" ChaoLi asked.

"No. I would be surprised if it did, actually. I think we are going to have to convince Mr. Wilson to our point of view in another way."

"With some help from our friend."

"Yes," JieMin said. "Mr. Wilson has convinced himself through a sophistry that it is acceptable to take our things – because they actually belong to Earth, you see – and give them to people on Earth."

"It's Avalon all over again."

"Yes, on an even larger scale. And it never works. The only

way out of poverty is education and work. But Mr. Wilson is unlikely to be moved from his current position through any sort of diplomatic effort. His worldview will have to be much more shaken to experience a transformation like that. Simply offering to be friends is unlikely to be enough."

"Should we even proceed with the mission then?" ChaoLi asked.

"Oh, yes. He needs to start thinking in this direction. The direction we want him to go. The change we want in his worldview will be simpler if he has been primed, I think."

ChaoLi nodded.

"I just worry about our people being exposed," she said.

"They will likely be fine. And they have powerful tools, not the least of which is their wits."

ChaoPing attended JieMin and ChaoLi in ChaoLi's tearoom. Once she was seated and tea was served, ChaoPing bowed to each of her parents in turn.

"Chen Zufu. Chen Zumu."

"You are authorized to proceed with the diplomatic mission to Earth as outlined in your most recent plan," JieMin said.

"Thank you, Chen Zufu."

JieMin nodded, just once, like a little bow.

"It is important that you understand something about this mission, ChaoPing," ChaoLi said.

"Yes, Chen Zumu?"

"We do not expect it to be successful. We also do not expect it to be unsuccessful. We have no expectation either way, but we must give the Earth – and by that we mean Chairman Wilson – the opportunity to be friends.

"That said, this mission is not do-or-die. If it fails, we have several other ways of dealing with Earth. Do not be unclear on this point. The primary goal of this mission is to return the crew safely to Arcadia. The secondary goals are, in order, to present Chairman Wilson with a different way of thinking about his duties to his citizens and how to carry them out, and to sign the Earth up to the trade agreement.

"Putting the crew in serious danger to try to achieve the secondary goals when Chairman Wilson is not amenable to them would be a failure of the worst kind."

"I understand, Chen Zumu."

ChaoLi caught ChaoPing's eye and held it for several seconds.

"Be certain that you do, ChaoPing. If Chairman Wilson wants to be friends with the colonies, all well and good. Sign the trade agreement with him.

"If he does not wish to be friends, however, you are to return safely to Arcadia. *We* will deal with him."

"Yes, Chen Zumu."

ChaoPing repeated the conversation to JuMing later that day.

"What did she mean, we will deal with him?" JuMing asked.

"I don't know, but the way she said it sent ice down my back."

"Yeah, no kidding. What have your parents got up their sleeves, I wonder."

"No way to know," ChaoPing said, "but don't forget what they've accomplished already. When they're sitting as the Chen, they're scary as hell."

ChaoLi and JieMin also met with Rob Milbank in the days leading up to the departure of the *Endeavour*. They had been friends for twenty years, beginning in the early days of the design and development work on the hyperspace project.

Milbank came to visit them personally, in response to their invitation. They met in ChaoLi's tearoom, where Milbank had met several times during his prime ministership with Chen MinChao and Jessica Chen-Jasic.

With Milbank seated and tea served, the three old friends sipped, as always, in order of priority, the guest first.

"JieMin, ChaoLi, it's good to see you. I haven't seen much of you since all the hoopla surrounding the *Wanderlust*'s return."

"Yes, and now we meet about another diplomatic mission, on another ship," ChaoLi said.

"A much different mission, though," Milbank said. "We always knew where Earth was, but not how to approach it. For *Wanderlust*'s mission, we knew how to approach a colony planet, just not where they were."

"Yes, Rob, and that difference is why we wanted to talk to you," ChaoLi said. "While ChaoPing is the head of mission, as she was with the *Wanderlust*, you will be the most experienced politician on this mission. We expect that you will once again play a critical role in accomplishing the mission's objectives."

"And what, for you, are the mission's objectives, ChaoLi?"

"The first and primary mission goal is to bring everyone back to Arcadia safely. We must approach Earth with the trade agreement, but that is merely our opening gambit. Chairman Wilson may be amenable to such an arrangement, but the early signs are not hopeful. World Authority Chairmen have been pretty reclusive for the last century, and we simply don't know enough about him to predict him with any confidence.

"So we have no expectations with respect to his response. At least no solid ones. If he is open to talking about potential relationships, of course, engage him. Try to get him to see our point of view. Our vision for the future, and if he wishes to be friends and to sign the trade agreement, by all means, execute the agreement.

"However, if Chairman Wilson decides not to be friends, then return safely to Arcadia. We will deal with him."

Milbank raised an eyebrow at that and looked back and forth between them.

JieMin stirred.

"There are things we know, things we can do, that we cannot share with you, Rob," he said. "Trust me when I say that we can deal with Chairman Wilson."

"And his navy, JieMin?" Milbank asked. "I assume he will build one if he decides not to be friends."

"Yes, and his navy. He cannot prevail, or even be more than a minor annoyance."

The hackles rose on Milbank's neck at JieMin's quiet assurance. The genius mathematician had discovered hyperspace and formalized its mathematics in thirteen years from a standing start. That work had been the foundation of the trading network among the colonies for the past twenty years.

But in those twenty years, JieMin had been no more than a part-time adviser to the hyperspace project. What else had he come up with in the past twenty years? The mind boggled.

One thing Milbank knew for sure. The Chen did not make big mistakes on major issues. JieMin, in particular, had never been caught out on something about which he was so sure. If he said he could deal with Wilson – and a potential Earth navy – then he could, pure and simple.

Milbank nodded.

"Given that, I understand the strategy," he said. "We would rather be friends with Earth than conquer it. If we conquer it, we own it and all its problems."

"Yes. Exactly," JieMin said. "And we make those problems worse. Ruling over a conquered planet is not a bowl of flowers. It would be a bleaker future for us all."

"So you need to convince Wilson that he cannot win," Milbank said.

"That we can do," JieMin said. "But first we need to get him at least thinking about an alternative. If he is primed for it, it will be easier for him to accept such a solution later."

"All right," Milbank said. "I understand now. If he is not amenable to friendship now, we can at least get him thinking in that direction. Pondering it before rejecting it."

"Yes," ChaoLi said. "And then come home safely. That may present its own difficulties, but I think Chairman Wilson and his minions will discover that *Endeavour* and her crew are more capable and resourceful than initial appearances might suggest. That will also help in priming him for his later epiphany."

The day before *Endeavour*'s departure was as for the *Wanderlust* mission. A final briefing for the whole crew was held in a meeting room in the hotel. This was followed by a lunch attended by Prime Minister Julia Bianchi and the Chen, JieMin and ChaoLi.

After lunch, the entire *Endeavour* crew went to the beach for the afternoon. They tarried until sunset, so the robots put on a light supper. While some people enjoyed the water that afternoon, Rob Milbank and Loukas Diakos were content to sit on the beach with their cigars and cognac.

"So no pool this time," Milbank said.

"No, but I understand that. The ship is so much lighter than a hyperspace liner, it's hard to compensate the off-center mass. And it is a much shorter trip. We do have the gardens, though. And a cigar room."

"Two cigar rooms. One with a hot tub."

Diakos nodded.

"That'll be nice," he said. "Nothing for relaxation like a hot soak and a cigar."

"And fresh fruits and vegetables all the way there and back."

"Won't be much different than being at home."

Milbank nodded.

Except for whatever reception we get at the other end, he thought.

On the day of departure, mindful of the upcoming zero gravity transfer from shuttle to ship, the crew of *Endeavour* had a light breakfast together at the hotel. A shuttle bus took them and their personal service robots to the Arcadia City spaceport.

At the spaceport, JieMin and ChaoLi showed up for a last farewell to their daughter, ChaoPing. They were in parent mode, and not in their personae as the Chen.

"Take good care of yourself," ChaoLi said.

"I will, Muqin."

They hugged, and things got a little teary. Then everyone else was aboard the small passenger container under the shuttle, and it was time to leave. One last hug from ChaoLi and a hug from JieMin, and ChaoPing got on board.

As they got on board, Diakos nudged Milbank with his elbow. When Milbank looked at him, Diakos nodded to the nearby corner of the passenger container. There was a fire extinguisher there, mounted to the wall. Milbank looked around, and there were a total of eight of them, two at each end in the corners and four more spaced down the side walls.

"Huh. Looks like they liked the idea," Milbank said.

"Armed and loaded for bear," Diakos said.

"That's probably a good idea," Milbank said, remembering his conversation with the Chen. "Actually, that's probably a really good idea."

The robot pilot got his takeoff clearance and spooled up the engines. When they were at rpm, he focused the thrust of the eight engines and the overpowered shuttle fairly leapt off the pad.

ChaoLi and JieMin were watching from the observation window in the terminal.

"I hope things go well for them," ChaoLi said.

"If it really gets bad, I will call on our friend for assistance," JieMin said.

ChaoLi started at that, and then nodded. She hadn't considered that Janice Quant could intervene even at this point if things got really bad for the diplomatic mission on Earth.

"That makes me feel a lot better, actually."

Endeavour floated free of the Arcadia freight transfer station, the normal situation for a ship taking on passengers. All the slow maneuvering had already been done to minimize the time passengers had to spend in zero gravity.

The ship was departure-ready, awaiting only her human crew.

The shuttle trip was nothing new for her experienced crew. All had made shuttle-to-ship trips a dozen or more times by this point, on the *Wanderlust* mission, on trips to Tahiti for anti-aging treatments before the planetary clinics opened, or during their careers with Jixing Trading. Some people actually napped on the way into orbit.

The shuttle approached *Endeavour* and the gravity dropped away. The parasite maneuvered the containers – a four-wide, one-high stack of passenger container, two JATO bottle containers, and a standalone QE radio container – into the latches of four additional containers aboard *Endeavour*. Unlike on a hyperspace liner, this was on the front of the shortened hull of *Endeavour*, the after space being used solely for JATO bottles and weapons containers.

When the containers were latched, Moore received a VR message from the robot second officer, Number Two, on the bridge of *Endeavour*.

"Orders, Captain?"

"Begin spin. Prepare for departure. Request departure clearance."

"Aye, Captain."

Moore felt the horizontal acceleration as the ship began to spin. It was significantly stronger than on a hyperspace liner due to *Endeavour*'s lower mass. Moore expected that, but it did get a comment from the crew.

"Wow," Diakos said. "That's a lot harder spin acceleration."

"Yes," Moore said. "*Endeavour* is a lot lighter, so she comes up to spin faster with the same maneuvering thrusters. Couple of minutes, we can go on aboard. Just remember to walk carefully, especially when going around corners."

Diakos nodded. The acceleration was still nowhere like that of a groundcar, for instance. The outer surface of the station rotated at about sixty miles an hour at one gravity, and took minutes to get there, as compared to seconds for a groundcar to go from zero to sixty miles an hour. One still needed to be careful when walking, however.

They went on board *Endeavour* a few minutes later. By the time they got to their cabins, they were nearing one gravity. One addition was obvious: the armchairs in the living rooms of all the cabins had seat belts.

Moore and McKay went directly to the bridge.

"Captain on the bridge."

"We ready, Number Two?"

"Just about, Captain. We're waiting for acknowledgement that all human crew are strapped in for departure."

He pointedly looked at Moore's waist, and Moore laughed.

"OK, I hear you, Number Two. C'mon, Gavin. Belt up."

Moore and McKay belted themselves into their own seats on the bridge.

"I have final acknowledgment, Captain."

"We have departure clearance?"

"Yes, Captain. Our discretion."

"Very well. Let's go ahead and get started, Number Two. Two thrusts to the hyperspace limit."

"Aye, Captain."

Endeavour fired up her main engines, then ignited the first round of JATO bottles. Straight ahead in her orbit at first, then she made her precession turn to open space.

When the first round of JATO bottles burned out, *Endeavour* fired a second set and continued to accelerate. Three hours out of Arcadia orbit, the ship passed the hyperspace limit, powered up its hyperspace field generator, and disappeared from normal space.

Endeavour

They all had dinner together in the dining room that evening. The robots did a credible job on a menu despite having only had access to the kitchen for a few hours after the JATO-bottle thrust of their departure was over.

"I have to say that was a quick departure," Julia Whitcomb said.

"Yes," ChaoPing said. "I was wondering if Jixing ought to offer passenger service on such ships. Not much cargo room, but only a few minutes in zero gravity and here we are in hyperspace hours later."

"But it doesn't speed up the six-week hyperspace trip at all," Milbank said. "Maybe a day or so on either end. That's it. And without cargo for revenue, the fares would be expensive."

"Some people might be willing to pay it," Diakos said. "Is there any way to shorten the hyperspace time for the lighter ship."

ChaoPing shook her head.

"No," she said. "We looked at it. The problem is that it's a hydrodynamics problem. Like air resistance. The shape of the hyperspace field determines the drag, and we've already optimized that."

"Pity," Diakos said. "Because that's where the time is."

"Speaking of time," Milbank said. "What are we going to do with the next six weeks?"

"Play out scenarios," ChaoPing said. "See what we can come up with as responses for various moves Wilson might make."

"Sounds productive," Milbank said. "I assume you've been

EARTH

working up scenarios and options."

"Yes," ChaoPing said, "but I want everybody's input and ideas now that we're all together. See what we can come up with."

Milbank and Diakos tried out the hot tub that evening. Cigars and cognac supplemented the experience.

"Ah, this is the life," Diakos said.

"Indeed," Milbank said. "Tom, one more degree, I think."

"Of course, sir," the robot said.

The robot did not move, accessing the controls in VR. Milbank could have accessed the controls in VR as well, of course, but he wasn't confident of himself with the VR controls and didn't want to turn himself and Diakos into soup.

"So we start working out scenarios tomorrow?" Diakos asked.

"Yes."

"I wonder what sort of scenarios she's looking at?"

Milbank gave Diakos a look, and Diakos shrugged.

"I haven't been able to pay a lot of attention to the latest range of possibilities," he said.

"Everything from 'Hail, fellow, well met,' to 'Lock them up,' I think," Milbank said.

"Really. They haven't been able to narrow the range more than that?"

"I don't think so. We don't really have a lot of information about Chairman Wilson."

"Ah."

Diakos sipped his cognac and considered.

"Well," he said. "Should be interesting."

They held the first meeting in the dining room the next

morning. Breakfast brunch was spread out, and, as people moved to coffee or tea, ChaoPing called them to order.

"OK, we're all here, we're all fed, and we're on the way," she said. "Time to get into the detailed planning on this mission. There are a number of things you weren't told before we left, because we needed to make sure these things stayed quiet. We'll go over those things now, and then we are going to get into some serious nuts and bolts about the Earth mission. Especially the landing party.

"Rolf, why don't you start us off?"

"Happy to, ChaoPing," Dornier said.

He stood and looked around at the group, the same nine couples who had set out on the *Wanderlust* mission, now eleven years before.

"We were all on *Wanderlust*, so we all know what the robots are capable of."

He nodded to the personal service robots, including Bob and Tom, who stood by around the outside of the group.

"For this mission, though, we have asked them to hide even their day-to-day abilities. To appear more primitive by far than they are."

Dornier nodded to Bob, and he came up to the table at Diakos's side. He walked slowly, with a primitive robotic stiffness.

"MORE COFFEE, SIR?" Bob said in a flat, mechanical voice.

"Yes, please," said Diakos, clearly amused.

Bob reached out for the coffee pot, but it was not the smooth motion of the robots – or a human – in their normal mode. Each joint seemed to adjust one at a time, and multiple times, as Bob reached for the pot. There was a noticeable pause as his fingers slowly closed around the handle. This type of motion continued through lifting the pot, pouring the coffee, and replacing the pot. Bob then stiffly walked back to where he had been, turning around to proceed forward, then slowly turning around again, as if he couldn't simply step back.

"Oh my God," Julia Whitcomb said. "They'll never buy it."

"Of course, they will," Dornier said. "Never having seen one of our robots before, they will learn from and incorporate what they see. We want them to be surprised when they learn differently."

"Some surprise," Paolo Costa said.

"Indeed. You are also all familiar with the handguns the robots used on the *Wanderlust* mission. We commissioned new handguns for this mission, based on the earlier model. These firearms have built-in suppressors. In addition, the new ammunition for use in these firearms has been redesigned to be subsonic. The mass of the projectiles is unchanged, and will be sufficient for anti-personnel use."

"What about vehicles, Rolf?" Wayne Porter asked.

"Two-thirds of the handguns will be the suppressed version, loaded with sub-sonic ammunition. The other third carried by the robots in the landing party will be the previous, full-power version. They will have the same ballistics as before, and will be effective against light vehicles and aircraft."

"That's all well and good, Rolf, but how do we get the weapons to the surface, and how do we keep them from being confiscated?" Paolo Costa asked.

"The weapons and ammo bags are sewn into the seat backs of the last half of the seats on the shuttle. If they inspect seats closely enough to find the weapons – which would require ripping them apart, basically – we believe they will inspect one or two of the seats closer to the door. If they go no further than halfway, they don't find anything. When the time comes to arm themselves, the robots will simply tear open the seatback in front of them."

"Has that been tested?" Milbank asked.

Dornier nodded to Bob.

"Yes, sir," Bob said. "We had no difficulty whatsoever accessing the weapons."

Milbank nodded, and Dornier continued.

"The one other thing I should mention is that the robots can make a steady twenty miles per hour on a hard surface while carrying an adult human in their arms. If we have to make a run for it to get to the shuttle, the robots will be the vehicles for the landing party. Other robots will run along with them, covering our escape."

"All right. Thanks, Rolf," ChaoPing said. "Wayne, do you want to cover the changes to the ship and the shuttle."

"Of course, ChaoPing."

Dornier sat down and Wayne Porter stood up.

"First, you have probably all noticed that the shuttle now has eight engines and not just four. The four-engine version has a lift capacity of twelve containers, but the eight-engine version we take down to the surface will be carrying only eight. Further, if we need to flee, we will leave two of the bottom four containers on the surface.

"Second, the upper tier of containers will carry a standalone QE radio and the passenger container in the outboard positions. The two inboard positions will contain four JATO bottles each. These are smaller than the JATO bottles on *Endeavour*, but will accelerate the shuttle at three gravities of acceleration for up to an hour."

Milbank let out a slow whistle.

"Yes," Porter said. "The shuttle can make the hyperspace limit from the surface of the planet in just over an hour."

"Why the hyperspace limit?" Dornier asked.

"The lower tier of containers will contain a container of gifts for Chairman Wilson, a weapons container, a hyperspace field generator, and an extra container of thruster fuel."

"The shuttle is hyperspace capable?" Diakos asked.

"Yes," Porter said. "If we need to flee, we're all going to get the hell out of there without trying to match velocities in orbit and dock the shuttle and all that. The two ships will proceed independently to a spot in the Alpha Centauri system and meet up for the trip home."

"Why Alpha Centauri, Wayne?" Milbank asked.

"It will be much easier to locate the meeting point for both ships if we have multiple, close reference points to navigate from. As a multiple-star system, it will be much easier to find each other in."

Milbank nodded, and Porter continued.

"The weapons container holds over fourteen hundred bomblets. These are explosive charges surrounded by a hundred thousand of these, and with a tiny rocket motor. When dropped behind the shuttle in groups of ten, twenty, or forty, the bomblets will use their rocket engines to scatter and then explode on signal."

Porter took a little plastic box out of his pocket and opened it. He dumped out a little white-metal tetrahedron with one-inch sides.

"These each weigh an ounce and a half. A cloud of them will be destructive of any craft or weapons trying to fly or space through them with any sort of velocity. They will also have the velocities imparted to them by the explosion of the bomblet."

"So we burn straight up from the planet for the hyperspace limit, dropping these behind us anytime we have to, and then go into hyperspace?" Dornier asked.

"That's the plan," Porter said.

"And any targets in front of us?" Dornier asked.

"We try to evade as best we can. The maneuverability of the shuttle with that much extra horsepower is pretty startling."

Dornier nodded.

"That's it for the shuttle," Porter said. "Let's talk about *Endeavour*. You all noticed how quick the ship was to spin up to speed for one gravity. That is due to its decreased mass. One-third the length of a hyperspace liner, and without significant cargo aboard, the ship is much more maneuverable and quick than a hyperspace liner.

"In particular, the *Endeavour* has the same engines as a hyperspace liner, so it accelerates much more quickly. The ship also has a large number of JATO bottles for higher acceleration when needed. *Endeavour* can make the hyperspace limit in under an hour from orbit, with three gravities of acceleration.

"You may have noticed the fore and aft thruster towers on *Endeavour* as we approached the ship in the shuttle. These are to give the steering thrusters more leverage. Like a gyroscope, the spinning *Endeavour* makes precession turns. When the fore and aft thrusters point to opposite sides, the ship pitches up or down. When the fore and aft thrusters point up and down, the ship turns left or right.

"*Endeavour* is much faster on the helm than a hyperspace liner. One evasive course we used in testing is to fly a corkscrew path through space, by rotating the steering thrusters as they fire."

"Is that the one that broke the ship?" Costa asked.

"Yes. It was a set of stresses we did not anticipate. That has all been cleaned up, and some extra safety precautions have been implemented as well.

"One of those safety precautions is the air-tight emergency doors at either end of this corridor. If *Endeavour* suffers a hull breach, we will hole up in this section of the ship while the robot crew takes us home. We have sufficient emergency rations in this corridor to sustain us for the trip.

"In addition to her speed and maneuvering capability, *Endeavour* carries significant weapons systems. We carry dozens of explosive containers. These are much like the bomblets of the shuttle, but they are whole containers. They have steering thrusters and a large JATO bottle for propulsion.

"There are multiple charges within each container that allow us to steer the shrapnel in the desired direction to provide the most potential for impact with the target.

"Each of the container weapons has two hundred million of those."

Porter gestured to the platinum tetrahedron sitting on the table.

"Two hundred *million*?" Dornier asked.

"Oh, yeah," McKay said. "We were aboard for the testing. Those are nasty."

"Any more questions?" Porter asked.

He looked around, but there were no questions for the moment.

"OK," ChaoPing said. "Thanks, Wayne. JuMing, do you want to talk about the fire extinguishers?"

Porter sat down and JuMing stood up.

"You all saw the fire extinguishers getting on the shuttle passenger container, I think. We've never had them before, because the passenger containers all have an automatic fire suppression system on board.

"There's not much to say about the fire extinguishers, actually. They are each gas canisters. Two are poison gas – a very quick-acting nerve agent that is fatal. Four are knockout gas. A good whiff from one of them, and you're out for about four hours. Two are antagonists for the knockout gas, to revive our own crew if they get hit with the knockout gas. Each canister contains enough agent for a small building.

"We disguised them as fire extinguishers because they're so innocuous as to be invisible."

JuMing sat down.

"Thanks, JuMing. All right, everyone. Now let's get down to cases."

ChaoPing sent them each a list, in VR, of the possible outcomes of their mission.

"So we might not be allowed to meet Chairman Wilson at all. We could just be jailed as soon as we get off the shuttle. Or we could be welcomed with open arms. Or it could be anything in between.

"We need to game these out. We know what our tools are. So where do we start?"

"What if we're jailed right off, such that the robots can't get us out?" Costa asked.

"My orders in that case are to call Chen Zufu. He said he will deal with it."

"He said that? But what can he do?"

"I don't know."

Eyebrows rose around the table, and ChaoPing shrugged.

"I was afraid to ask."

One of the initial questions they had to answer was who went on the landing party and who stayed with the ship.

The list they decided on was driven by both need and politics:

- Chen ChaoPing, the head of the mission and Chen family representative.

- Rob Milbank, the only one aboard with the experience, like

Chairman Wilson, of ruling a planet.

- Loukas Diakos, the official, accredited ambassador of the Arcadia government, giving the mission diplomatic status.

- Rolf Dornier, the person most knowledgeable about the capabilities of the robots and best able to direct them.

- Marie Legrand, one of *Endeavour*'s two doctors.

Everyone else would remain aboard *Endeavour* when the initial landing party went down to the surface.

The Chairman

Endeavour dropped out of hyperspace a light-month short of Earth to take its bearings. With the course for the remainder of the trip laid in, they were about a hundred seconds hyperspace cruise from their destination.

"We're all set," Moore said to ChaoPing in VR.

"We emerge one and a half times the hyperspace limit from Earth?" she asked.

"Yes. As specified."

"Good. I want to keep them in the dark about where the hyperspace limit is for us."

"We're ready when you are, ma'am. Should we proceed?"

"Well, we aren't going home without stopping in to say Hi, Justin. Whenever you're ready."

"Yes, ma'am."

Moore turned to the robot second officer.

"All right, Number Two. Proceed when ready."

"Aye, Captain. Entering hyperspace."

The forward viewscreen blanked out, then came back on less than two minutes later. Centered in the screen was a blue planet with a large satellite.

"Comm?"

"Channel open, Captain."

"*Endeavour* to Space Traffic Control."

"Space Traffic Control. Go ahead *Endeavour*."

"Hyperspace passenger ship *Endeavour* announcing arrival in Earth space from colony planet Arcadia. Requesting approach and orbital clearance."

EARTH

Unlike the colony planets when first discovered, Earth had a large space-based infrastructure, much of it put in place during the colony project. They should be on the Earth space controllers' radar. *Endeavour* was squawking her ID on the correct frequency, determined by the data capture probes.

"Roger that, *Endeavour*. We have you. Estimated time of arrival?"

"*Endeavour* here. We estimate arrival in seventy-two hours."

"Roger that, *Endeavour*. You are cleared for a direct approach to Earth from your position for the next forty-eight hours. You're pretty alone out where you're at. Contact at forty-eight hours for further instructions."

"Roger, Space Traffic Control. Direct approach for forty-eight hours, then contact for instructions. *Endeavour* out."

Moore gestured to the comm officer.

"Channel closed, Captain."

"Pretty cut and dried so far," McKay said.

"Yeah. Let's see what happens next."

Moore turned to the robot second officer.

"Standard approach, Number Two, but at one-half normal deceleration."

"Aye, Captain. One-half thrusters on deceleration. Flipping ship."

The forward and aft steering thrusters began firing, and the *Endeavour* slowly flipped end for end, to point its after aspect toward the planet.

"Main thrusters engaging at one-half normal deceleration, Captain."

They felt the small shift in apparent gravity from the main thrusters.

"All right, Number Two. Steady as she goes. You have the conn."

"Aye, Captain. I have the conn."

Moore and McKay went to the dining room for dinner.

It was just after breakfast on Chira Island, in Costa Rica, Central America administrative region, when Chairman Wilson's chief of staff, Antonio Braida, called on the big screen display in his office. It was not the time for their normal status call.

"Good morning, Mr. Chairman," Braida said.

"Morning, Tony. What have you got? Something come up?"

"Yes, sir. A ship contacted Space Traffic Control asking for approach and orbit clearance. They claim to be the hyperspace passenger ship *Endeavour* from the colony planet Arcadia."

"Really," Wilson said.

"Yes, sir. They show up on radar far off our normal space traffic routes, to the Moon and the asteroids. Sunward, rather than away from the Sun."

"Could they have come from somewhere else?"

"I don't think so, sir," Braida said. "There's nothing else out that way. Space Traffic Control would have seen them coming. They weren't there, and then they were."

"Interesting. So this hyperspace things works, and the colonies have it."

"At least one of them does, sir."

"Right," Wilson said. "This Arcadia. Is that one of the colonies established in 2245?"

"Yes, sir."

"But the ship. *Endeavour*, you said? That sounds more like a warship than it does a passenger ship."

"Actually, the *Endeavour* was Captain Cook's ship, sir," Braida said. "It was an exploration vessel."

"But it was originally a warship, right?"

"Yes, sir."

"All right, Tony," Wilson said. "Let's see if we can ask them for some briefing materials. Who's on board? What's their purpose here? All that sort of thing."

"Yes, sir."

"Whatever they send back, send a copy to Morten Andersen as well."

"The vice chairman? Of course, sir."

Wilson cut the connection and sat back to consider.

If the colonies had true hyperspace passenger ships – ships on which people could book travel between planets – they were probably ten, fifteen, maybe even twenty years ahead of Earth in their hyperspace activities. They already knew the answers to many things Earth was still puzzling out, like how to make the damn thing move once it was in hyperspace.

It also meant the colonies – at least one of them, anyway – were doing well enough to spend manpower and resources on such an effort. No small thing.

Whatever their goals for this mission, Wilson's goal was clear. Find out as much as he could from them. About the colonies. About the hyperspace ship. More information was always good.

Not through coercive measures, however. Wilson had always found being pleasant and friendly got him more information in the end.

For right now, though, he had to await developments.

It was about three hours after they contacted Space Traffic Control that Moore got a VR message from the robot second officer.

"We have a request from Space Traffic Control for more information, Captain."

"Go ahead and send the package, Number Two."

"Aye, Captain. Transmitting now."

When the package came in, Wilson studied it with interest. There was a lot of information there, but there were things that were obviously missing as well.

The package did mention that the twenty-four colony planets were all involved in this trade agreement of theirs. All appeared to be doing well by it, and all had higher average standards of living than Earth.

Well, of course. They were given a free restart, an opportunity to begin again without any of Earth's historic baggage.

The list of items most frequently traded among the planets was interesting as well. They were mostly what Wilson considered luxury goods. That is, they were not trading bulk staple items, like corn, wheat, soybeans, rice. So each planet must be making its own way pretty well as far as the basics.

One thing the package did not include was the colonies' locations. Wilson had had people looking for that information for months, since he had become World Authority Chairman last year, and they hadn't found anything.

The only reasonable conclusion was that they had been deliberately hidden by the colony project, and the colonies apparently – at least for the moment – weren't going to tell him, either.

Wilson met with Braida and Andersen that afternoon. It was a video meeting, of course, as neither was located on Chira Island. Braida was in Naples, Italy and Andersen was in Copenhagen, Denmark, both in the Central Europe administrative region.

"Thanks for joining us, Mort. I really wanted more insight here."

"Sure, Jon. Not a problem," Andersen said.

"Have you both had a chance to look at the package they sent us?"

Both Braida and Andersen nodded.

"Let's start with you, Mort. What do you think? What do we know at this point?"

"First thing, aside and apart from the package, I asked if anyone had gotten any imagery of this ship, or if they could get any imagery. It's out there, all right. From the images, using size references on the ship, it's about five hundred feet in diameter and two hundred and fifty feet thick. It's hollow on both ends, with containers and parasites in the hollows."

"Parasites?" Braida asked.

"They have several shuttles aboard, Tony. I don't think the ship itself would ever go down to a planet surface."

"Ah."

"Five hundred feet in diameter and only two hundred and fifty feet thick?" Wilson asked. "What's with that, Mort?"

"The ship is spinning about three and a half RPM. Call it sixty miles an hour at the outer circumference. That's what you need for one gravity at the outermost point."

"I see. That dimension is fixed by the need for internal gravity at a realistic rate of rotation, so the thickness would depend on the volume you wanted."

"That's right, Jon," Andersen said. "And the pictures of their freighters in the package look like they're the same diameter, but more like six hundred or six hundred and fifty feet long, again mostly hollow."

"Which is where they put the cargo containers. I saw that."

"They can carry thousands of containers on one of those

ships, Jon. One other interesting note. None of the freighters they show in those pictures have the same name. They all have the same Chinese characters below them – ji and xing – but the names are all different."

"Could they be faking that, Mort?" Wilson asked.

"We looked into it, analyzing the pictures, and we don't see any evidence of tampering."

"So they have a lot of them."

"Well, there are a dozen pictures or so, so they have at least a dozen of them, but they could have hundreds of them," Andersen said. "They mention that they are doing freight runs between all the colonies, in a hub-and-spoke model, and you need a certain number of ships to make that model work across twenty-four destinations."

"What about the passengers on this ship?" Wilson asked.

"They only give us bios on three of them. One is Loukas Diakos, who is the accredited ambassador to Earth of the Arcadia colony government. They claim diplomatic status."

"Which is nonsense if they're under World Authority sovereignty."

"Yes," Andersen said, "so it looks like their formulation of the relationship isn't the same as ours. The other two people we have bios on are Chen ChaoPing, who is listed as the representative of the Chen family, which owns Jixing Trading Company, and Rob Milbank, the former prime minister of Arcadia."

"Anything else interesting in those bios, Mort?"

"The ages are interesting. Chen ChaoPing is somewhere in her mid forties, which is in the range for an executive like that. But Loukas Diakos must be approaching eighty years old. And Rob Milbank must be closer to ninety."

"Which is awfully old to be gallivanting around the galaxy,"

Wilson said.

"Yes, Jon, unless one of two things is true. Either travel aboard one of these passenger ships is a pretty comfy trip and not a particular danger to someone that old, or they have some significant life extension technology, or both. Probably both."

"All right, Mort. Thanks. What about you, Tony?"

"Staff and I concentrated on the colonies, Mr. Chairman. The first thing we noticed is that they have apparently established relations and trade among all twenty-four of the colonies established by the colony project in 2245.

"I think what's significant about that is that they united all twenty-four of the colonies before sending a delegation here.

"Another thing that stands out to us is that all twenty-four of the colonies retain their own planetary government. Those governments vary a bit in their composition, but all are some form of democratic government with an elected legislature. There has apparently been no attempt to craft some sort of unifying political structure across colonies."

"Which makes them weak," Wilson said.

"Not necessarily, sir. The history of Europe has numerous cases where fractious independent countries joined in a tight alliance to fight a large invader. They often won, particularly in the modern era. That the colonies are all united in trade suggests such an arrangement may emerge here as well."

Wilson nodded. He was a student of history, and several such cases occurred to him.

"Another thing we saw was that the colonies all seem to be doing pretty well. We saw modern cities, but without slums. We wondered if that might simply be a case of judicious camera angle, but we don't think so. Some of the overview shots of their cities make it unlikely.

"Contributing to that conclusion is that the trade goods

listed between the colonies are all luxury and technology items, including medical technology. We don't see shipments of corn, wheat, soybeans, rice, and other staple crops between colonies. Coffee, tea, chocolate, cigars, wine, liquor – none of these are things one trades for if people are starving. The colonies must be independently capable of producing their own staple crops."

"Yes, I saw that as well, Tony, at least in the information they gave us. They're clearly holding information back as well, however."

"Yes, sir. In particular, some of the descriptions of the technology items are deliberately vague. What does 'personal communications technology' mean, for example. Better communicators, or more than that? Or 'cancer treatments'? Do they have a cure, or simply the next generation of some therapy we're familiar with?"

"What's your take on that, Tony?"

"I think they are probably hiding the level of their advancement, sir, and I would err on the side of thinking they are much further along in all these areas than they are letting on.

"There's two reasons I think that. First, if we take the hyperspace ship as a pacing item, they're clearly well ahead of us there. Is that an outlier, or does it apply elsewhere as well? Second, one of the technologies listed is 'anti-senescence research.' Then it turns out one of their emissaries on this mission is likely ninety years old. If we meet with them, Mr. Milbank's and Mr. Diakos's apparent ages should tell us a lot."

Wilson nodded, and Andersen stirred.

"About that last, Jon," Andersen asked, "will you meet with them?"

"Yes, of course. I can't see it will hurt anything, and I need more information. I'll likely have their delegation come here."

"You'll meet with them personally then?"

"Oh, yes," Wilson said. "This sort of video meeting is all well and good, but we have all known each other for years. To get the best information from them, and the best read of them, I really need to meet them personally."

"What about your personal security, Jon?"

"Oh, I don't worry about that at all, Mort. I think my security people here are up to the task."

Andersen nodded.

"Anything else?" Wilson asked.

Braida and Andersen both shook their heads.

"All right. Thank you both. If you think of anything else, let me know. I need the best analysis and insight you can give me on this."

"Sure, Jon."

"Yes, Mr. Chairman."

The input from Anderson and Braida was helpful, but Wilson felt hemmed in by the lack of information. He needed to know much more to make reasonable decisions.

Hopefully he would learn a lot more from the Arcadia visitors, particularly if they stayed on Earth for a while. Then again, once they were off their shuttle, they weren't going anywhere until he let them leave.

Oh, Wilson would be a wonderful host, but delaying their departure would not be a problem once he had their shuttle. Even better would be if he could get more information on that ship of theirs, but it would of course remain in orbit.

Wilson began to consider how he might get a hold of that ship anyway.

Earthfall

Justin Moore and Gavin McKay were on the bridge when they contacted Space Traffic Control again.

"*Endeavour* to Space Traffic Control," Moore said.

"Space Traffic Control, Go ahead, *Endeavour*."

"Now projecting twenty-four hours to Earth Orbit. Request clearance."

"Roger that, *Endeavour*. Our orbitals are pretty crowded, but we have an equatorial slot for you at five thousand two hundred miles. You are cleared on your current vector to that orbit. Steer clear of the geosynch orbit at twenty-two thousand two hundred miles."

"Roger, Space Traffic Control. Cleared on current vector to five thousand two hundred miles equatorial, steer clear of geosynch. *Endeavour* out."

Moore made a cutoff gesture to the comm officer.

"Channel closed, Captain."

"Five thousand miles?" McKay asked. "That's a ways out."

"Who knows?" Moore asked. "Maybe their orbitals are that crowded."

"Huh. Or maybe they want the shuttle that far away from the ship to foil any easy escape."

"Yeah, there's that, too. What are the chances, do you think?"

"Pardon me for being cynical," McKay said, "but I don't like it. Not in terms of what it may signal of their intentions."

"Yeah, but given our plan, it's actually better. *Endeavour* is closer to the hyperspace limit, with a lot less stuff to maneuver through to get out of here."

"Yeah, there's that. They think it's better for them, but it's actually better for us. I kinda like that. Sticks it to 'em."

"We'll see," Moore said.

"All right, everybody," ChaoPing said, standing. "Can I have your attention for a minute?"

Everybody looked up from their places at table. It was just after dinner in the dining room.

"Thank you. Well, we're moving into orbit over the next day. We expect we'll get invited down to meet with whoever they think is appropriate. We don't know yet whether it'll be Chairman Wilson or not.

"So the landing party should start wearing their communicators and using them. We'll try not to use VR except for private communications on the surface. That means we need to get back into practice.

"Those staying on *Endeavour* should stay alert. You should also stay in this corridor, on this side of the air-tight emergency doors. We might all have to get out of here in a hurry, and they might try to stop us.

"For those of us going down to the surface, *Endeavour* is going to be orbiting at five thousand miles, so it's going to take a while to get down, especially since we won't be using the full capabilities of the shuttle. To keep them in the dark about our capabilities, we can't use them all, and that means it will be several hours to the surface from orbit."

"ChaoPing, why do they have us orbiting at five thousand miles? Do we know?" Costa asked.

"We don't know, but we can make some guesses. One could be that they don't want the Earth population to be able to see us in orbit. Or they could really have as crowded of orbitals as they said. Or it could be something darker, like trying to get the shuttle far enough away from the ship to make it hard to rendezvous for departure before they can catch us.

"Since our escape plan doesn't include meeting up with the ship in-system, it actually helps us if *Endeavour* is farther out of their gravity well, so I don't have a problem with it.

"Any other questions?"

ChaoPing looked around.

"All right. Thanks, everybody."

"*Endeavour* to Space Traffic Control."

"Space Traffic Control. Go ahead, *Endeavour*."

"*Endeavour* in stable orbit at five-two-zero-zero miles."

"Roger that, *Endeavour*. We have you on radar. Stand by for incoming file."

"Go ahead, Space Traffic Control."

A file transfer followed, then Space Traffic Control signed off.

ChaoPing met with the landing party in the dining room.

"It's an invite," she said. "We are invited to bring down whomever we think would be best, to be the guests of the chairman at his private residence."

"Where is that exactly?" Rob Milbank asked.

"Chira Island, in Costa Rica. We have coordinates for the shuttle pad."

"What's the climate like there? What season is it currently?"

"It's winter in North America at the moment, but that hardly matters. Costa Rica is in the tropics, and has a climate much like Arcadia City."

"Ah. Excellent."

"Are we good on our plans?" ChaoPing asked. "Anybody

see any need for changes?"

"I think we're good, ChaoPing," Dornier said.

Milbank and Diakos nodded. ChaoPing looked to Marie Legrand and raised an eyebrow.

"Oh, I'm good, ChaoPing. I just feel useless on this landing party."

"Let's hope you stay that way, Marie. If you don't, it would be bad."

ChaoPing looked around at them all.

"All right. I'll accept the chairman's invitation, and we'll depart whenever the robots decide is the right time to hit the landing."

Endeavour's orbit was nearly five hours long at this altitude, so they had to wait several hours until they were in the right position to begin their descent. There were five humans in the landing party, plus twenty robots in the small passenger compartment.

The upper tier of containers was the small passenger container, two containers of four JATO bottles each, and the QE standalone radio. The lower tier of containers was a container of gifts for the chairman, the hyperspace field generator, a container of bomblets, and a container of additional oxidizing thruster fuel.

The shuttle released the latches on the bottom containers and separated from *Endeavour* with its engines aimed forward, toward *Endeavour*, and on minimum thrust. The shuttle backed out of the forward cargo space and drifted away from the big ship. *Endeavour*'s maneuvering thrusters immediately began firing at maximum declination in the spin direction, beginning to bring the onboard gravity back up.

As the shuttle backed away, the shuttle's engines rotated up, pushing the shuttle below *Endeavour*. When it was sufficiently clear of *Endeavour*, the shuttle's robot pilot rotated the shuttle engines to the rear and brought them up to one-third thrust. The shuttle began to slow down in its orbit, and fall toward the planet.

The shuttle pilot was only using the shuttle's engines at one-third to disguise the shuttle's capabilities. A normal four-engine shuttle could do half again the deceleration they were showing now. The modified eight-engine shuttle of the *Endeavour* could do three times as much.

The robot pilot kept the thrust up, continuing to push against the shuttle's orbital direction. He watched the vertical velocity grow as the shuttle came down. They had five thousand miles of altitude to lose, so he let the velocity climb to reduce the time to re-entry, which would begin at about the sixty-mile mark. Pushing back against the orbit kept his passengers pushed back in their seats.

After over an hour of burn against the orbital rotation, with the shuttle falling faster and faster, the robot pilot shut the engines down to low thrust and rotated them to first flip the shuttle over end-for-end and then roll it. The shuttle was now oriented nose forward in its orbital direction, with its lower side toward the ground.

The engines were rotated down and slightly forward, and the robot pilot brought the thrust up again. The goal now was to reduce the vertical velocity and continue to push against the orbit. He was well within the shuttle's flight envelope for landing at Chira Island.

Coming in from the high orbit and constrained by the desire to hold thrust to one-third what the shuttle was capable of, it was an eight-hour descent. The landing party tried to sleep on the way down, the occasional intervals of zero gravity notwithstanding.

It was six in the morning in *Endeavour*'s ship time when the shuttle landed on Chira Island. It was ten in the evening local time, and it was already dark.

"We're down, ma'am," Bob said to ChaoPing. "A vehicle is approaching. It looks like a small bus."

"Very well. Get the fuel transfer started."

"Already in progress, ma'am."

"And disguises in place."

"YES, MA'AM," Bob said in the mechanical voice.

As she got up from her seat, if she listened carefully, ChaoPing could hear the fuel-transfer pumps running. They were refueling the now-depleted tanks of the shuttle from the thruster-fuel container immediately, so the shuttle was ready to go whenever it became desirable or necessary.

They would also leave that container behind when they left.

As ChaoPing and the rest of the landing party, including five robots, came down the ladder the pilot had extended from the small passenger container, a young man in a business suit walked up to the bottom of ladder. A half-dozen security men also got off the bus and began to deploy in a perimeter around the shuttle.

"Hello, my name is Nathan Blaisdell. I am a senior aide to Antonio Braida, the chairman's chief of staff. Welcome to Earth."

"Thank you, Mr. Blaisdell. I am Chen ChaoPing. These are Rob Milbank, Loukas Diakos, Rolf Dornier, and Marie Legrand."

"Excellent. It's good to meet you all. The chairman hopes to meet with you in the morning. In the meantime, we have guest accommodations prepared for you."

"Thank you, Mr. Blaisdell. It was a long descent from our ship, and we could really use some sleep."

"We weren't prepared for the additional, er, guests, however," Blaisdell said, gesturing to the robots.

"Oh, these are our valets, Mr. Blaisdell. They need no additional accommodation."

"Ah. Very good, Ms. Chen. This way then."

The bus took them about a mile and a half to a small hotel that had apparently been part of the tourist business on Chira Island before the World Authority had purchased the island for the chairman's residence. It now served as a guest quarters. As they got off the bus, they could see that a beach ran across behind the hotel.

"Very nice," Milbank said, looking around.

"Thank you," Blaisdell said. "It is our goal that you be very comfortable here."

He led them into the hotel, the robots following behind carrying their luggage. The robots were in full disguise, walking their mechanical walk.

A hotel employee came up.

"Your rooms are all ready," he said, "and the kitchen is open twenty-four hours if you would like to order dinner."

"I believe the chairman hopes to meet with you after breakfast," Blaisdell said.

"Breakfast will be available here in the morning as well," the hotel staffer said. "I might suggest the veranda for breakfast."

"Sounds lovely," ChaoPing said.

"Let's plan on ten o'clock tomorrow for your first meeting with the chairman, Ms. Chen. In the meantime, I wish you all a good evening."

130

"Thank you, Mr. Blaisdell."

Blaisdell nodded to the others, then left, and the hotel staffer showed them to their rooms.

Once in his room, Loukas Diakos nodded to Bob. Bob clunkily walked around the room, pretending to stare at the pictures on the wall one at a time.

When he had finished his circumambulation of the room, Bob caught Diakos's eye and nodded once.

Diakos sent a short message in VR.

"Careful, everyone. The rooms are bugged."

ChaoPing and Dan, her valet robot, came down to the veranda on the back of the hotel about half past seven. She was wearing a lavalava and flip-flops, quintessential Arcadia wear.

ChaoPing noticed a lavalava tossed over the railing of the veranda by the steps down to the beach, flip-flops lying nearby. She looked out over the beach and saw Milbank standing in waist-deep water smoking a cigar. He turned around to look at the hotel and she waved. He waved back, and started out of the water for the hotel.

Milbank walked up to the steps and climbed them onto the veranda, then put on his lavalava and flip-flops before joining her at a table set for five.

"Nothing like a dip before breakfast," he said.

"How's the water?" ChaoPing asked.

"Perfect. Warm like Arcadia and no surf."

ChaoPing nodded. The island was in a shallow, protected bay, and the beach was around the corner from the bay exit to the ocean, so that only made sense.

"You worried about upsetting the locals?" she asked.

"You mean, with Arcadia standards of swim dress? No.

What are they gonna do? Arrest me?"

In VR he sent her a message, "After all, I'm already in custody."

"The guards at the shuttle?"

"Of course. Why are they there? Not to protect the shuttle. They're there to prevent us leaving."

"They don't know we already have a short platoon inside their perimeter."

Milbank nodded. He took a deep draw on his cigar.

"Life is good," he said aloud.

Diakos, Dornier, and Legrand walked out onto the veranda from the hotel.

"Ah, there you are," Diakos said. "Ready for breakfast?"

"Indeed," Milbank said.

A waiter brought them a menu, and it had breakfast basics peppered with items from around the world.

"Our host obviously tries to make his guests feel at home," Diakos said.

"Yes," Milbank said. "At the same time, I would stick to the basics or the local cuisine. Local kitchen staff may not be up to par on items from the other side of the world. I would not rely on the Chinese, for instance. We're spoiled in that regard."

ChaoPing agreed, and selected the Denver omelet with a side of toast, orange juice and coffee. The others made selections from breakfast basics – eggs, bacon, sausage, and such – except for Milbank, who copied her omelet order.

When the food came, it was very good, prepared perfectly.

"I must admit, the chairman has excellent staff for his guest quarters," Diakos said.

"I suspect he doesn't entertain much here," Milbank said. "The cook this morning is probably someone detached from his own kitchen."

EARTH

They talked about trivia during breakfast, though there was a tension about the upcoming meeting. They stayed off the VR channels, both to keep their capabilities hidden and because there was nothing more to say.

At a quarter to ten, the shuttle bus showed up. The five of them got aboard and the bus driver set off for the meeting.

The robots didn't like being left behind, but ChaoPing told Dan in VR that they would stay in touch in VR. If they needed help, they would let them know and they could come running.

"Very well, ma'am," the robot transmitted back, "but we don't like it. Do take care."

The actual residence of the chairman was only a mile or so away. It couldn't be much further given the size of Chira Island, which was perhaps five miles long and two and a half miles wide. It was on the southeast corner of the island, on a headland that gave breathtaking views out over the water. An elevator car on tracks down the cliffside gave access to a private beach.

The building itself was low and narrow, stretched along the ridge. Bends and ells in the building formed private niches and balconies along the cliffside. There were multiple porticos along the front wall.

"Nice digs," Dornier said as the bus pulled up to one of the front porticos.

"It's good to be the chairman," Diakos said.

The bus driver remained silent, but opened the doors when they were stopped. Blaisdell was waiting under the portico and greeted them as they got off the bus.

"Good morning. I hope you all had a good night. Please come this way."

Meetings

It was not a long walk to the meeting room on the back of the house, narrow as the house was. The chairman, dressed in an off-white summer-weight suit, was looking out the picture windows down the Colorado Gulf to the passage into the Gulf of Nicoya, some fifteen miles distant. The Gulf of Nicoya opened into the Pacific Ocean perhaps fifty miles to the southeast of Chira Island, invisible over the horizon.

Wilson turned as they entered. He was tall, tanned, and once muscular, with short hair and a ready, welcoming smile.

"Ah, my guests. Come in, come in," Wilson said.

Wilson identified them all quickly from their bios. That had to be Milbank, who looked to be about seventy years old, dressed in tropical shirt and khaki trousers. Diakos, the ambassador, was dressed, like Wilson, in a tropical suit. He looked to be maybe sixty. Dornier, the youngest of the men and also in tropical shirt and khakis, looked to be in his early thirties.

There was no difficulty identifying the women, either. Surely that was Chen ChaoPing, all business in a suit that would have been at home in New York City or London. She was in her mid thirties, or appeared to be. The other, then, would be Marie Legrand, the doctor, in a summer-weight jacket and trousers that would have been at home in any hospital in the tropics.

Wilson went straight to the head of mission and shook her hand.

"Madam Chen, welcome to Earth."

"Thank you, Mr. Chairman."

"Mr. Ambassador, welcome."

"Thank you, Mr. Chairman."

"It's good to meet you, Mr. Prime Minister."

"And you, Mr. Chairman."

"I hope we have no need of your services, Dr. Legrand."

"I as well, Mr. Chairman."

"And Mr. Dornier. Welcome to my home."

"Thank you, Mr. Chairman."

"Please, be seated, everyone."

Wilson waved to a conversation circle of armchairs and sofas, selecting one armchair for himself. Milbank and Diakos sat on a sofa, as did Dornier and Legrand. ChaoPing sat on an armchair.

"How remarkable to have you all here," Wilson said. "Of course, we've all known space travel was possible. The World Authority solved that problem once, then lost the solution in the tragic loss of the colony transporter with all aboard, including the scientists who invented the technology. We have to this point been unable to replicate their achievement.

"And now here you are. How exciting that is, that someone has again unlocked the secret."

Diakos nodded.

"It is a different secret, however, Mr. Chairman," he said. "We do not have the means to simply pop someone from here to there as the colony transporter did. It has taken us some weeks to cross several thousand light-years to meet with you."

"So I understand, Mr. Ambassador. You identified your ship as a hyperspace ship in your communications with Space Traffic Control, and you appeared at several days' travel from the planet, not simply popped into existence here. I presumed, therefore, a different mechanism. A more rigorous one."

"Indeed, Mr. Chairman. It was not instantaneous transport, but more of a voyage."

"With all the hardships that represents, with which I am personally familiar. Which brings us to the question of why you have endured the rigors of such a trip to come here. What is your mission, Mr. Ambassador?"

"We wish to invite the Earth to join a free trade agreement we have implemented among the twenty-four colony planets, Mr. Chairman."

"I see. And do you have a copy of this agreement for me, Mr. Ambassador? It was not included in the package you sent me."

"Of course, Mr. Chairman. Together with my own credentials."

Diakos pulled the formal document naming him Arcadia's ambassador to Earth out of his inside jacket pocket, as well as a copy of the free trade agreement. He handed them across to Wilson. Wilson glanced at the ambassadorial credentials, then read the free trade agreement carefully.

"A remarkable document, Mr. Ambassador. No protected markets, no preferences, no limits."

"That's correct, Mr. Chairman."

"And this has been in place how long?"

"Among its oldest signers, for twenty years, Mr. Chairman. It's newest signers have been on board for seven years now."

"And it is working as it stands, Mr. Ambassador?"

"Yes, Mr. Chairman. Oh, there have been some teething issues. Some planets who imposed protections of one sort or another, and dropped them when they found that reciprocal sanctions by other planets permitted under the agreement made them worse off. But the agreement has proven itself over the years."

"Remarkable, Mr. Ambassador."

"I can claim no credit for the document, Mr. Chairman. Prime Minister Milbank and Earthsea Planetary Director Valerie Laurent wrote the document at the very beginning, some twenty years ago."

Wilson raised an eyebrow to Milbank.

"How did this document come about, Mr. Prime Minister?"

"Arcadia and Earthsea each had items the other wanted, that had no local equivalents, Mr. Chairman. Trading our excess in these items to each other made us both better off. As we contacted more colony planets, we discovered they each were in a similar position. The colonies had each excelled in some area or another, and each had products to trade that were unmatched anywhere else."

"Yes, I saw some of these products in the package you sent, Mr. Prime Minister. Cigars, liquors, chocolate, wine. Also technology expertise in various areas. Medical items. A varied list, to be sure."

"Yes, Mr. Chairman. It is into this agreement, which has worked so well among us, that we would invite Earth. We have brought a container of goods from various planets as a gift to you, so that you can sample some of these trade items for yourself."

"Thank you, Mr. Prime Minister. The gift is appreciated. I am not sure this agreement of yours is appropriate for Earth, however."

"How so, Mr. Chairman, if I might ask."

"Of course, Mr. Prime Minister. This agreement is structured as an agreement between and among equals. That is clearly inappropriate in the Earth's case."

Milbank raised an eyebrow to Wilson, and Wilson continued.

"You said it yourself, Mr. Prime Minister. 'Colony' planets.

The twenty-four signees to this agreement now are colonies of Earth. They are subordinate to Earth. To the World Authority, for that matter. The World Authority financed the colonies from the start, at tremendous cost. The World Authority has not abrogated its sovereignty over them."

"Ah, but it has, Mr. Chairman. At the very start. The contracts the colonists signed with the World Authority before setting out in 2245 were explicit on this very point."

"Our interpretations of that agreement are clearly at odds, Mr. Prime Minister. That is a legal matter, for the courts to decide."

"Your courts or our courts, Mr. Chairman? I would aver that there is no court of competent jurisdiction to decide the issue. In fact, the wherewithal to decide the issue is here, in this room, and here only."

"The World Authority courts are, of course, the correct venue, Mr. Prime Minister."

"Only if one starts from the assumption that the World Authority has jurisdiction, Mr. Chairman, which is making the decision before considering the issue."

Wilson considered. Milbank was clearly no lightweight, and was not intimidated by the setting or Wilson's status. It was clear he could debate this issue endlessly. At the same time, Wilson's own plans needed some time to come to fruition. It was therefore time to lighten up the conversation, to turn away from the essential issue for the moment.

ChaoPing was watching Wilson intently. She saw his mental shift of gears, and anticipated what would come next. He would change the subject. He would not sway in his position, but he would go back to information gathering, which had all been one-sided, or stalling. Wilson had given them no information whatsoever, other than his opening position, but had instead concentrated on eliciting from them whatever he could learn. If he switched to stalling instead, one had to wonder what he was planning.

"This is all a matter for further discussion, obviously," Wilson said. "In the meantime, you are my guests, and you should feel free to explore the island. Mr. Blaisdell can assist you with anything you require. For the moment, I must get back to my other duties, but I hope to speak with you again tomorrow."

"Of course, Mr. Chairman," Diakos said.

Wilson stood, as did the others. Blaisdell returned, and the chairman said goodbye to each in turn, shaking their hands. As the visitors followed Blaisdell out, Milbank held back.

"A word, if you would, Mr. Chairman," Milbank said once he and Wilson were alone.

"Of course, Mr. Prime Minister."

"If you were to attempt to assert World Authority sovereignty over the colonies, Mr. Chairman, it would quickly escalate to war. I have one piece of advice in that regard."

Wilson motioned him to continue.

"Do not underestimate the Chen."

Milbank nodded to him and turned to follow the others out.

Blaisdell took them out to the shuttle bus, which took them back to the hotel. They had a superb lunch on the veranda. They did not discuss the meeting with Wilson.

That afternoon, they all went out on the beach. ChaoPing and Legrand sunned themselves, laying out on their lavalavas on the sand. Milbank and Diakos stood waist deep out in the warm water, smoking cigars. Dornier swam out to an islet and back, doing laps.

This was camouflage. They were all logged into a VR

meeting, in which their avatars sat around a table.

"I don't trust him," ChaoPing said. "He's stalling. Which makes me wonder what he's up to."

"What do you think he's planning?" Diakos asked.

"Some way of getting hold of the ship and the shuttle," ChaoPing said. "In his mind, he already has us."

Milbank's avatar nodded.

"I think you're right. There's clearly no day-to-day business that should keep him from meeting with us further until tomorrow. He's stretching this out."

"Which means he's up to something," ChaoPing said. "I'm going to warn the ship to keep their eyes open up there."

"Couldn't he have already seized the shuttle?" Legrand asked.

"Not without exposing his hand," Dornier said. "Seizing the shuttle would scare away the bigger prize. He has the shuttle under guard, so there's no need to do anything more there for the moment."

"Is there no chance for negotiation then?" Diakos asked.

"I don't think so," Milbank said. "The difference is too fundamental. His position as stated need not even concede our standing to negotiate. We are under his authority. It could not be a negotiation between equals in his mind, and he said as much."

ChaoPing's avatar nodded.

"I was watching him closely throughout the meeting. His goal was clear. To learn as much as he could from us while giving us no information in return. But he was deadly earnest when discussing his authority over the colonies. That is a position he will not abandon without much more pressure than we can bring to bear with this visit."

"A shame, really," Diakos said. "There is such potential in

the relationship."

"Yes, but it's a relationship he doesn't want. At least not yet," ChaoPing said.

Her avatar turned to Rolf's avatar. He was swimming yet another lap out in the gulf.

"Rolf, what's our status?"

"We're good to go anytime you give the word, ChaoPing."

"All right. I'll get *Endeavour* on alert. Have them looking for some move up there. In the meantime, be ready to depart on a moment's notice."

Everybody nodded around the table, and ChaoPing dropped the VR meeting.

She rolled over on her lavalava on the beach and sighed.

Why couldn't it be easy?

Justin Moore was in bed when he got the VR call from ChaoPing.

"Yes, ma'am. Go ahead."

"Sorry about the hour, Justin, but I need you guys to be super vigilant up there. The chairman is stalling in our negotiations. I think it's a front, and he's going to try for the ship."

"Roger that, ma'am."

"So keep everybody on alert up there. Keep the human crew in the air-tight corridor and its rooms. And be ready to get the hell out of there."

"Yes, ma'am. And you guys?"

"We're ready to go as soon as it's clear what he's up to."

"All right, ma'am. You take care."

"You, too, Justin. We'll see you in Alpha Centauri if it goes as I expect."

World Authority Chairman Wilson was in a meeting that afternoon as well. Vice Chairman Morten Andersen and chief of staff Antonio Braida joined Wilson for a call on the big display in his office.

"So how did the meeting go?" Andersen asked. "Did we learn anything?"

"Some," Wilson said. "Apparently Arcadia is thousands of light-years away, and it took them weeks to get here. And they gave me a copy of this free trade agreement of theirs."

"I saw that," Andersen said. "Thanks for sending it on. It's remarkably short."

"Yes, and they say it's been working for twenty years. They want Earth to sign on as well, which is clearly ludicrous."

Andersen nodded.

"Yes," he said. "That would ignore Earth's sovereignty over its own colonies."

"Exactly. I made that point to them myself."

"And got some pushback, I expect."

"Oh, yes. Not from Diakos. He was all ambassador. Not a power player. Milbank, though, is. Very skilled. And he wasn't at all intimidated by me."

"An act, you think?" Braida asked.

"Not at all," Wilson said. "And he hung back when everybody else left. He told me if I tried to assert World Authority sovereignty over the colonies, there would be war. And then he told me not to underestimate the Chen."

"The Chen?" Andersen asked. "This Chen ChaoPing woman? Did she say anything?"

"No. Nothing. Nothing at all."

"A lightweight, do you think?" Andersen asked.

"No. The opposite, I think. She's the real power player."

"Really. And she's the Chen?"

"I may be able to shed some light on that, sir," Braida said.

Wilson waved him to go ahead.

"It's in the materials they sent us. The Chen-Jasic family owns Jixing Trading, the interstellar shipping firm that is the backbone of the trade agreement. The Chen are what they call the couple that heads that family. I got the impression they were very rich and powerful. That couple is who's calling the shots. Chen ChaoPing is their daughter."

"OK, that explains a lot," Wilson said. "Daughter of the big shots. Sent on this mission as the real leader. Sat back and let her minions spar with me while she watched. She's the one with the power here."

"Really?" Andersen said.

"Yes, really," Wilson said.

"Huh. So what now?" Anderson asked.

"I have a plan to take that ship. Then we can reverse engineer whatever they're doing. Another day or so to get into position."

"And in the meantime?"

"I put off the next meeting until tomorrow."

"Ah."

"After that, it won't matter."

Making A Run For It

It was well into the next day ship's time – in the deeps of the night on Chira Island – that anything of note happened. It was the robot second officer who brought it to Moore's attention.

"Captain, I think you should take a look at this."

"What's that, Number Two?"

"Well, at first we didn't think anything of it, Captain, but it's starting to take on a certain structure."

The forward viewscreen turned into a three-dimensional display, with the *Endeavour* in the middle.

"This is our orbital position, Captain. When we first made orbit. The other objects in orbit near us are shown."

"Yes, I see."

"This is our orbital position now, Captain. New objects near us in orbit are highlighted."

The other objects from before were still present, but half a dozen new objects were highlighted.

"They're trying to hem us in," McKay said.

"Are there more on the way, Number Two? Other things moving toward us?"

"Yes, Captain. There are another half dozen objects moving closer slowly. They all look to be shuttles."

"Is our polar escape still available, Number Two?"

"Yes, Captain. They appear to be concentrating on our orbit, both ahead of and behind us. They are keeping their distance, and appear to be spacing themselves based on our earlier-displayed acceleration."

"They want to block a standard departure forward, and also

block the shuttle coming up to meet us from behind," Moore said.

"And they're trying to be subtle about it, but they're using our earlier acceleration to decide where to position themselves," McKay said.

"Which means they will not be in position to intercept us if we use our actual capabilities," Moore said.

"That's currently true, Captain," the robot second officer said, "but the distances are slowly falling."

Moore called ChaoPing in VR.

"Yes," her avatar said.

"I'm sorry about the hour, ma'am, but I think it's show time. They're trying to hem us in up here, and we don't have long to make a clean exit."

"All right, Justin. We'll start things going down here, then I'll give you the go once the alarm is up."

"Thank you, ma'am."

Moore cut the connection.

"Keep an eye on things, Number Two. We're getting out of here soon. Acceleration warnings to everybody right now."

"Aye, Captain."

ChaoPing sent an emergency wake-up call to the entire landing party, including the robots.

"They're trying for *Endeavour*. We're getting out right now. Rolf, implement the plan."

"Yes, ma'am," Dornier replied.

The fifteen robots remaining in the rear seats of the shuttle, who had been sitting heads down as if powered off, sat up suddenly. They ripped the seat backs in front of them open and withdrew their weapons. Six of them handed their weapons off to their fellows, and exited the small passenger container, climbing down the ladder.

The guard nearest the ladder heard them and turned around. He accosted them.

"What are you up to?"

"ROUTINE INSPECTION, SIR. IT'S BEEN OVER TWENTY-FOUR HOURS. WE NEED TO ENSURE THE INTEGRITY OF THE EXTRA FUEL TANKS."

"All right, then. Get about it."

"THANK YOU, SIR."

The six robots clunkily walked around the shuttle, ostensibly inspecting the lower-tier containers, but actually distributing themselves behind the guards. When all the guards were once again facing outward, the six rushed up behind them and punched them in the back of the head. All six went down.

The six robots picked them up and carried them to a nearby building. The other nine robots exited the small passenger container. Three carried fire extinguishers as well as their firearms. Six took up the previous guards' positions – from a distance it would look like the guards were still on post.

The other three robots joined the prior six robots in the building where they had taken the unconscious guards. They dosed the guards with knockout gas from one of the fire extinguishers to ensure they stayed out. They also handed out firearms and ammo bags to the first six.

The first six robots now headed out at a dead run to the hotel. It was just a mile or so away, on a paved road, and they were there in three minutes.

The other three robots ran to the guards barracks, located between the airport/shuttleport and the chairman's residence, half a mile in the other direction. When they got there, they climbed to the roof of the single story buildings. They opened the fire extinguishers and placed them under the buildings' ventilation inputs, then jumped down and headed back to the shuttleport.

They stopped at the edge of vegetation and the shuttleport tarmac, to form a defensive line against any guards who hadn't been gassed.

"Our escort is almost here, ma'am. Time to saddle up," Dan said.

"All right, Dan. Let's go."

The robot swept her up into its four arms and headed for the front door of the hotel. When they got to the lobby, the other four landing party members were already there, also cradled in the arms of their 'personal valet' robots.

"Now," Bob said. "Hang on, everybody."

The five robots ran out the front door of the hotel, leapt to the ground without use of the three steps up to the porch and took off down the road at a dead run of twenty miles an hour. ChaoPing saw the escort robots, armed with the suppressor version of those big hand cannons of theirs, running alongside them.

It was three minutes to the shuttle. Halfway there, ChaoPing heard an alarm sound somewhere off to the southeast, toward the barracks and the chairman's residence.

"Justin, the alarm's up. Get out of there," she VRed to Moore.

"We're gone, ma'am."

"Helm, full power to main thrusters. Hard turn to port, one hundred twenty degrees."

"Aye, Captain. Thrusters firing. Hard turn to port."

Its fore and aft steering thrusters firing, the spinning

Endeavour precession turned across its west-to-east orbit and beyond, pointing north and a bit back against its orbital velocity.

"When your turn is complete, fire JATO bottles."

"Aye, Captain."

"Shuttles nearby are turning toward us, Captain."

"Turn complete. Firing JATO bottles."

Endeavour went to three gravities of acceleration, pushing against her orbital velocity and piling on the velocity parallel to the Earth's surface, heading north.

"Shuttles are under acceleration now, Captain. They're behind us, but making four gees. They'll cut our angle."

"Stand by weapons launch."

"Standing by, sir."

"Number Two, make the call on the weapons launch and detonation."

"Aye, Captain. Tracking trajectories."

Either forward or behind *Endeavour* in her orbit, the World Authority shuttles had to make their own turns for the unexpected direction. They also had to angle toward *Endeavour* as the big ship bolted at ninety degrees to her prior orbit. Being small, they had the acceleration advantage, but they had some catching up to do.

They broke out onto the shuttleport tarmac, and ChaoPing could see the shuttle looming ahead, when shots rang out from a nearby hangar building on their right. Shots pinged off the robots.

"Ow!" ChaoPing said as she took a hit in the thigh.

She heard someone else grunt as well.

The responding fire from their escort, as well as from the robots around the shuttle, was immediate, and she heard

148

screams from the building. They made the shuttle, and the robots carrying them virtually ran up the ladder, followed by their escort and finally the guards.

The robot pilot already had the engines running. He cut loose the latches on the two outboard containers on the lower tier while the engines were spinning up. Then the over-powered shuttle, under the full thrust of her eight engines, leapt into the sky. The robot pilot brought her nose up and aimed for the stars.

"Medical check," Legrand said.

They had practiced this in their scenario planning.

"Dornier fine."

"Diakos fine."

"Chen. Hit in the thigh. Two wounds. It went through. Bleeding heavily."

There was no answer from Rob Milbank.

It was impossible for any human to move around in the shuttle under acceleration. Between the planet's gravity and the shuttle's vertical acceleration, there was two gravities in the cabin right now, and it was oriented toward the rear.

A robot clung to the seat frames like a ladder, making its way down the aisle as the shuttle accelerated upwards. Reaching ChaoPing, it handed her two trauma patches, one at a time. She placed the first four-inch by four-inch pad on the exit would and activated it. It sealed and released nanites into the area. He handed her the second, and she placed and activated it as well.

Another robot made its way to the unconscious Milbank. It patched its vision into Legrand's VR, then, under her instruction, placed a trauma patch on his entry wound.

Then the shuttle pilot hit the JATO bottles, and ChaoPing blacked out.

The air defense batteries on Chira Island and the mainland around it were unaffected by the robots' gassing of the guard barracks, and their orders were clear in case of an alarm. No unauthorized flights over Chira Island, in, out, or otherwise.

Surface-to-air missiles took off after the fleeing shuttle.

The shuttle's robot pilot saw twelve incoming SAMs, and tracked them closely as they screamed after the shuttle. At the opportune moment, he rolled forty bomblets and let them scatter themselves.

When the robot pilot detonated the bomblets by remote control, the forty explosions distributed four million platinum tetrahedrons in the shuttle's wake.

The SAMs ran into that cloud of sharp metal debris and shredded. Most of them exploded, and their shards fell back to Earth.

Awakened by the alarms, Chairman Wilson walked over to his bedroom windows and looked out. He couldn't see anything to the southeast, but he could hear screaming jet engines in the distance. He walked out onto the patio and turned toward the northwest, looking over the roof of his residence, just in time to see the shuttle rising up into the sky, lifting its nose toward orbit.

There was a sudden glare of rocket flames from under the shuttle and it streaked up into the air. There were also a dozen streaks of surface-to-air missiles rising after the shuttle. They would easily catch it.

But as the SAMs closed with the shuttle there were dozens of explosions behind it. Wilson could see a cloud of silver particles in the reflected light from the shuttle's rockets. The SAMs hit that cloud and came apart, many of them exploding, and flaming debris started falling.

Wilson ran back into his bedroom and watched as debris rained down outside his window, heard it impacting on the roof.

What the hell was that?

Endeavour's first set of JATO bottles burned out and they ignited another, continuing to run from the pursuing shuttles.

"We have six in pursuit, Captain. They've made up their deficit and are beginning to gain on us."

"Weapons free. On your order, Number Two.

"Aye, Captain."

They waited and watched the traces in the schematic displayed on the forward viewscreen. Several minutes went by.

"Container one release now."

There was a slight shudder that passed through *Endeavour* as she ejected the weapons container while under spin.

"Container two release now." .

Again the shudder. Two containers now shot back away from *Endeavour* on their own JATO bottles. They diverged east and west as the ship continued to flee toward open space, in the direction pointed by the Earth's north pole.

Moore watched on the schematic as the weapons headed toward the pursuing shuttles. The later they detonated, the denser the cloud when the shuttles hit them. Wait too long, though, and the cloud wouldn't be big enough to envelop all six shuttles, three coming up from the east and behind, three from the west and behind.

"Detonation."

The schematic showed the size of the dispersal cloud as the two weapons containers each shot out two hundred million platinum tetrahedrons in the path of the pursuing shuttles.

Unable to avoid them at their velocity, the shuttles slammed into the expanding clouds of sharp metal debris and disintegrated.

"Targets destroyed, Captain."

ChaoPing woke to an emergency VR call from Legrand. She had only been out for a few seconds.

"Hi, Marie. I'm here."

"ChaoPing, Rob is in bad shape."

"How bad?"

"He took a bullet in the chest."

"Can you help him?" ChaoPing asked, already knowing the answer.

"Not here. Oh, with a full surgical suite in one gravity, it would be no problem, but here? ChaoPing, we don't have a full surgical suite on *Endeavour*, and in any case, we're three hours from meeting up with the ship in Alpha Centauri."

There was a long pause.

"I'm sorry, ChaoPing, but we're going to lose him."

ChaoPing pounded her hand on the seat arm, or tried to in the three gravities of acceleration. It was unfair! Rob Milbank would die from a gunshot wound they could fix anywhere else but here. All because of that asshole Wilson.

They had all known it was a dangerous mission, but it just wasn't fair.

Not knowing what else to do, ChaoPing called her parents.

Emergency

"We must act," JieMin said.

"For one man, JieMin?" ChaoLi asked.

"Yes, for one man."

He looked at her.

"Would you have me live without honor?"

"Never."

When JieMin presented his plan to her, Janice Quant had the same question.

"You would risk exposure for one man, JieMin?"

"Yes, Janice. We must. Else if we are later exposed, your ruse will no longer work. Because I would risk exposure for one man, and everyone knows it. Therefore it could not be me who passed up the chance to save him. Now it is you who are exposed."

Quant sat at her desk, her stylus rapping in staccato rhythm.

"Very well."

She cut the connection.

"Kim, attend me," ChaoLi said through the open tearoom doorway.

A robot came around the corner.

"Yes, ma'am."

ChaoLi stood up, gathering her robe about her, and put on her sandals.

She stood waiting.

One thing Janice Quant had been working on during the

past century was a way to disguise her transporters. Not to make them look like something else, but to make them invisible, or nearly so.

Quant had perfected a non-reflecting coating. A perfect non-reflecting coating. It was a perfect black, and completely radar absorbent. Against the blackness of space, it was the next thing to invisible. All of her transporters were now coated with this material.

She had also learned how to suppress the blue flare, and to increase the cycle time of her transporters. They didn't so much turn off and restart between cycles, they just stayed on at a reduced level.

She used these advances now to perform the impossible.

On the shuttle, now on its second set of JATO bottles and hurtling northward to the hyperspace limit, Rob Milbank disappeared. Only Milbank's clothes were left behind.

On the *Endeavour*, Julia Whitcomb disappeared, clothes and all.

In JieMin's tearoom, standing next to him, ChaoLi and her personal robot disappeared.

In an aisle of the Chen Emergency Services Center in the Arcadia City Hospital downtown, Rob Milbank appeared, nude, on a hospital gurney. Julia Whitcomb appeared in a chair along the aisle. And Chen ChaoLi and a robot appeared alongside the gurney.

"Kim, bring the gurney," ChaoLi said.

"Yes, ma'am."

ChaoLi strode down the aisle to triage, the robot following behind, pushing the gurney. Julia Whitcomb tried to figure out what was going on, but seeing Rob on the gurney headed down the aisle, she followed in a daze.

ChaoLi, in her silk robe with dragons rampant, walked up to the triage desk.

"Emergency surgery. Gunshot wound. Right now."

"Who are you?"

"I am Chen Zumu. *NOW MOVE!*"

Nobody needed to tell the head triage nurse in the Chen Emergency Services Center who Chen Zumu was.

"Code Red, Surgery Two. Code Red, Surgery Two."

ChaoLi nodded to the robot, who wheeled the gurney with the unconscious Milbank through the door and down the aisle to the surgery rooms.

Julia Whitcomb made to follow, but ChaoLi held her back.

"No, Julia. Let them do their jobs."

"But, but how? Where are we? This is Arcadia, isn't it?"

"Yes. But you must never speak a word of this to anyone. It will ultimately leak out, but it will be as hearsay. A myth. A legend."

"But how?"

"Chen Zufu is a remarkable person."

Whitcomb nodded numbly.

"Will Rob be OK, ChaoLi?"

"We think so, Julia. Now is the difficult part."

Whitcomb raised an eyebrow.

"Waiting," ChaoLi said.

"Where did Rob go?" Legrand asked ChaoPing in VR.

They were still under three gravities' acceleration to the hyperspace limit, but Legrand had been keeping an eye on Milbank through the robot's vision.

"To a full surgical suite," ChaoPing messaged back.

"But how?"

"Shhh."

After receiving a message from her father, ChaoPing also sent a message to Moore, letting him know Whitcomb was no longer on the ship.

To his question about how, she gave the same answer she had given Legrand.

"Shhh."

It was four hours before the doctor came out of surgery to talk to them. He didn't recognize either of them, and spoke to them both.

"He's going to be OK. For a normal round in that location, he would have died. It must have been a mostly spent round, like a ricochet, or maybe it passed through something else first. It'll be a few weeks of recovery, but he'll be alright."

"Excellent. Thank you, doctor," ChaoLi said.

"One thing for the paperwork, ma'am. For a gunshot wound, I need to file a report with the Arcadia City police. Where, when, who – all of that."

"Do you have that report with you, doctor?"

"Yes, ma'am."

"Let me have it."

The surgeon put the proper form on the top of his clipboard and handed it to her.

On the top of the form, under 'Patient Name', she wrote, 'John Doe.' Underneath that, she drew a line diagonally across the report, and wrote 'Waived' in big letters along the line.

"Ma'am," the doctor began.

ChaoLi held up one finger and he stopped. She pulled a small stamp and sealed inkpad out of the pocket of her robe. She unscrewed the top of the pad, then inked the stamp on it. Under 'Signature' at the bottom, she stamped a single Chinese character, in red. Chen.

陈

ChaoLi handed the clipboard back to the doctor. He took one look at that stamp and his eyes widened. Only Chen Zufu or Chen Zumu would dare sign any document with the Chen family name only. He bowed to ChaoLi.

"Yes, Chen Zumu. That will do nicely. Thank you."

"No problem, doctor. Thank you so much."

At ChaoLi's instruction, Milbank was carried on the hospital's records as John Doe. She also made arrangements for 'Jane Doe' to stay on a rollaway bed in his private room.

"Thank you so much, ChaoLi," said Whitcomb, finally on the verge of tears after having been so strong. "I don't know what to say."

ChaoLi gave her a hug.

"You just did," ChaoLi said and smiled. "Now remember. Just between us."

"Yes, of course."

"And now I must be going."

"Thank you, ChaoLi. And thank JieMin for me."

ChaoLi and Kim left the hospital by the front door, where a family car was waiting for her.

"That was well done," ChaoLi said to JieMin when she got back to his tearoom five hours after she had left.

"It was the only honorable course."

In the Alpha Centauri system, two ships dropped out of hyperspace within minutes of each other. They were light-minutes apart, but found each other easily. The problem with that is that it was too far to space in a reasonable time under thrusters, and too close to use hyperspace toward each other.

Instead, they used hyperspace to both go off in nearly the same direction, a little jump at a time, edging toward each other. When they were within an hour's spacing apart in normal space, they did the same thing under thrusters, edging toward each other as they went. This kept them from building velocity toward each other they would have to take time to decelerate away.

After a couple hours of such maneuvers, *Endeavour* stopped her spin, the shuttle docked, and the ship resumed spin.

Dan carried ChaoPing into *Endeavour*. Justin Moore and Giscard Dufort were standing in the entrance corridor from the small passenger container hatch.

"Orders, ma'am?" Moore asked.

"Take us home, Justin."

"Yes, ma'am."

"And I have orders for you, ChaoPing," Dufort said. "Sick bay. Right now. Unless, of course, you want a limp for the rest of your life."

"Yes, doctor," ChaoPing said meekly. "Lead on."

Endeavour energized her hyperspace field generator and disappeared from normal space.

After-Action Reviews

It was afternoon the day after the overnight escape of the Arcadia diplomatic mission that Jonathan David Wilson called a video conference to find out what had happened the night before. Attending were Morten Andersen, Antonio Braida, and Max Kalbe, the chief of the World Authority Police.

"All right. Let's start with you, Tony. What's our status on Chira Island right now?"

"Yes, Mr. Chairman. Two of the surface-to-air missiles fired at the departing shuttle, while disabled by the shuttle's anti-missile weapons, had surviving warheads. These warheads exploded when they hit the ground, scattering shrapnel. They did not do any physical damage because Chira Island doesn't have a lot of infrastructure. They just chewed up some vegetation.

"A lot of burning debris from the SAMs rained down on the island and the waters nearby, some starting small fires. Those were vegetation fires, not building fires, as no buildings were hit. All those fires have now been put out.

"The other thing that rained down on Chira Island were these metal tetrahedrons from the shuttle's antimissile weapons. The metal it turns out is platinum, which I've learned can be a byproduct of space manufacture depending on the composition of the asteroids used.

"There were a lot of these metal fragments. We estimate a couple of million of them. They all fell on the island. There were a couple of deaths and several injuries on the ground from people in the open getting hit by them. Those were mostly security people.

"There are also a number of broken windows from those metal fragments bouncing when they hit the ground. We're trying to get an accurate count of the windows broken, but, for the ones we have inventoried, replacements have already been ordered."

"Thank you, Tony. Mort, what have you got?"

"Mostly about the action in orbit, Jon. Their ship, this *Endeavour*, initiated its departure after the alarm went up on the ground. Rather than take a standard departure route, thrusting forward in its orbit, *Endeavour* departed to the north, at ninety degrees to its orbit.

"That would not have been possible with the observed acceleration capability we had previously calculated for the ship, so our assets were poorly placed. *Endeavour*, after she ignited rocket engines in addition to her chemical thrusters, was making almost three gravities. Nevertheless, our shuttles gave chase, and they were closing on *Endeavour* when they were destroyed.

"*Endeavour* deployed a similar weapon to that used against the SAMs above Chira Island, but on a much larger scale. We estimate a total of half a billion of these platinum shards were ejected by the explosions of the two weapons *Endeavour* deployed. Our shuttles hit those clouds of shrapnel with closing velocities in the thousands of miles per hour. They were shredded.

"The ongoing and bigger problem is those shards. A number of them have fallen to Earth already. When they come in from that altitude, they're really moving. Atmospheric drag has some effect on them, but they're sharp-edged, dense, and are coming in from ten thousand miles out.

"We've had a number of deaths and injuries on the ground

from people getting hit by these things. Some infrastructure damage, too. Probably the most serious is a large fire started by a high-tension power line that got taken down by a direct hit.

"The ones that haven't come down yet fall into two camps. Some of them will continue to come down over the next several months, though at a reduced rate. But we could have some of these coming down now and again for years.

"The other group is almost worse. They're now in orbit around the Earth. These orbits are, by and large, wildly eccentric, depending on the velocity and vector the original explosions gave them. The orbits are generally north-south, which means they pass through the more common east-west orbits twice each time around the Earth.

"Those orbital periods range from about two hours to more than ten, and the debris now forms a cloud of tens or hundreds of millions of projectiles just randomly flying around out there, taking out anything they hit. That will include, over time, many of our satellites and spacecraft."

"Lovely. Absolutely lovely. We're going to have to actively go after rounding them up, I suspect."

"Yes, but part of the problem is that they're so small."

"I understand. I've seen them. I have several hundred samples spread around on my lawn at the moment."

"Yes, sir."

"All right. Thanks, Mort. Max, how about you?"

"Yes, sir. The action on the ground began when the security guards around the shuttle noted that six of these robots of theirs came down the ladder from the passenger compartment under the shuttle. They claimed to be doing some sort of safety check of spare fuel containers.

"The guards resumed their outward observation, because their job was to establish a perimeter around the shuttle."

"But the robots were already inside their perimeter."

"Yes, sir. The robots seemed so clumsy and limited, however, it was not a worry. The robots, though, snuck up on the guards and clubbed them to the ground. Robots also deployed gas canisters on the barracks buildings. It was a knockout gas, not a lethal gas, but the guards in the barracks were out of the rest of the action.

"Robots ran to the hotel, then formed an armed escort for the robots that were already with the Arcadians, who carried the Arcadians to the shuttle."

"The robots carried them? They didn't run on their own?"

"No, sir. From some of the security footage, we have the robots running to the hotel making thirty miles per hour on the road from the shuttleport. The robots carrying the Arcadians to the shuttleport from the hotel were running about twenty miles per hour, even so laden."

"Remarkable."

"Yes, sir. Their robots are much more capable than they initially acted. Upon arrival at the shuttleport, the escaping group was fired upon by several guards who had not already been rendered ineffective. The robots returned fire with large handguns they carried, and all of those guards were killed, all with several bullet wounds apiece.

"Those heavy bullets went right through their body armor. We speculate that the robots have infrared vision, and they are very good shots with a firearm. Those firearms have the ballistics of a crew-served weapon. I doubt a human could even fire one and hang on to the gun, but the robots carried them as pistols.

"When their shuttle lifted, it lifted with about three times the thrust we had calculated from earlier observed accelerations when it came down for re-entry and landing. It then fired off rockets in addition to its thrusters, and achieved no less than three gravities of acceleration.

"Both the shuttle and the *Endeavour* headed due north – parallel to the Earth's axis of rotation – where our space-based assets are thinnest. *Endeavour* dispatched our pursuing shuttles as you heard, and no assets were in position to pursue the shuttle."

"Did the *Endeavour* and the shuttle then rendezvous before departing the solar system?"

"No, sir. They proceeded independently to about the same distance from Earth before they each, separately, disappeared. That distance was two-thirds of the distance they were from the Earth when they initially appeared in the system and contacted Space Traffic Control.

"So that shuttle is hyperspace-capable."

"Yes, sir. That's all I have."

"Who ordered the firing of the surface-to-air missiles, Max?"

"That was standing orders, sir, in case of an alarm on Chira Island. No aircraft to land, depart, or fly over. The ordered response is to shoot them down."

"And the orders to shoot to kill at the escaping Arcadians?"

"That was part and parcel of your orders to maintain an armed perimeter on the shuttle and not let any pass, sir."

Wilson nodded. Once the Arcadians made a break for it, everything was on automatic. He had no place in the chain of command there, but no one had acted without authority.

What a disaster. He had underestimated the Arcadians at every turn. Of course, they had obscured their full capabilities from the start. The clumsiness of their robots. The accelerations of their ships, both with and without the extra rockets they had mounted. The distance of the hyperspace limit from Earth – for his science and engineering people had already determined there was some limit, just not, yet, what that limit was.

Again and again, they had obscured their true capabilities, and again and again he had taken what he saw at face value. And he couldn't say he hadn't been warned.

Chen ChaoPing was the head of the mission. Her parents ran the family that built, owned, and operated those ships. That had likely been Chen ChaoPing's plan, start to finish.

Milbank's words rang in his head: 'Do not underestimate the Chen.'

"We got out-snookered," Wilson said.

"Yes, sir," Andersen said. "We sure did."

Chen ChaoPing didn't hold her own after-action review until they had been underway back to Arcadia for several days. Giscard Dufort had performed an arthroscopic surgery on her thigh to repair the buried muscle damage from the bullet that passed through her leg. With nanites in place, the healing was accelerated, but healing still took time.

Everybody was in the dining room for the review, all eighteen of them. At the main table sat the landing party, plus Moore and McKay. The five robots from the landing party stood along the wall.

"All right, Justin. You kicked this off. Why don't you start?"

"Yes, ma'am. After you told us to keep an eye out because you thought Wilson was up to something, I made sure we were tracking all the objects in orbit around us. My second officer brought it to me that they were sliding assets into orbit both in front of and behind us."

"To stop *Endeavour* from making a standard departure and to forestall any rendezvous of the shuttle with *Endeavour*," ChaoPing said.

"That was our conjecture, ma'am. They were trying to hem

us in, no doubt about that. I let you know, then when you told me the alarm had gone up on the planet, we made a hard left turn and got out of there.

"Well, those assets they were sliding into place were shuttles, all right. Fast ones. Even with our maximum acceleration and the fact we got the drop on them with our direction change, they were catching us. So we deployed two of the container bombs. We detonated them right in front of them, and they couldn't miss them. Took them all out.

"Then we continued hightailing it for the hyperspace limit. Nothing else came after us, and we went into hyperspace bound for Alpha Centauri.

"That's about it, I guess. Except we left a hell of a mess behind. Four million pieces of shrapnel in their high orbitals. They're going to be forever cleaning that crap up. And if they don't, it'll randomly take out satellites, shuttles, and spaceships into the indefinite future."

"Serves them right," Carla Maier said.

ChaoPing nodded.

"On our end," she said, "when you told me they were hemming you in, I gave orders to Rolf to initiate the plan to leave. The robots overpowered the guards at the shuttle, gassed the guard barracks, and came to the hotel. Our robots in the hotel carried us to the shuttle with the others as armed escort.

"I could hear that the alarm went up before we got to the shuttle, and told you to get out of there. As we neared the shuttle, some group of guards we had missed opened up on us, and the robots returned fire and killed them. We got on the shuttle and got out of there.

"I've heard from the robots that they fired surface-to-air missiles at us from the ground, and the pilot took them out with one drop of forty bomblets. We proceeded to the hyperspace limit and headed for Alpha Centauri."

"And you took casualties, ma'am," Moore said.

"Yes. I was shot through the thigh, and Rob took one round to the chest. We're both doing fine. Also, several robots were damaged."

"Those units have been repaired, ChaoPing," Dornier said.

"Where is Rob, ChaoPing?" Wayne Porter asked.

"And where is Julia?" Denise Bonheur asked.

"OK, I will tell you, but this is the deepest secret you have ever heard. You must keep this quiet. Forever. Agreed?"

ChaoPing looked around the table, catching assents and nods. She looked to the robots.

"That goes for you guys, too."

"We understand, ma'am," Bob said

ChaoPing nodded.

"When Marie told me we were going to lose Rob, I called my parents and told them the situation. They had said to be in touch if it all fell apart, and they would deal with it. I had no idea what they could do, but with Rob dying, I called them.

"Rob Milbank is now recuperating from emergency surgery in the Chen Emergency Services Center of Arcadia City Hospital. He's going to be fine. Julia is with him. He's listed in hospital records as 'John Doe.' And that's all I know."

There was a noise from one of the robots standing along the wall. Almost a sob. ChaoPing looked at Bob and raised an eyebrow.

"That's Tom, ma'am. Mr. Milbank's robot. He has been blaming himself for Mr. Milbank's injury. And was afraid he was dead."

"Tom," ChaoPing said.

The robot looked up.

"Yes, ma'am."

"Rob is fine. I've talked with him. You can contact him in VR yourself if you wish."

"I don't think I could face him, ma'am. I failed to protect him."

The robot was fidgeting his arms, and ChaoLi noticed something. A hole in his upper arm.

"Is that a bullet hole in your arm, Tom?"

"Yes, ma'am. It does not interfere with function, so I did not have the arm replaced."

"Well, that solves one little mystery. The surgeon told my parents that the bullet that hit Rob was nearly spent. It must have ricocheted or passed through something else first. If it had been full power, it would have killed him instantly.

"And now we know. The bullet that hit Rob passed through Tom's upper arm first, then hit Rob. You didn't fail him, Tom, you saved him, by blocking the full power of the bullet that would have killed him."

"I did, ma'am?"

"Yes, you did, Tom. Rob is alive because you were there for him, shielding him in your arms. I wouldn't repair that upper arm, either. I would wear it as a badge of honor."

"Yes, ma'am. Thank you, ma'am."

The robot sounded as if he were about to cry. The other four robots all gave him high-fives then, and clapped him on the shoulder.

ChaoPing turned back to the table and saw Dornier staring at the robots.

Ha! Your little inventions are evolving in front of your eyes, aren't they? she thought.

"Back to the topic here," ChaoPing said. "What Chen Zufu did, I don't know. All I know is that I called my parents and told them what was going on, and then Rob disappeared. I got a message back that he was in surgery on Arcadia, and then that he was going to be fine. Like I say, I've talked to him myself since.

"And all of that must be kept deeply secret."

"But what about when we show up on Arcadia and he's not aboard?" Paolo Costa asked. "Everybody knows he left with us."

"I suspect he and Julia will rejoin us when we come out of hyperspace."

Costa stared at her, but Diakos nodded.

"That makes sense," he said. "Take him out, put him back. What about the Earth mission, though? It's a failure."

"No, it's not," ChaoPing said, "in several ways. First, we offered a peaceful accord with Earth. We had to do that to have clean hands in whatever happens down the road.

"Second, we showed them we can and will walk away from negotiations in bad faith, and there's nothing they can do to stop us.

"And third, hopefully we got them thinking that maybe that friendly agreement is a better option."

"Better option than what, ChaoPing?" Helen Calder asked.

"Better, say, than having us light off several dozen of those containers of debris in their orbitals."

"Ouch," McKay said. "That would take out their entire orbital infrastructure."

Moore nodded.

"Yeah," he said. "They now know, if they want to get nasty, we can get nasty, too. Really nasty."

EARTH

Homecoming

Endeavour made the trip back to Arcadia in six weeks in hyperspace. It was a quiet trip, subdued both because they had all had the experience of 'being shot at and missed,' and because Rob Milbank and Julia Whitcomb were not among them.

As a small example of the dislocation, Loukas Diakos had to recruit a new hot-tub-with-cigar-and-cognac partner. Rolf Dornier was not old enough to get full enjoyment – and Diakos was afraid of Carla Maier – but he found a willing and enjoyable companion in Gavin McKay, whose wife Sinead Doyle was already familiar with his vices. Diakos appreciated McKay's offbeat and sometimes black sense of humor as appropriate to the trip.

Such small dislocations in the camaraderie of the crew were widespread on the long trip.

When *Endeavour* emerged from hyperspace at the hyperspace limit for the Arcadia system, they called in their arrival to Arcadia Flight Control, and were assigned an approach path and orbital. Thirty minutes later, Rob Milbank and Julia Whitcomb emerged from their cabin as if nothing had happened.

Milbank, Diakos, and McKay were all in the hot tub with their cigars and cognac.

"So what happened?" Diakos asked.

"I don't know," Milbank said. "I was unconscious the first

time. This time, I was there, in the hospital bed, then I was here, in the bed in our cabin. I asked Julia about it, and she said, 'I was here, then there, and there, then here.' No nothing. Just blip, and there she was. Same with me."

"Remarkable," McKay said.

"You guys do know all this is secret, right?" Milbank asked.

"Oh, yes," Diakos said. "You were wounded, but you made it back to *Endeavour* with Marie's help, and Giscard did a great job on you in sick bay."

"Yep," McKay said. "Tremendous doctors, Marie and Giscard. Both of them."

"OK. Good," Milbank said. "Never look a gift hospital in the mouth, or something like that."

"Here's to that," Diakos said, and they all tinked glasses in a toast.

Moore was on the bridge when the robot second officer came up to him.

"Excuse me, Captain."

"Yes, Number Two. What is it?"

"Well, Captain, you know we maintain camera surveillance around the ship at all times."

"Yes, of course."

"We picked up something on the forward camera that we don't understand, Captain. I can show you on the viewscreen."

The viewscreen changed, but subtly. They were a bit farther from Arcadia. Moore looked at the timestamp. It was about thirty minutes after *Endeavour*'s emergence from hyperspace.

"I don't see anything unusual, Number Two."

"No, Captain. Not in this shot. But let me step it forward one frame at a time."

Moore could see the timestamp inch along in the hundredths

of seconds digit. The screen remained unchanged each frame until– What the hell was that? It was there one frame and then gone.

"Back that up to that frame again, Number Two. The one with whatever the hell that was."

"Aye, Captain."

The viewscreen timestamp inched backwards until that one single frame and then stopped.

There was Arcadia. If one looked closely, one could see the massive interstellar freight station and its ships. But in this one frame there was something else. A massive geodesic sphere, with thousands of facets, enclosing the planet. It looked to be half again the diameter of the whole planet, even enclosing the low-orbiting freight station well within its scope.

The geodesic sphere was black, and only showed where it was silhouetted against the planet or where it was seen in tangent, on the edges.

"It's dead black, Captain. I don't think anyone inside of it could even see it against the blackness of space beyond."

"Were there any other ships in the system at the time, either on the way to the hyperspace limit or on the way in from it?"

"No, Captain. *Space Master* transferred into hyperspace on its way to Samoa fifteen minutes before. There were no other ships in the system outside the geodesic sphere when it appeared."

"So we're the only ship that could have seen it."

"Yes, Captain."

"And it was gone in the very next frame?"

"Yes, Captain."

Moore stared at the screen. That was just before Rob Milbank and Julia Whitcomb had emerged from their cabin. They had not appeared immediately once *Endeavour* emerged from hyperspace, only half an hour later, once *Space Master* was safely gone.

Moore could add two and two and get four. This was more like adding two and two and getting fifteen, but still....

"Number Two, can you substitute the frame before or after for this one, and diddle the timestamp so it matches?"

"Falsify the record, Captain?"

"Yes, Number Two. And then forget about this frame, this whatever-the-hell-it-is, and editing the record. Instruct the entire crew to forget about them as well."

The robot second officer looked at him for several seconds, processing that.

"Check with Bob, Number Two. Tell him what we have on camera, and what I ordered," Moore said.

Another two seconds of motionlessness, and then the robot second officer stirred.

"Aye, Captain. Will comply."

Moore eschewed using JATO bottles to speed *Endeavour's* return to Arcadia orbit, instead making a standard approach. They had all had quite enough of high acceleration, thank you very much, and, with Milbank and Whitcomb back aboard, the old friends were a full crew again.

From this dangerous mission, they had all made it back alive after all.

It was something of a non-stop party for the day it took to get to Arcadia orbit.

The shuttle settled down on the pad with a delicate touch. The hyperspace field generator and the weapons container had been left aboard *Endeavour*, so the small passenger container was on the ground once the shuttle landed.

ChaoLi and JieMin walked out from the terminal building

once the engines shut down. ChaoPing was first out the door, and she and ChaoLi hugged.

"I was so afraid for you when it all went into the dumper," ChaoLi said. "How's your leg doing?"

"It's fine, Muqin. Giscard did a really nice job cleaning it all up. I hardly even limp anymore."

ChaoLi let her go, then she and JieMin greeted each of the eighteen crew and their nine personal service robots and welcomed them back to Arcadia.

There wouldn't be a lot of details about the trip made public, but Arcadians never needed a lot of details to justify a parade. It was the first trip to Earth, humanity's ancestral home, and that's all that mattered.

The *Endeavour* crew all rode into town in open cars down Quant Boulevard, with JieMin, ChaoLi, ChaoPing, and JuMing riding in the last car. The cars pulled up one at a time to the reviewing stand to debark their passengers.

The *Endeavour* crew mounted the stairs to the reviewing platform in Charter Square, which was completely full of cheering people. Luisa Bianchi, the prime minister, was there, as was the mayor of Arcadia City and Miss Arcadia City.

The crowd waved their lavalavas in the air and cheered. Caught up in the moment, Carla Maier, the youngest of the crew, whipped off her lavalava and waved it in the air, too. Miss Arcadia City followed suit, and the crowd went nuts.

It was the best parade ever.

When Giscard Dufort and Marie Legrand got home to their house in Arcadia City, Francoise ran up and hugged them both.

"I was so worried about you," she said.

"You told us we had to go," Legrand said.

"Yes, and you did. Did you have to help anyone? Did you

save anyone's life?"

"Oh, yes."

"Who?" Francoise asked.

"Rob Milbank and Chen ChaoPing."

"Oh, my gosh. You see. If you had not gone, and one of your friends had died, you would have blamed yourselves forever."

When ChaoPing and JuMing got home, GangLi and GangJie were both unpacking. After the first week, they had gotten too lonely in the big apartment and had gone to live with LingTao and Antonio Costa and their kids.

After three months in that dynamic household, though, they were happy to be back home.

"We saw you in the parade," GangLi said.

"We watched in VR," GangJie said.

"We told you that you had to go."

"No one will question you as Chen Zufu and Chen Zumu now."

ChaoPing laughed.

"Well, that's a long way off, we hope," she said.

"Yes, there is much to learn before we can hope to replace your Gramma and Grandpa," JuMing said.

"Are they really that good?" GangLi asked.

ChaoPing squatted down in front of him for a better hug.

"GangLi, they're so good, they're scary."

The day after the parade, Rob Milbank visited his old friends, ChaoLi and JieMin. They sat in ChaoLi's tearoom, the site of so many memorable meetings in his past. With tea poured and sipped, Milbank jumped right in.

"ChaoLi, JieMin, it's good to see you both."

"It's good to see you looking so well, Rob. We were very

worried about you."

"Yes, but I'm fine and healing well, thanks in no small part to you."

"We had no part in it, Rob," ChaoLi said. "Any statement to the contrary is hearsay and myth."

"Oh, I understand," Milbank said. "And so I thank you for all the things you didn't do for me."

Milbank winked, and JieMin chuckled.

"So what is now to become of Mr. Wilson?" Milbank asked.

"We will not soon forget his perfidy in this matter," ChaoLi said. "When the time comes, we will deal with him."

"When will that be?"

"That is a time of his own choosing. But we will be waiting."

JieMin nodded.

"Sooner or later, he will see the best path forward," JieMin said.

"He will?" Milbank asked.

"Yes," JieMin said. "For there is no other path open to him."

One nice thing about the six-week trip back. ChaoPing had had plenty of time to prepare her mission report. The After-Action Report on their escape, the video recording and a transcript of their meeting with Chairman Wilson, which she had stream-recorded in VR, multiple videos and pictures of Chira Island, the videos and pictures of the escape, the videos and pictures of her and Rob Milbank's wound.

ChaoPing had it all together by the time *Endeavour* had emerged from hyperspace, and she had sent it in to Chen Zufu and Chen Zumu.

Two days after the parade, ChaoPing received a request to meet with the Chen.

With tea poured and sipped, ChaoPing bowed to her parents in turn.

"Chen Zufu. Chen Zumu."

"You performed well on this mission, ChaoPing," ChaoLi said. "The goal was to present the trade agreement and a friendly relationship to Chairman Wilson, who we expected to be dismissive, and then to bring everyone back safely. You have achieved this goal."

"We failed to conclude the agreement, Chen Zumu," ChaoPing said.

"Concluding the agreement was always a possibility, though a faint one, and not under your control in any case," ChaoLi said. "You did well. Your plan was well conceived and well executed."

"We are very proud of you, both for ourselves and for the family," JieMin said.

ChaoPing blushed and bowed to her father.

"Thank you, Chen Zufu."

"I note you did not mention anything about the resolution of Rob Milbank's wound other than that he survived and returned with you aboard *Endeavour*," ChaoLi said. "That was well done, as well."

"Thank you, Chen Zumu."

"There will come a time when you and Chen JuMing will learn what really happened, and how. It is not yet that time."

"I understand, Chen Zumu."

ChaoLi sipped her tea. JieMin looked lost in thought.

"Chen Zumu?"

"Yes, ChaoPing?"

"What will happen with Earth now, Chen Zumu? What will they do? What will we do?"

"We will wait, ChaoPing. Earth will work out the secrets of

hyperspace. They will build a navy. Then they will come looking for us. In five years. Perhaps ten."

"And what will we do then, Chen Zumu?"

"We will prove to them that they cannot win against us."

"Will we build a navy as well, Chen Zumu?"

"No, ChaoPing. We already have everything we need."

Outside of the Port of New Jersey, there was a large space where empty cargo containers were stored. These may be used again at some point, but usually were not. For the time being, they sat idle, stacked five high in rows thousands of feet long.

No one noticed that, one night, another container simply appeared there, at the end of the current row being filled. The next day when workers returned, they continued stacking empties in that row. The new container was quickly buried.

None of the workers paid any attention to the Earthsea markings, or what those might mean.

RICHARD F. WEYAND

Worldview

Jonathan David Wilson, World Authority Chairman, was working in his office when he got a call request. He did not recognize the calling address, which was strange in itself. All his calls were screened at multiple levels, and an unknown address should not have been able to get through to him.

Wilson ignored the call request. He had many things on his mind. The continuing losses of satellites and other orbital infrastructure from collisions with the debris of the Arcadians' weapons continued to mount. Oh, it was a small percentage – so far, at least – but annoying. They were cleaning up all the crap as fast as they could, but those projectiles were annoyingly difficult to track down and pick up.

Wilson also continued to push on his hyperspace project. They should have been able to learn something from observation of the Arcadians' ships in the confrontation two months ago, but progress was annoyingly slow. He thought again about how he might kick the project into high gear. The Arcadians had made a fool of him, and he didn't like it.

The call request came again, and he dismissed it.

Then the most astounding thing happened.

Wilson's display lit up anyway.

"Good morning, Mr. Chairman."

Wilson's display showed a small man of mixed heritage – Asian, surely, as well as some European, and perhaps some Indian and African thrown in as well – in tailor seat on a pillow. He looked maybe forty-five years old, and wore some sort of sari or wrap-skirt. He was naked from the waist up, his long black hair pulled back, perhaps in a ponytail behind.

He was seated before a heavily framed teak doorway that opened out onto a beautiful garden. It was located in a tropical zone, not unlike Wilson's own residence in Costa Rica.

"Who the hell are you?" Wilson asked.

"I am the Chen."

"What does that even mean? There are millions of people named Chen."

"I am Chen Zufu of the Chen-Jasic family, on the colony planet Arcadia. The leader of the family. As such, people simply call me the Chen."

Wilson tried to cut off the display, but, even though he turned the display off, the image persisted.

"You do not control your display, Mr. Chairman. I do."

"But how?"

"Do you wish to discuss computers and display technology, Mr. Chairman? I think you and I have more important things to discuss."

Wilson struggled to get his mental feet under him. He sat back in his desk chair, and waved to JieMin.

"Very well, then," he said. "Proceed."

JieMin nodded.

"I am not sure whether you will be relieved or annoyed to hear this, Mr. Chairman, but Prime Minister Milbank and my daughter, Chen ChaoPing, both survived the gunshot wounds they received in your attempt to kill our diplomatic mission."

"That was a misunderstanding of their orders by my security people."

"You are not responsible for the actions of people acting under your authority, Mr. Chairman? That is an interesting concept of leadership."

"Your people were in a secured area without authorization."

"But you invited them to move about the island, did you not, Mr. Chairman? And the shuttle was my property, to which my daughter and her associates should not have been denied access. Unless of course you intended to steal my shuttle, as you tried to hijack my hyperspace ship, the *Endeavour*."

"*Your* ship?" Wilson asked.

JieMin sighed.

"Mr. Chairman, I am the leader of the Chen-Jasic family, which owns Jixing Trading, and all its ships and properties across human space. As such, I am currently the wealthiest and most powerful human being in history. You tried to steal my property and very nearly killed my daughter and my friend, who were on Earth as your guests under diplomatic immunity. I am not amused."

"Not more powerful than me."

"Mr. Chairman, I could poison your orbitals with billions of projectiles of the kind you are even now struggling to clean up from *Endeavor*'s minimal use of its defensive weapons. I could lock you onto your own planet by making space flight from Earth impossible. Can you do the same to me? No. I am controlling the display in your own office from here, thousands of light-years away. Can you do the same to me? No."

"But the colonies are under my authority. The World Authority has sovereignty over the colonies."

"You persist in this fantasy, Mr. Chairman? The legal documents the colonists and the World Authority executed in 2245 are clear on this matter, and they do not agree with you."

"No court has made such a determination."

"No court has jurisdiction, Mr. Chairman. There is no competent judicial authority to make that decision. So *I* have made the decision."

"Who are you to decide?"

EARTH

"As I said, before, Mr. Chairman, I am the Chen."

"You have no authority over me," Wilson said. "You can't just make such a decision and bind me to it. The World Authority will go out into space and find you. You'll see. I am the Chairman of the World Authority. I am the ultimate authority over every human being, everywhere."

JieMin considered. Janice Quant had done an exhaustive search of police records in Kolkata from the period before 'Jonathan David Wilson' had signed aboard a tramp freighter as cook's boy. It had taken years, but she had found a facial and genetic match to Wilson in those records, with multiple arrests for petty theft. JieMin decided to use that now.

"The persistence of your worldview in defiance of the facts is not unexpected. But the behaviors and attitudes that served you so well in the slums of Kolkata will not avail you now, Anup Patel. You cannot simply steal whatever you want. I will not permit it."

Wilson started as if struck. He had buried all the records. How did this quiet little man know any of this? Once again, Milbank's warning echoed in his head. 'Do not underestimate the Chen.' The Chen. It was *this* man Milbank had warned him about.

"There is but one relationship Earth may have with the colony planets, Mr. Chairman," JieMin said. "Just one relationship I will permit. And that is as friends and equals. Had you accepted that relationship two months ago, food and technology would already be flooding into Earth, bettering the lot of everyone, especially its poor.

"But in your arrogance you have rejected that relationship to persist in this fantasy. Very well. Then Earth and its poor can do without. As the planetary chairman, it is your decision.

"If you change your mind, Mr. Chairman, you can contact

me via the address on this call request. I would be pleased to extend the same relationship to Earth that my daughter extended to you two months ago. Then we could begin to address the plight of Earth's poor together.

"Until then, Mr. Chairman, good day."

JieMin cut the connection.

"So did that make any difference, do you think?" ChaoLi asked after JieMin's call to Wilson.

"Not yet, I don't think. As issues pile up, it should hopefully give Mr. Wilson doubts about the wisdom of his chosen path."

"I think it may be more difficult than that," Quant said. "Mr. Wilson is sure of his prerogatives and confident of his methods and approach. Not without reason. He did become World Authority Chairman."

ChaoLi nodded.

"You would know a great deal more about that than us, Janice, given that you were World Authority Chairman yourself," she said.

"It seems such a simple matter," JieMin said. "We just need him to accept that the World Authority's sovereignty extends only over the Earth and its system. That the colonies lie outside of its borders."

"And you are correct, JieMin, that the colonist agreement with the World Authority spelled that out in precise legal terms," Quant said. "I drew up that agreement myself, and there is no ambiguity."

"Well, we shall see where all this leads," JieMin said. "Thank you, Janice, for you assistance."

"I'm happy to help, JieMin. With you as a front, I am finally able to do something about Earth and its problems."

EARTH

"I'm sorry, Mr. Chairman," Antonio Braida said, "but that mail address doesn't resolve to anything. It's not in the system."

"How can that be, Tony?" Wilson asked. "I got a call request and had a conference call with that address. Can't you trace it back from the call request or the call itself?"

"That's just it, sir. There is no record of the call request or the conference call."

"I thought all of my communications were recorded for my use."

"Yes, sir," Braida said. "And, as far as the system is concerned, no such call request or conference call took place."

"What about my display status?"

"The system shows your display as idle all morning, sir."

How the hell did that little bastard pull that off? Wilson didn't know, and he wished he did. Braida continued.

"We do not even know how he was able to communicate in real-time across interstellar distances, sir."

"And nobody has any ideas?" Wilson asked.

"Guesses, sir. Some sort of quantum-entanglement device, we suspect. Nothing for sure."

"That would mean a device in this system, right? Don't those have to be a matched pair?"

"Yes, sir, and we haven't found that, either. I do have several other items today, though," Braida said.

"Go ahead, Tony."

"Yes, sir. We lost another two satellites last night. We assume from projectile impacts. They just went off-line with no warning."

"Shit," Wilson said with feeling. "How are we doing on cleaning that crap up?"

"We are making progress, sir. The estimate is that we have

183

about half of them now."

"Those bastards. Poisoned our orbitals on their way out."

"Excuse me, sir," Braida said, "but it could have been much worse."

"How is that?"

"We got some pretty good pictures of their ship's after aspect, sir. We can tell the difference between containers with rockets and containers with weapons. They were carrying ninety-six rocket containers. They used them eight at a time. They used four rounds of rockets to get to the hyperspace limit, or about a third of their onboard inventory."

"And the containers with weapons?" Wilson asked.

"That's just it, sir. The other sixty containers were weapons containers. They used two of them, which we now estimate contained two hundred million of those little projectiles apiece. Those weapons also have their own rockets aboard, and can be steered."

"So?"

"If they had wanted to poison our orbitals," Braida said, "they could have fired the other fifty-eight containers on their way out of the system. They could have steered them into the most crowded orbitals, or into elliptic orbits that would sweep through the whole stack of orbitals. That would have been twelve *billion* projectiles, sir."

"But they didn't."

"No, sir. They fired two weapons at the shuttles that were chasing them. But it would have been thirty times worse if they had fired off the rest. We wouldn't even be able to get spacecraft up there to clean them up. We'd just lose the spacecraft."

"You almost sound sympathetic to them, Tony," Wilson said.

"Just stating the facts, sir. They fired the weapons they had to fire to get away, and then stopped."

Wilson nodded. That had to have been Chen ChaoPing's decision. Her plan, anyway. If she'd been wounded in their getaway, she might not have been giving the orders at that point. If she had been wounded but was still giving the orders, he had to admit that showed remarkable discipline and restraint. She could have fired off the rest of their weapons out of pique at that point.

"All right, Tony. What else have we got today?"

"We do have some progress on the hyperspace project, sir. One thing we did learn from the Arcadian ships is that they do not have any indication of a propulsion system not designed for normal space. Rockets and chemical thrusters is all we saw. We know – or we think, at least – that those won't work in hyperspace, but there were no other propulsion means we could see."

"How do we know those don't work?

"They've tried them, sir," Braida said. "They send the probe into hyperspace with the computer programmed to fire the rocket or thruster for a few seconds, then come back."

"And the probe doesn't move?"

"No, sir. And when it comes back, it's surrounded by hot exhaust gasses, in the shape of the hyperspace field. The camera recordings make it clear that all the gasses stay in the field, and the thrust doesn't actually serve to move the ship at all."

"But the Arcadians have to be doing something," Wilson said.

"Yes, sir. But the lack of anything on their ships we didn't understand got the engineers and scientists wondering if they weren't manipulating the hyperspace field itself."

"In what way, Tony?"

"As I understand it, sir," Braida said, "if you generated the hyperspace field with some kind of fins or ridges on it, and then rotated that, it would act like a propeller. There's also some talk about generating such fins or projections in the field and moving them from front to back."

"Like oars on a boat?"

"Yes, sir, in a sense. But they're working up how to do that. They hope to have something they can build and test soon."

"Excellent," Wilson said. "Progress at last. Keep me informed on how that goes, Tony."

"Of course, sir."

"We'll see if that Chen bastard is as cocky when our ships show up in his system."

Wilson sat back and looked out his full-height office windows, across the veranda and the forever pool, down the gulf. The ladies were playing in the pool this afternoon, but neither the view down the gulf nor the view of the naked lovelies in his pool calmed him this afternoon.

He puffed on his cigar, one of the ones from the container of gifts the Arcadians had left behind when they departed so abruptly. They had not reneged on the gifts they had given him, but left them behind when they lifted. The hell of it was that it was an excellent cigar. Better than any he had ever had, and he had access to all Earth's products, cost no object.

The liquors, the cheese, the wines, the beef, the chocolate – all were as good or better than the most expensive luxury brands available on Earth. In Earth terms, that container of gifts was worth a small fortune by itself.

But even the finest cigar he had ever had couldn't relax him.

The conversation with the Arcadian – Wilson couldn't bring

himself to call him the Chen, even in his thoughts – had upset him more than he liked to admit. Who was the Arcadian to lecture the chairman of the World Authority about the plight of Earth's poor? Wilson knew much more about being poor than he would ever admit.

More than that pampered Arcadian bastard did, that's sure.

But they were on the verge of a hyperspace drive now, and, once they had it, Earth would be dominant. No colony planet could match Earth's manufacturing capacity. Wilson would build a navy the colonies could never hope to aspire to, and the World Authority would be supreme again.

It was characteristic of Wilson's worldview that he did not spend time considering what that manufacturing capacity could do to aid Earth's poor if he applied it to that goal instead of to building military power in order to steal what he wanted.

And he never gave a second thought to partnering with that arrogant Arcadian prick to work together to solve Earth's problems.

Even if it meant having a regular supply of great cigars.

Intermezzo

The planetary executives that had signed the trade agreement over the past twenty years were generally long-serving. The surge of prosperity that had resulted from free trade had made them popular, and they usually served until they retired, as Rob Milbank and Sasha Ivanov had. Turnover, though, was low.

Still, twenty years is a long time, and many of the original signers had retired. One who had not was the planetary chairman of Playa, Oliver Nieman. He generally liked the job, which most people on Playa would find distasteful. All that dealing with people all the time, even in VR. Yuck.

Nieman's long tenure, his sense of humor, and his rational, non-confrontational approach had made the epicure something of a de facto leader among the planetary executives.

As the chairman of Jixing Trading through its explosive growth period, ChaoLi had established and maintained excellent relationships with all of the planetary executives, including especially Nieman, whose planet supplied the robots that had outfitted Jixing Trading's ships and contributed so much to the general prosperity.

So it was not surprising that it was Nieman who first contacted ChaoLi about the *Endeavour* expedition.

"Hello, ChaoLi."

"Hello, Oliver. It's good to see you."

Nieman sipped a red wine – likely from Bali, the colony planet whose specialization in fine wines had produced superb results – then remarked on it.

"Excuse me, please. I know it is morning in Arcadia City, but it is after dinner in the evening here, and I do so love the Bali Merlots."

ChaoLi laughed her little bells laugh.

"Not a problem, Oliver."

"Thank you for that," Nieman said and wiped his mouth delicately with his napkin. "The reason for my call today is to discuss this *Endeavour* mission of yours, and learn if there is anything we must do in light of it."

"Of course, Oliver. I rather expected you to call, actually."

"Yes, like a bad credit, I keep turning up."

ChaoLi laughed again, and Nieman used the opportunity to sneak a tiny and exquisite Aruba chocolate from the plate of after-dinner treats in front of him.

"But there are a lot of rumors floating around about what did or did not happen on this expedition, ChaoLi. I thought I would clear those up with you if I might. And, once the facts are clear, we must decide what, if anything, we do about it."

"I understand, Oliver."

"First, I understand that ChaoPing offered the planetary chairman the same trade agreement we all are parties to, inviting him to the party, as it were."

"It was actually Loukas Diakos, the Arcadia ambassador to Earth, who offered the agreement during their meeting, Oliver. If the Earth government – in the form of the World Authority Chairman, Jonathan Wilson – had agreed, Diakos would have executed it on Arcadia's part, and then it would have been forwarded to all of you for your consideration."

"As we had all agreed for the prior *Wanderlust* mission. I understand, ChaoLi. But am I right that the Earth planetary chairman rejected the agreement with some nonsense about

Earth having sovereignty over the colony planets?"

"Chairman Wilson did assert the sovereignty issue, Oliver, and said the agreement was inappropriate because it was structured as an agreement between equals. Our delegation pointed out the terms of the colonist agreement of 2245, which he waved away. He did, however, schedule a meeting for the next day to discuss matters further."

"Disturbing. I have reviewed in some detail the terms of that agreement in this context, ChaoLi, and he has not a leg to stand on. They are most explicit, and are binding on the parties, their heirs, successors, and assigns."

"I agree with you, Oliver. The problem is that there is no appropriate venue to decide the issue. The Earth courts are not independent. They are subordinate to the chairman."

"Yes. As always, an agreement is only as binding as the honor of the parties. A trait the chairman seems to have slipped the constraints of, if he in fact ever felt bound by them at all."

Nieman sighed, and consoled himself with another chocolate dainty.

"There's some evidence he has a longstanding slippery relationship with the rules, Oliver."

Nieman nodded.

"We were asking the leopard to change its spots. Unlikely. So your delegation then left, once the chairman's position was clear?"

"Not quite, Oliver. They were prepared to remain on Earth as the chairman's guests and continue negotiations. But the short meeting, with another scheduled for the next day – rather than a longer session immediately – made ChaoPing believe he might be delaying."

"Which raises the question of what he was delaying for."

"Exactly. So they kept close watch, both on the ground and

on the ship. And they found that Chairman Wilson was moving assets into place around the ship. It looked like a play to seize the *Endeavour*."

"Which it likely was, ChaoLi. He would lust after such a prize. And that is when your delegation made the logical decision to decamp the premises?"

"Yes, Oliver. ChaoPing made the call."

"Always did have a good head on her shoulders, that one," Nieman said, nodding. "Now the rumors get somewhat fuzzier, ChaoLi. There was a gun battle for them to regain the shuttle? Is that right?"

"Yes, Oliver. Your robots against the chairman's security forces."

"Oh, my. That can't have gone well for them. How many robots?"

"Twenty, not including the shuttle pilot, against several hundred of the chairman's security people."

"Ah. They were outnumbered then. That is, the chairman's security people were outnumbered."

"Yes. The robots immobilized the greater part of the chairman's forces with a knockout gas, then simply ran past most of the rest, carrying the delegation. Only one group got off any fire, and they were quickly dispatched."

"And I heard some of your people were wounded, ChaoLi?"

"ChaoPing and Rob Milbank were both wounded. ChaoPing took a round through the muscle of the thigh that missed both the bone and the artery, and Rob was hit in the chest by a mostly spent round that passed through his robot's upper arm first."

"Lucky. I'm very happy that turned out as well as it did, ChaoLi. If the chairman had created that large a blood debt between us, it would have made going forward even more

191

difficult."

"If he had killed them, I would have seen Chairman Wilson drawn and quartered in Charter Square. We can always deal with his successor."

Nieman nodded. He had known ChaoLi for twenty years. She was one tough cookie, but had a soft spot for her children and close friends. Hit that soft spot, and you could get a really large helping of tough in return. Nieman had no doubt on that score at all.

"But they regained the shuttle and both ships escaped undamaged, or that's the hearsay."

"Yes, Oliver. ChaoPing had hidden their capabilities on the way in, both with *Endeavour* and the shuttle. They had planned their deployments around the performance envelope they had seen, and were seriously out of position. The forces that were able to respond were dispatched with defensive weapons."

"Shrapnel grenades, I heard."

"That's a serious understatement, Oliver. The shuttle dropped forty bomblets, each containing a hundred thousand sharp platinum tetrahedrons, to defeat their surface-to-air missiles. *Endeavour* deployed two much larger devices, each containing two hundred million such projectiles, and exploded them in front of their pursuing shuttles, with the results you would expect."

"My heavens!"

"Oh, yes. Then both ships independently went into hyperspace and rendezvoused in Alpha Centauri, the system next door. That was also a surprise for them, I think. Their strategy looked designed to keep the shuttle from getting back to the *Endeavour* in-system, but that wasn't necessary."

"A remarkable story, ChaoLi. But we now have this dishonest and dishonorable person, this snake, in command of

Earth's resources. I also heard they are working on hyperspace capability of their own."

"That's true. That was the motivation for initiating contact now. To gauge their intentions."

"And I think you gained a good picture of them, ChaoLi. This fellow is going to build a hyperspace navy and then come out here and try to lord it over us."

"That's our read as well, Oliver."

"What do we do then, ChaoLi? Do we begin building our own navies?"

"No, Oliver. There is no need, and a great deal of danger. Such structures are self-sustaining. To be so, they need war. The bedecked and bedazzled senior officers, safe behind the lines, push war as the quickest way to acclaim and promotion.

"One needs a military when faced with a threat, but we have no threats among us. Were we to build up such space navies, however, they would create such threats to justify their existence."

"I understand, ChaoLi. That has been our position for twenty years. But we now face a threat from Earth."

ChaoLi shook her head.

"No, Oliver. We don't. Earth and its potential navy are no threat to us at all. They cannot prevail against us. They can't even harm us."

"Truly? How can that be, ChaoLi?"

"JieMin will not allow it."

"JieMin can defeat their navy? All by himself?"

"Oh, yes."

Nieman gave her a skeptical look.

"Oliver, do not forget who JieMin is. He came up with hyperspace when he was fourteen years old. He formalized all the mathematics by the time he was twenty-seven. He has not been idle in the more than three decades since, and he has had access to the family's considerable resources as heir to Chen Zufu for the last twenty years.

"Earth cannot harm us. The Chen will not permit it."

Nieman sat back and considered. He had known ChaoLi for twenty years. He had spoken with her almost weekly until she had recently become Chen Zumu. During that time, she had said some amazing things, committed to some amazing things, and had never been wrong, had never failed to make good on her commitments.

Not once.

"Very well. When in doubt, bet the horse that is winning," Nieman said. "You have never committed what you could not produce, ChaoLi, and I will not bet against you now, even on such an existential issue. Playa will build no navy, and I will use my influence, such as it is, with the other planetary executives as well."

Nieman understated his own influence, ChaoLi knew. He had tremendous and well-earned clout with the other planetary executives.

"Thank you for your confidence in me, Oliver. It means a great deal to me."

Nieman raised his wine glass to her, nodded, and cut the connection.

A probe, assembled into six shipping containers as a structural platform, appeared in the Alpha Centauri system. It stayed there thirty minutes, taking pictures and monitoring radio frequencies, then disappeared.

"They've done it, sir," Braida said. "Sent the probe to Alpha Centauri and back."

"Finally," Chairman Wilson said.

He had chafed for over a year at the slow progress. It had been fifteen months since the Arcadians had visited, then left so abruptly.

"There's no colony there, by the way. The probe listened for radio and power emissions, and there was nothing."

"We expected that, though, right?"

"Yes, sir," Braida said. "One of the three stars is a G-type star, but the known planets are all unsuitable for one reason or another. But we did want to check out the equipment."

"A negative check is no check, though, Tony."

"That's correct, sir, so we had it monitor Earth as well when it returned, and it picked up both our radio emissions and our power-grid emissions."

"Ah. Excellent," Wilson said. "That is a check. We can start building these then?"

"Yes, but the engineers say they can refine the design. The current design is a bit brute-force in their opinion, sir."

"Yes, they would tinker with it until doomsday if we were willing to wait. I'm not willing to wait. So let's start building these and sending them out. When they have a refined design, we can start building those."

"Very well, sir," Braida said. "How many do you want to build?"

"As many as it takes, Tony. I want a probe to visit every single G-type star, working outward from the Earth."

"That's a lot of stars, sir. One in thirteen stars in this part of the galaxy is a G type, and the galaxy as a whole is a hundred billion stars."

"I don't give a damn. They can route each probe from one to the next to the next, if they want. But when a probe finds a colony, it comes right back here and tells us. We have the manufacturing capacity to build tens of thousands of these probes, Tony. Let's get on with it."

"Yes, sir."

"And get the designers working on those warship designs. They have a working probe now. It doesn't really need tinkering. What I really want them working on is my navy."

"Yes, sir."

In the Asteroid Belt, millions of miles from Earth, thousands of factories generated raw materials and manufactured products for Earth and its space-based platforms. Established by Janice Quant a hundred and fifty years before for the colony project, they had continued replicating themselves at need.

Two hundred of those factories now shifted their production to hyperspace probes. As each probe was completed, the factory that built it ejected it with a small mechanical launcher.

When the probe was far enough from the factory, it transitioned into hyperspace.

In the engineering departments of dozens of manufacturers on Earth, thousands of engineers worked at producing warship designs. They took a cue from the *Endeavour*, building ships that would house their crews in the outer volume of a spinning cylinder five hundred feet across.

Just as Wayne Porter had on Arcadia, they worked through all the environmental issues, the supply issues, the provisioning issues. Earth, though, had been in space a long time in its own system, and they were not starting from scratch. Progress was rapid, helped along both by their prior experience and the willingness of the World Authority to throw money at the project.

They worked in provision for the refined hyperspace drive,

provision for rocket assist, like the Arcadian ship had, provision for steering thrusters.

And they built in provision for weapons. Lots of weapons.

There had never been a space navy before, and only one space battle, between *Endeavour* and her parasite and the Earth shuttles and missiles that had targeted them.

So the engineers built in a lot of different things as weapons. Similar weapons to the Arcadian ships, which had proved so effective. Missile launchers, mounting modified surface-to-air missiles with either conventional or nuclear warheads. Even high-powered lasers and electromagnetic projectile guns.

They also built in provision for space-to-surface missiles. Big ones, suitable for carrying large multiple independently targetable nuclear weapons.

The design work went quickly, as the engineering firms were in a race with each other. The World Authority had committed to paying royalties on some of each design, but finishing your design sooner meant they would build more of your design, and you would get more royalties.

The Asteroid Belt factories would build the ship hulls, then they would be outfitted for their crews in Earth orbit. That would be a much smaller effort than the Arcadian hyperspace liners, however, as the crew quarters would be much more spartan than the Arcadians' comfortable passenger cabins.

Janice Quant kept a watchful eye on their progress.

The Search

In star system after star system after star system, a probe would appear, sit for an hour or two, and then disappear. As they did, the radius of Earth's search for its colonies increased.

It was slow going. There are a lot of stars in the galaxy, even in the less dense outer area of the Milky Way the Earth occupied. And one of every thirteen was a G-type star.

What Earth did not know, having no initial information on the locations of the colonies, was that Janice Quant had separated all the colonies from Earth and each other by a minimum of three thousand light-years.

Earth would not find the first colony planet until its search radius was out three thousand light-years. A six thousand light-year diameter sphere is over a hundred billion cubic light-years. There were hundreds of millions of stars in that large a volume, and tens of millions of G-type stars.

An exhaustive search working outward from the Earth was going to take a very long time to find even a single colony.

Of course, they did not know that when the search started. They continued to build more and more probes, sending them out with long itineraries of stars to check.

But four years had passed, and no probe had ever come back to report it had found a colony. Probes continually came back to get a new itinerary, having finished their route, or to have their power plants refueled, but never to report they had found a colony.

In the meantime, designs had been approved, factories assigned, and the Earth's interstellar battle fleet was under construction and growing rapidly. Dozens of completed hulls orbited the Earth, and were being outfitted. Dozens more had made their first voyages to nearby star systems and practiced with their weapons systems.

There was only one problem.

They had no place to go.

More than five years after the Arcadians had visited, the tide finally turned. Jonathan David Wilson was now a recorded sixty-three years old – in actuality, Anup Patel was fifty-nine years old – and his motives and his attitudes had mellowed with age.

He sometimes wondered now if he had been wrong not to accept that deal. After five years of trade, of cooperation, where would Earth be now? Instead he had sunk huge resources into his navy and into finding the colonies, and to what end?

Nevertheless stubborn pride had kept him going, had kept him from calling the Chen and requesting the deal after all. He would keep on, because he had sunk so much into this path already.

Finally, he got a break, and these doubts vanished.

"Sir! Sir! Mr. Chairman," Braida's voice broke into Wilson's thoughts.

Wilson pushed the acceptance for the video call and Braida's flushed face appeared on the display.

"Yes, Tony. What is it?"

"They did it, sir."

"They found a colony?"

"Yes," Braid said. "Actually, two of them, sir."

"Two of them?"

"Yes, sir. Arcadia and Dorado. They're just over three

thousand light-years away. That's why it took so long. They're nowhere close to here."

"Three thousand light-years?" Wilson asked. "Wow."

"Yes, sir. Curiously, they're also three thousand light-years from each other."

Braida's face moved to an inset as he put a star chart on the display. Earth, Arcadia, and Dorado were marked, forming an equilateral triangle on the chart.

Something clicked in Wilson's head as he looked at it. Three thousand light-years, hmm?

"That's it, Tony. Three thousand light-years. I want new probes, and probes coming back in for a new itinerary, sent out to check the G-type stars near three thousand light-year distances from the rest of the planets."

"But, sir, that will leave a lot of closer G-type stars unchecked."

"Which we can come back to later, if necessary. Let's go, Tony. Change the selection criteria for the probes' routes. Assume all the colonies and Earth are at least three thousand light-years apart."

"Yes, sir."

Wilson cut the connection but had frozen the chart on the screen. He looked at it as he thought.

Why three thousand light-years? Wilson didn't know, but it sure looked deliberate.

And in any case, they had found Arcadia, to spinward of the Sun and toward the center of the galaxy, in the gap between the Orion Arm and the Sagittarius arm. Which meant he could move against the Chen at last.

Wilson would not move immediately, though. Oh, no. He wanted all the colonies found first, or at least most of them. He wanted to move against them in an organized way, not hit or miss.

Wilson started reviewing the readiness status of his navy, and the schedule for new ships coming on-line.

He sent out orders accelerating some activities, delaying others, and increasing the working-up schedules of ships that would be available in a year.

JieMin and ChaoLi got a video call request from 'JQ'. They both accepted and dropped into VR.

"Hello, Janice. Long time no see. Something up with our friends on Earth?" ChaoLi asked.

"Yes, ChaoLi. They've found two of the colonies, Arcadia and Dorado."

JieMin nodded. That made sense. The two of them were both in the group closest to Earth.

"So is Mr. Wilson's navy going to be paying us a visit soon, Janice?" ChaoLi asked.

"I don't think so. They're not working up their navy yet. Instead, Wilson has ordered an increased staffing and training schedule. He's also sped up some things, like outfitting existing hulls, while delaying others, like working up new hulls. I think he's aiming at more like a year out. That's when his new schedule would result in a navy."

JieMin shook his head.

"Such a waste of effort," he said.

"Janice," ChaoLi asked, "where do you think they will strike first?"

"Arcadia," Quant said. "Wilson will want to strike at the Chen first."

"Good," JieMin said.

"Yes," Quant said. "It will be easier if we know where his navy is most likely to come out of hyperspace."

"And it will be a bit easier for me to keep the 'no navies' position in place in the colony governments if it is Arcadia that is first threatened," ChaoLi said. "Luisa Bianchi is no blushing flower, and she trusts us to handle it. Some of the others may not stick to the plan if the Earth fleet were to show up there first."

"Yes, his navy would be pretty intimidating without a counter to it," Quant said.

"How big is his navy, Janice?" JieMin asked.

"It looks like it will be around a hundred ships," Quant said. "A bit more, I think. Mounting, among other things, space to surface nuclear weapons."

"Is he insane?" ChaoLi asked. "Two can play that game. Then nobody wins."

"Bear in mind the history of Earth, ChaoLi," Quant said. "Horrific casualties were common. Slaughtering millions, military and civilian alike. This is not unusual at all in that context. Wilson's more of a reversion to type."

"We will deal with his navy when the time comes," JieMin said.

More colony finds came into Wilson's office over the following months as his tactic paid off. On three thousand light-year centers, the map began to grow. Aruba, Earthsea, Playa, Olympia, Westernesse. As they came in, they were added to a three-dimensional star map.

Soon they had only five colonies left to find. Wilson stared at the map, trying to see the opportunities for new finds in the gaps.

"Only five more to go, sir," Braida said.

"Yes," Wilson said. "But it's hard to see the pattern."

Wilson rotated the map around. Was that gap big enough, in

the middle of those three colonies?

"Tony, can you shade in a three thousand light-year diameter ball around each of these?"

"I think so, sir."

Braida manipulated some controls.

"Ah, yes," Wilson said when the display changed. "Much better. Like a stack of cannonballs."

Wilson started setting pins in the three-dimensional display.

"Let's send some probes to look here, here, here."

Wilson rotated the display a bit more.

"And here, here, and here. Oh, and here."

Wilson rotated the display again.

"Let's see. Here, here, here, here, and here."

Wilson rotated the display on the other axis.

"And here, here, here, and here. Get some probes heading out to those locations, Tony. They have to be in some place like that."

"Yes, sir. It is pretty obvious when you map them like that. I'll get people right on it."

Wilson continued to stare at the map and play with it off and on that day. He added five more possible locations, and sent those off to Braida.

Meanwhile Wilson's space navy was working up. The hardest part had been staffing it. Wilson was able to move some people, especially the more senior officers, from the World Authority's sea navy.

While there were no other nations with which to fight naval battles on Earth, there was always the problem of piracy. As long as men had been plying the sea in boats, other men had gone to sea to steal from them. So the World Authority maintained a navy sufficient to suppress piracy, though they could never get rid of it all.

One problem with using wet navy officers in his vacuum navy ships is that a lot of officers' first reaction was to think of five hundred or a thousand men on a ship. Wilson couldn't staff that size of crews in the time he had, and they wouldn't all fit aboard anyway.

Wilson thought of the ships more as destroyers than cruisers. Maybe even frigates. A hundred spacers total. No more. What would they do all day in space?

Wilson suspected the senior officers were worried there wouldn't be enough people aboard to salute them sufficiently often.

And they couldn't say Wilson didn't know what he was talking about. He had spent six years at sea.

He had found a senior officer he liked, however. A rear admiral in the World Authority's navy. Not so far from captain that he didn't still have salt air in his lungs, but experienced at thinking in terms of multiple ships and bigger missions.

Wilson promoted him and put him in command of World Authority's space fleet.

Vice Admiral Dennis Stevens was at that moment going over the latest readiness reports on the ships reporting to his new assignment. It was taking some getting used to.

First thing is that the ships were so fragile. They were more like the air assets under his command in the navy than they were like warships. One solid hit from something like those platinum tetrahedrons the Arcadians had deployed against the World Authority shuttles and surface-to-air missiles six years ago could take out a ship.

Of course, armoring the ship against projectiles – like those or even bigger – could be done, but then you ended up with a brick. A heavy, slow target with limited military utility. It would just end up being the backstop for the weapons fire of smaller, more maneuverable assets.

Second thing is the ships were not small exactly, but had limited volume. The Arcadians' design of a spinning wheel or cylinder was well considered, Stevens thought, because it gave you full gravity without coriolis forces being so high as to make life aboard difficult. Spin a smaller ship faster to get the same gravity, and it was hard to pour a cup of coffee.

So it wasn't so much that they were small as that they had limited volume. Crew sizes had to be small because you needed enough room not just for them, but for all the supplies they would need, plus some things you usually took for granted. Air, for example. The result was a hundred ships had a total crew of barely ten thousand.

Third thing was that they would be carrying nuclear weapons. Nuclear weapons had been around for four hundred and fifty years, but they had previously had limited or no utility for the World Authority. One just didn't need that big of a piece of ordinance to deal with pirates.

They also had the disadvantage of spreading a lot of radioactive crap everywhere, and so it wasn't something you wanted to use on your own planet if you could avoid it.

For this mission, though, against an insurrection against World Authority sovereignty by entire planets, there may be a mission profile that would require their use.

The fourth thing was that there was no communications method from the fleet to home shorter than twelve weeks at a minimum. This had been the case in Earth navies in the past, of course, up until 1900 or so.

Ship's captains then had been used to being out of contact with home for months at a time. They had their orders and their mission, and they also had the training and experience, by then in their careers, to make the tough calls on their own.

Stevens did not have that experience. He had always been able to contact headquarters for clarification or guidance. In this assignment, however, the fastest he could get any input or feedback was to dispatch a ship back to Earth and wait a minimum of three months for the round-trip reply.

Looking into the history of wet navies on Earth, Stevens found that large fleets often did just that, maintaining contact with a small group of ships that continuously relayed messages, and decided he would do something like that himself.

It did, in fact, take the best part of a year to find the remaining five colonies. Earth's manufacturing capacity had allowed it to send out thousands of probes. Once the three thousand light-year 'rule' had become known, the problem had been reduced in size enough they simply swamped the possible spaces with probes until they found them.

Wilson now knew where all the colony planets were, he had his navy, worked up and exercised, under a competent commander, and he had his plan.

It was time to act.

It was the year 2398 on Arcadia's calendar. Chen JieMin and Chen ChaoLi had been Chen Zufu and Chen Zumu of the Chen-Jasic family for seven years. They were sixty-seven and sixty-eight years old respectively, but, thanks to the Tahiti anti-aging treatments, looked to be in their late forties.

It was the year 2404 on Earth's calendar. Jonathan David Wilson, nee Anup Patel, had been World Authority Chairman for the same seven years. Wilson was now sixty-four years old in the records, though he was sixty years old in actuality, and he looked and felt it.

It was the year Earth would finally move against its colonies, forcing them to acknowledge World Authority sovereignty over them or be destroyed.

Wilson expected them to choose survival.

He did not at all expect what actually happened.

Assault On Arcadia

"Chairman Wilson has found all twenty-four colonies now, and his navy is provisioning for space," Quant said.

"You're all prepared, Janice?" JieMin asked.

"Oh, yes. I'm good."

"Do we need to make any changes to our plans?"

"No," Quant said. "I have the design documentation for all of his ships, so I should be able to pull it off."

"Excellent. Keep an eye on them."

"I will, JieMin. I'm monitoring their communications frequencies in all twenty-four systems already, so I should see them communicating as soon as they emerge from hyperspace. You should be watching for them, too, ChaoLi."

"All Jixing assets in every system will be watching for them once they go into hyperspace, Janice," ChaoLi said. "We have at least one ship in orbit around every planet non-stop now, so we're good there. And the planetary executives of every planet have agreed to let me know as soon as they see anything as well."

"Sounds like we're all good," JieMin said.

"Oh, this is going to be fun," Quant said, smiling broadly. "Reminds me of the good old days."

JieMin chuckled and shook his head.

Quant was just, well, Quant.

One of Admiral Stevens' problems in taking a fleet from Earth to Arcadia in hyperspace is that his ships had no way to communicate or navigate while in hyperspace. One sort of lined up on one's destination and went, counting off the time in hyperspace based on known acceleration and velocity curves.

The result of that is that his fleet would emerge from hyperspace all higgledy-piggledy, and that was assuming they didn't simply run into each other when they emerged.

It was the equivalent of taking a wet navy all the way across an ocean with no navigation on the way, in radio silence, and without looking out the windows.

Stevens' solution was to have his fleet make the bulk of the journey in one hop, emerge close to Arcadia, regroup, then make the much smaller hop to the planet. That smaller hop would not be enough to jumble his fleet.

And all of this had to be arranged, documented, briefed to the crews, and exercised ahead of time, because, once they went into hyperspace, there was no inter-ship communication.

As for supplies, unlike a commercial ship, which expects to be able to resupply at a friendly destination, a military ship has to have enough supplies aboard to make it back home again without resupply. Stevens' mission plan also assumed multiple destination planets before ships could return to Earth for resupply.

One thing Wilson's urgency for lots of warships had done is cause him to ignore the need for fleet supply ships. Such ships ply back and forth between the deployed fleet and the friendly port or ports supplying the fleet. They were the equivalent of an army's logistic train, the fleets of supply trucks that kept the army eating, moving, and fighting.

Stevens' knew that, but he had not been involved in the early decision making, and he had no fleet supply ships. No logistic train. He compensated for this weakness by jury rigging an extra six weeks of supplies on all his ships.

Crews strapped or latched containers to anything available, and welded cleats on the vessels if nothing else availed. Some of his enlisted personnel had been drawn from Earth's existing space-based construction industry, so they had the expertise to perform those sorts of modifications.

The plan was to shed empty or mostly empty supply containers, and full or mostly full waste containers, once they got to the rendezvous point. They would then use the shuttles they had along to move the temporarily mounted containers to the locations provided in the original designs. They would thus arrive at Arcadia fully provisioned.

On an ongoing basis, Stevens' would get to the point where he would have to rotate a quarter of his fleet at a time through Earth for resupply, and operate at seventy-five percent of his nominal fleet strength more or less continuously. It was a waste of warships, but that's the choice he had.

Until Arcadia or one of the other planets surrendered, at least. Then he could commandeer colony-planet freighters to be his fleet supply ships.

Stevens met with Wilson one final time in a video call before the fleet set out for Arcadia. He was already aboard his flagship, the World Authority Ship (WAS) *Gunter Mannheim*.

"You're clear on your mission, Admiral?" Wilson asked.

"Yes, sir. Require a recognition of World Authority sovereignty from each planetary executive, who can then remain as director of the administrative region that planet represents."

"And do not take No for an answer, Admiral. Use whatever force you have to in order to get that recognition."

"Yes, sir," Stevens said. "Including nuclear weapons."

"That's right, Admiral. Oh, not their capital cities, but you can make sure they understand that No is not an option. And if you have to make an example of one of them, well, then the others will be more likely to fall into line. There's only fifty million people or so on each planet, so casualties will be light in any case."

"I understand, sir."

"You can also do things like drop a full waste container on their downtown from a hundred miles up. Hell of a mess, apart and aside from the destruction. That sort of thing.

"What you absolutely cannot do, Admiral, is let one get away with its defiance. That will embolden the rest and we'll never get them under control. Not without a lot more effort and a lot more casualties."

"Yes, sir."

"Then you need to liquidate or commandeer any military assets they have. You cannot leave an independent armed force behind. That's just asking for trouble. If they won't surrender, then destroy them, but don't leave any military assets outside your control."

"Absolutely, sir."

"Very well, then, Admiral. Good luck and good spacing."

"Thank you, Mr. Chairman."

The *Gunter Mannheim* was one of half a dozen ships in Stevens' fleet with a flag bridge. The others were also named after past World Authority Chairmen. One of them was even named the WAS *Janice Quant*. The irony that these ships would be going out to abrogate the agreement that World Authority Chairman Janice Quant had written and executed with the colonists was lost on her builders and crew.

On his flag bridge, Stevens turned to his chief of staff, Rear Admiral Atsuki Mori.

"All right, Atsuki. Let's get everybody under way."

"Aye, Sir."

Mori nodded to the comm officer and the message went out.

"Message from the Flag. Prepare for departure. All squadrons report when ready."

Ninety-seven ships. A bit short of Wilson's one-hundred-ship target, but that had always been an arbitrary number. Six ships had simply not been ready, for a number of reasons. Engineering failure on their space trials was the most common.

But squadron commanders all responded within minutes. All ninety-seven ships reported ready.

"Message from the Flag. All ships depart orbit."

In clusters by squadron around the world, the ships of the fleet engaged thrusters. They thrust in the direction of their orbits and thirty degrees to port or starboard so that their spiral departure from their two-hundred-mile orbit would not intersect the equatorial band of the more crowded orbits above them.

The World Authority space fleet was under way.

The fleet formed up as it continued to build velocity toward the hyperspace limit. They were only thrusting at one-quarter power because of all the extra supply containers and their jury-rigged attachment to their ships. It would take them five days to get to the hyperspace limit.

On a six-week transit, however, that didn't seem excessive, and it was more important to arrive at Arcadia fully stocked than it was to cut three or four days off their departure.

When they got to the hyperspace limit, the ships of Stevens' fleet engaged their hyperspace field generators, and, in squadrons, disappeared from normal space-time.

There was very little to do on a ship during a hyperspace crossing. Yet what needed doing had to be done properly. If it wasn't, you risked dropping out of hyperspace with no way back and no way to tell anyone what had happened to you. You were marooned, tens or hundreds of light-years from anyone who could receive your speed-of-light radio message, with mere months of supplies on board.

It was a really complicated way to kill yourself.

Cognizant of the risk, ship's officers tried to keep the crew on their toes as the weeks stretched out, not wanting to be the first ship's crew to prove just how helpless one could be made by the simplest of errors or omissions.

After six weeks in transit, fleet elements began emerging from hyperspace two light-months distant from Arcadia. They had plenty of time in two months – the time it would take their radio communications to reach Arcadia – to swap their supplies and form up as a fleet. It should take only days.

When the *Gunter Mannheim* showed up at the rendezvous, Stevens began assessing their status.

"Squadron commanders are beginning to report in, Sir," Mori said within minutes of their arrival announcement to the fleet.

"Status when you have it, Atsuki."

As reports came in, it was a mixed bag. Two squadrons had interpenetrated when the second's arrival passed through the first's position. Two ships had collided with the loss of all hands. Emergency evasive maneuvers by the others had avoided further collisions, but several squadrons had to move to avoid the drifting debris.

There was no attempt made to recover the bodies.

As ship arrivals thinned out, it became clear three ships had not made the crossing successfully. They were missing and presumed lost in space. One of them appeared a day later, having repaired the problem that had cut power to its hyperspace field generator. They had successfully transitioned back to normal space on the residual available power, having been quick to respond to the problem.

It may have been the same mechanical failure in the other two ships. Perhaps their crews were not quite as quick.

Stevens ordered all ships to inspect for the issue, and two more power connections were found that had not failed, but were on the verge of doing so.

Hell of a way to shake down your ships, doing it on a real mission, but sometimes needs must, Stevens thought.

It took two days to safely jettison the empty supplies containers and full waste containers, on trajectories away from the fleet, and cycle their replacements into position.

Once complete, the fleet transitioned into hyperspace and made the final short transit to Arcadia.

Luisa Bianchi was working at her desk in the prime minister's office in the Administration Building in downtown Arcadia City.

They were all hyper-alert, because they knew the Earth fleet had set off in hyperspace a little over six weeks ago, and they weren't on a pleasure cruise. Everyone expected the call to come soon as to where they were, and Arcadia was the expectation.

Bianchi got a quick warning from JieMin – 'They're here, at the hyperspace limit. If they call you, make them angry if you can.' – and then she got a video call request. The call had been patched through from Arcadia Traffic Control.

EARTH

Bianchi accepted the call in VR and sat facing a man in his forties in some sort of uniform, three stars on his shoulders, seated in some sort of swivel chair with a safety harness. He looked very serious and also, somehow, prim and proper.

"Bianchi," she said.

"This is Vice Admiral Dennis Stevens of the World Authority Space Navy. Arcadia is being reorganized as an administrative region of the World Authority. I am here to ensure that outcome."

"Not likely, asshole. Not interested."

Stevens reddened, then his face hardened.

"I have my fleet here, and we are prepared to use whatever force is required to compel your cooperation, up to and including bombarding the planet."

He talked about bombarding a planet full of peaceful people minding their own business like it was dropping off laundry at the dry cleaners, and Bianchi completely lost it.

"Listen, *segaiolo*. You tell that *stronzo* Wilson to write his ultimatums down on a piece of paper, fold it until it's all corners, and shove it up his ass till he bleeds."

She accompanied this with the appropriate gesture, but she wasn't done.

"And as for you, *faccia a culo*, his little lap dog, with your cute little stars on your leash, you can just *mangia merde e morte. Vaffanculo, coglione*."

She accompanied that one with the appropriate gesture as well, then cut the connection.

"Well, that was fun," Bianchi said to her empty office.

She put in a call to JieMin.

"Hi, JieMin. Mission accomplished. He's probably pretty pissed at the moment. And if he knows any Italian, he's *really* pissed."

Arcadia Responds

When the Earth fleet emerged from hyperspace at the hyperspace limit, there were a lot of radio communications between ships as they got themselves organized.

Jixing Trading RDF probes with QE radios, not used since the last colonies had been found on the *Wanderlust* mission, had been stationed around the planet at the hyperspace limit to listen for them. JieMin, ChaoLi, and Janice Quant knew the Earth fleet was at Arcadia within minutes.

They all got together in a VR meeting.

"Well, they're here," ChaoLi said.

"Good," JieMin said. "Here is good."

"Yes, it's easier."

"I need to warn Luisa," JieMin said, and he made a quick call to Bianchi.

He went blank-faced for a couple seconds, then his attention was back in the meeting.

"I told Luisa they were here, and told her to make them angry if she could."

"You told Luisa to make them angry?" ChaoLi asked. "Oh, my."

Quant raised an eyebrow to JieMin.

"Luisa has a way with words," he said.

ChaoLi laughed like little bells.

"Oh, you might say that," she said, rolling her eyes.

"Good," Quant said. "It never hurts to have your enemy not thinking clearly."

"And you're ready, Janice?" JieMin asked.

"Oh, yes. They're sorting themselves out into fleet order now. I'm monitoring from nearby."

"Is that going to be a problem?"

"Not as long as they stay within twelve thousand miles of each other. And they're in a knot a couple hundred miles on a side at the moment."

"Good," JieMin said. "Excellent."

"I'll let you know when they begin moving toward Arcadia, JieMin."

"And then I'll talk to Admiral Stevens."

Vice Admiral Stevens did not, in fact, know Italian. But his communications computer translated foreign languages for him automatically. Earth still had a lot of different countries and regions speaking different languages, and such equipment was necessary.

It had done a marvelous job in rendering Prime Minister Bianchi's reply in perfect English, in her voice, and dripping with sarcasm and contempt, as she had said it:

"Listen, wanker. You tell that asshole Wilson to write his ultimatums down on a piece of paper, fold it until it's all corners, and shove it up his ass till he bleeds.

"And as for you, ass-face, his little lap dog, with your cute little stars on your leash, you can just eat shit and die. Fuck off, moron."

Then she cut the connection.

Mori had been monitoring.

"Personally, I think that sort of invective is more effective in Japanese," he said. "Mostly because it's so seldom used."

Mori's dry humor acted to defuse Stevens' anger a bit. He just wasn't used to being talked to that dismissively, and he didn't like it. Not one bit.

"Yeah, and in German it would sound like somebody cutting sheet steel with a chain saw."

"Yes, but in German, so does a lullaby."

Stevens nodded absently.

"I guess we do it the hard way. Get us under way, Atsuki."

"Aye, Sir."

"It'll be nice to make her eat those words. That's for sure."

"They're moving, JieMin," Quant said.

"Very well, Janice. Patch me in."

"Hello, Admiral Stevens."

There was no preamble, no call request. Suddenly, on the flag bridge display of the *Gunter Mannheim*, where Luisa Bianchi had appeared for her conversation with Stevens, this man appeared.

Stevens' caller looked to be in his late forties, was naked from the waist up, with his long hair in a pony tail. He wore a sari, and was seated tailor seat on a pillow before a teak-beamed doorway opening on a tropical garden.

With everyone's attention on JieMin, no one noticed the appearance of a twelve thousand mile diameter geodesic sphere around the Earth fleet. Over five thousand miles away at its closest point to the fleet, it was radar-absorbent, absolutely black, and nearly impossible to detect from inside against the blackness of space.

Janice Quant began ranging ships, collecting coordinates, tagging masses. She would be ready by the signal.

"Who are you?" Wilson asked the man in his viewscreen.

"I am the Chen," he said softly.

218

"What's that to me?"

"Are you here in peace or in conquest, Admiral Stevens?"

"I am here to assert the sovereignty of the World Authority over its colony Arcadia."

"As that is an abrogation of the agreement between the World Authority and the colonists of 2245, I take your answer as conquest of an independent planet, Admiral Stevens. I am sorry, but that is not permitted."

"Not permitted? Not permitted by whom?"

"By me, Admiral Stevens."

"And who are you to permit or not permit anything?"

"As I said, Admiral Stevens, I am the Chen."

"I've heard about you. From Chairman Wilson. You're on Arcadia. You're under my guns, and, quite frankly, you're not in a position to permit or not permit anything."

"You will not be allowed to approach the planet or harm anyone on it, Admiral Stevens. You are not welcome here. Go home, back to Earth, and leave the people of Arcadia in peace."

"Like hell I will. Your request is rejected."

"It was not a request, Admiral Stevens. You are going back to Earth. We can do that your way or my way."

"I'm not leaving, Mr. Chen. I intend to subdue this planet and assert World Authority sovereignty whether you like it or not."

"My way, then. Very well. Goodbye, Admiral Stevens."

JieMin raised his hands from his lap, where they had sat through the whole conversation, then clapped them together once.

The Chen disappeared from the forward viewscreen and a blue-green planet was once again centered in the display. Stevens turned to Mori to say something, but he was interrupted by a staffer who was looking at the viewscreen curiously.

"Admiral Stevens? Does Arcadia have a Moon, Sir?"

On the bridge of the *Gunter Mannheim*, alarm signals were sounding all over the bridge. Excited bridge crew started reporting to the captain.

"Captain, our hyperspace field generator is off-line, Sir. It shows no status at all."

"Captain, our ordinance racks are empty. All weapons systems show 'Ready for loading' and a zero ammunition level."

"What about the nukes?"

"The weapons magazines and racks are all empty, Sir. That includes the space-to-surface missiles."

It took the best part of an hour to figure out what had happened, inventory the fleet, and collect data back from all the ships.

First, the planet ahead of them was Earth, not Arcadia.

Second, they were the same distance from the hyperspace limit, bound for Earth at the same velocity, and their thrusters were firing at the same level of thrust, as they had been at Arcadia.

Third, the hyperspace generators on all the ships were missing. They were simply gone. Unlike Arcadian ships, whose hyperspace unit was modular and mounted on the outside of the ship, the Earth ships carried their hyperspace field generators internally, deep within the hull. They were integral to the ship.

Crews on all ships had gone to the engine room to inspect the hyperspace field generator and found it physically missing. There was a big open space in the room where it had been, in the very center of the ship. In ships with redundant hyperspace field generators, they were both missing.

Fourth, all weapons systems were empty. No missiles, no nukes, no projectiles. They were simply all empty, whether the ordinance was mounted externally or carried in magazines internal to the ship. There was no ammo for any weapons system in the entire fleet.

It had taken Admiral Stevens and his ninety-three surviving ships seven weeks to get to Arcadia.

The fleet had been returned to Earth in the blink of an eye, while being rendered toothless and incapable of hyperspace.

Doubling Down

"That was nicely done, Janice," JieMin said.

"Thank you, JieMin. You did a nice job with Admiral Stevens as well. Now we'll have to see what Chairman Wilson does."

"What did you do with their weapons and hyperspace field generators, Janice?" ChaoLi asked.

"I transported them to the chromosphere of Alpha Centauri A, where they constituted a minor solar flare. They're gone."

"So they can't come back out here and threaten us again," ChaoLi said.

"Not for a while, anyway," JieMin said.

The reports came in to Luisa Bianchi from her staff.

The Earth fleet – all ninety-some ships of it – had simply disappeared. Gone. Arcadia was safe.

Bianchi had no clue about whatever JieMin had done, but it reminded her of something Rob Milbank had told her long ago.

"Do not underestimate the Chen."

"What the hell are they doing back here?" Wilson shouted at Braida on his display. "Did they even go to Arcadia?"

"Yes, sir. As I'm trying to tell you."

Wilson tried to calm down, but it was hard. He had spent the last seven years – all of his chairmanship – on this project.

"Sorry, Tony. Go ahead."

"Yes, sir. Admiral Stevens called the prime minister of Arcadia and presented his position, and she told him, in no uncertain terms and laced with profanity, to pound sand. Admiral Stevens got his fleet in order and began his approach to Arcadia, when he received a video call from the Chen."

"The same guy as called me?"

"Yes, sir. The Chen told him he would not be able to approach Arcadia or harm anyone on the planet, and told him to go back to Earth. When Admiral Stevens refused, the Chen clapped his hands once, and the fleet was back here, the same distance from Earth it had been from Arcadia."

"That's unbelievable."

"I have the recordings for you, sir."

"And when they got back here, their weapons and hyperspace field generators were gone?" Wilson asked.

"Yes, sir. Well, the ammunition is gone, anyway. The weapons remain. And the hyperspace field generators are gone as well."

"Those are deep in the ship, Tony. Were there holes in the hull?"

"No, sir," Braida said. "Just empty engine rooms. Some of the weapons magazines are pretty deep in the ship, too. The magazines were there, but they were all empty."

"And full when they left."

"Yes, sir."

"So they spent seven weeks in hyperspace to go three thousand light-years, and the Chen clapped his hands and they were back here?" Wilson asked

"Yes, sir. The recordings don't have any transition at all. One frame they are there, the next frame they are here."

"Three thousand light-years?"

"Yes, sir," Braida said.

"Tony, how can that be?"

"We don't know, sir, but one of the staffers brought up the

Lake-Shore Drive that the World Authority used to transport the colonists in the first place."

"Of course! That must be it. This Chen character or his family has reproduced the Lake-Shore Drive."

There was a terrible symmetry to the idea. The World Authority under Janice Quant had used the Lake-Shore Drive to deliver the colonists, and now the colonists were using the Lake-Shore Drive to bottle the World Authority up in the Earth system.

The idea that Janice Quant herself was Wilson's nemesis never occurred to Wilson or Braida. After all, she died almost a hundred and sixty years ago.

"That could be it, sir," Braida said. "That's the only thing anyone here can come up with. And we've been analyzing the radio data Admiral Stevens downloaded from our probe in the Arcadia system. The Chen – variously called Chen Zufu or Chen JieMin – is the fellow who discovered hyperspace on Arcadia fifty-five years ago. Like Dieter Wagner did here on Earth."

"Not fifty-five years ago, Tony. He can't even be fifty-five years old."

"In Earth years, the Chen is seventy years old, sir. That's well established. He discovered hyperspace when he was fifteen. He's something of a mathematical prodigy."

"I still don't believe the age thing," Wilson said, "but the math prodigy lines up with the idea of him also discovering the Lake-Shore Drive."

"Yes, sir. On the age thing, I might mention that Rob Milbank, when he was here six or seven years ago, was ninety years old."

"And he didn't look a day over seventy. Yes, I see, Tony. They must have some sort of anti-aging technology as well. So this Chen guy could be seventy."

"Anti-aging technology would be nice to have, sir," Braida said. "We're not getting any younger."

"Yes, and I'm working that as hard as I can, Tony. You don't think they'll actually trade for that, do you? If we can assert sovereignty over the colonies, though, we get all that stuff."

"Against the Lake-Shore Drive, sir?"

"There must be a way to defeat them anyway. Have people looking into that. Maybe we can swamp their defenses. Those transporters back in 2245 were huge. How many such transporters can he have?"

"All right, sir. We'll look into it."

"And we need to re-equip the fleet. Get hyperspace field generators back on those ships. Resupply the ammunition."

"Engineering says it will take years to open up the hulls, reinstall hyperspace field generators, and close the hulls back up again, sir."

"Then they're thinking about it wrong. They don't have to put them back where they were. Just bolt the damn things on the outside of the ships."

"I'll tell them, sir."

Wilson stared out the picture windows of his office and down the Colorado Gulf toward the passage to the Gulf of Nicoya and the Pacific Ocean beyond. As usual on such a beautiful day, young local girls frolicked nude in his pool. Today it raised no desire in him. It just brought his age home to him.

Despite the records, Wilson was actually sixty years old, and his body had started reminding him of that on a persistent basis. His mortality was making itself known, and wasn't being subtle about it.

The Chen, however, was ten years older than Wilson was. Had discovered hyperspace when Wilson was only five years old. Before Wilson had set out on the journey that had taken him out of the slums forever.

Yet the Chen looked perhaps fifty. In the recordings, he didn't look much older than he had at their last confrontation six years ago, whereas Wilson had noticeably aged during the same period. Had aged a great deal, in fact.

Would the colonies actually trade such technology? What could Earth possibly offer them in trade? Wilson knew for a fact that their cigars were better than Earth products. Even the best Earth products. So was their chocolate, their wine, their liquor, their beef. The list went on and on.

Wilson shook his head. No. Earth would be a beggar at the colonies' banquet table.

He had promised himself decades ago never to beg again.

"I don't think Mr. Wilson has yet rethought his approach," Quant said. "In fact, I think he's doubling down."

"What are you seeing, Janice?" ChaoLi asked.

JieMin and ChaoLi knew that Quant was monitoring a lot of computer activity on Earth, through the use of her interstellar communications probes in the Asteroid Belt. She had built trap doors in the Earth's computer systems before she left in 2245, and had used that access to infect new systems as they were developed.

"He's ordered the fleet re-equipped, and fitted with new hyperspace field generators on the outside of the hulls."

"He still thinks he can prevail against us after that little demonstration you arranged, Janice?" ChaoLi asked.

"Apparently so," Quant said. "What's worrying is that they are also looking into the Lake-Shore Drive."

"Do they have any chance of reproducing that, Janice?" JieMin asked.

Quant waved the question away.

"No, JieMin," she said. "I don't even know how it works, at least in this persona. I have to switch into another, completely different context to even consider the problem."

"Then what's the problem?" ChaoLi asked.

"They're looking for ways to defeat me, even with the Lake-Shore Drive. The current favorite appears to be attacking all twenty-four colony planets at once, with four ships per colony, coming in from different directions."

"Could you handle that, Janice?" ChaoLi asked.

"I think so. I have three transporters, and the actual mathematics work can be assigned to groups of multiprocessor blades for independent action. It would be a little touchy, but I think I'm okay on that one.

"The second plan is more concerning. That one involves equipping the thousands of probes they used to find the colonies with nuclear weapons. That is a problem I'm not sure I can handle, especially since something as sturdy as a probe can transition much closer than the hyperspace limit."

"And that one's the problem."

"Yes, ChaoLi. It would be a very dicey situation. I might be able to get them all, but some might leak through."

"And the problem with nuclear weapons," JieMin said, "is that even one can ruin your whole day."

"Indeed," Quant said. "I think it may therefore be time to make one last effort to make Chairman Wilson change his mind."

JieMin nodded.

"One more confrontation," he said.

"Yes. What we talked about before."

"Do you think that will work, Janice?"

"I don't know. I think so. Especially if we do the good cop, bad cop version."

"Oh, that sounds like fun," ChaoLi said, clapping her hands. "I get to be the dragon lady."

Good Cop, Bad Cop

Wilson took a break from paperwork – a misnomer, as it was all done on his display – and smoked a cigar as he looked out the windows of his office. The young local women were playing nude in the pool today, except for Consuela, who had twisted an ankle. She was instead sunning herself on one of the loungers, her ankle boot being her one item of apparel this afternoon.

Such deliciously slender ankles turned out to be a weakness. Who knew?

He took another puff of his cigar, then put it in the ashtray and sighed. He missed the Spring cigars that had been in the container of gifts Chen ChaoPing, Rob Milbank and the rest had brought him six years ago. He was smoking one of Earth's best right now, but it wasn't the same.

"Good afternoon, Mr. Chairman."

Wilson started and turned around. On his display was the Chen, seated on his pillow before the teak-framed doorway into his garden. Wilson didn't try to turn the display off. He already knew that wouldn't work.

"I should have known," Wilson said. "The one thing that could spoil such a beautiful day."

"It's good to see you, too, Mr. Chairman," JieMin said. "For what it's worth, I, too, am disappointed. Disappointed that you have not yet dropped your attempt to conquer a billion free, independent people who are no threat to you at all."

"I'm not attempting to conquer anyone. I am going to assert World Authority sovereignty over the colonies it paid for."

"And which sovereignty it voluntarily signed away in legal documents with all two-point-four million colonists, Mr. Chairman."

"A legal point on which we disagree."

"In any case, you will not be allowed to succeed. I will not permit it."

"You have nothing to say about it. You have no official position, and certainly no official position over me."

"You have no official position over the colonies either, Mr. Chairman. Yet that does not prevent you from using force to impose your will. If that is your concept of government – who has the power has the right to rule – what is to prevent me from using force to impose my will on you?"

"You can't do anything to me. I can and will assert World Authority sovereignty over the colonies, however."

The Chen paused to consider.

"Perhaps this conversation would be more fruitful if conducted in person, Mr. Chairman."

"You're coming here?" Wilson asked.

"No, Mr. Chairman. You are coming here."

The Chen clapped his hands, and Wilson was sitting on a pillow across from the Chen over a tea table. The tropical garden was visible through the teak-framed doorway behind him.

Seated on another pillow alongside him was a woman, also apparently in her late fifties, and dressed in a silk robe decorated with embroidered dragons rampant. She was very pretty, with auburn highlights in her still-dark hair.

"Wha– Wait. Where am I?" Wilson asked.

"Welcome to Arcadia, Mr. Chairman," the woman said. "I am Chen Zumu. I am the other half of the couple known on Arcadia as the Chen."

EARTH

Wilson struggled to come to grips with what had happened. How had they done that? He had been on Earth. The one thing everybody had been clear about was that the Lake-Shore Drive could only transport objects within its field. Could they enclose the entire Earth? Or did they have some other mechanism entirely?

"You were saying, Mr. Chairman, that I could do nothing to you," JieMin said. "That is clearly untrue. I can do to you and with you anything I care to, and could have at anytime during these protracted negotiations. In contrast, you and your forces cannot approach Arcadia or any other colony. Nor can you do anything whatsoever to me."

A tea girl entered, set an additional cup before Wilson, and poured tea from the pot on the table. She also topped off JieMin's and ChaoLi's teacups. She bowed to Wilson, to the Chen, and left.

"However, you are my guest," JieMin continued, "and I am known for treating my guests better than you do. Please, have some tea."

JieMin waved to the cup on the table, one of a matched set with theirs. Wilson picked the cup up with trembling hands and sipped the tea. Once he had, ChaoLi and then JieMin sipped their tea as well.

Wilson had drunk his share of tea when he was young, in Asia. He had never been a fan, but this tea was extraordinary. The warm liquid calmed him, allowing him to collect his thoughts.

"You would conquer Earth, then?" Wilson asked.

"I could, Mr. Chairman. Or destroy it, for that matter."

"Destroying Earth would kill four billion people. The colonies together are only one billion."

"If four ruffians attack an innocent man – to mug him, to rob him – does he not have the right to defend himself, Mr. Chairman? Even to the use of deadly force? Or should he acquiesce because they outnumber him? The moral equation does not change when one scales up the problem.

"That is not my intent, however. I wish to leave the World Authority in place, under its chairman, as an independent planet, conducting free trade in friendship with the other independent planets, the colonies."

Wilson was regaining his wits from the shock of his sudden transport to Arcadia. Or was it? Was all this a ruse? A trick played through his display? Some sort of delusion, anyway. Was he not still sitting in his office on Earth, after all?

The Chen – Chen Zufu, Wilson supposed – sat looking at him benignly, but the woman – Chen Zumu – was watching him intently.

Wilson shook his head. It was a trick! He knew it. They simply couldn't do such a thing.

"No," Wilson said flatly. "The colonies are possessions rightfully the property of Earth and the World Authority. That is now and will always be true."

"I have heard enough," ChaoLi said. "You are clearly too stupid and arrogant to be World Authority Chairman. Perhaps your successor will not suffer from these deficits."

ChaoLi snapped her fingers, and Wilson was back on Earth. Or rather, above it. He looked down on his residence on Chira Island from five thousand feet in the air.

He began falling.

If this was a trick, it was a good one. Wilson began tumbling, and lost a shoe. He remembered seeing skydivers spread out their arms and legs and did so, stopping his tumble.

Wilson now looked down on his estate as it rapidly approached. He would impact on the concrete pool deck, where Consuela sunned on one of the loungers, wearing only the ankle boot, as he had seen her from his office.

He was at terminal velocity now, falling at a hundred and twenty miles an hour. He would die, he knew, and his life flashed before his eyes. Certain scenes of it. His childhood. His time at sea. His political career. All the compromises and accommodations to get to where he was.

And his ultimate goal all along: to stay out of the slums himself, at whatever cost, and to raise the poor up out of those slums if he could.

All to remain undone.

To come to an end.

Here.

Now.

Abruptly, from a hundred feet above the pool deck, less than a second from impact, he was back on Arcadia, sitting once again across from the Chen.

"I have been persuaded to give you a second chance, Mr. Chairman," ChaoLi said. "Or rather, a fifth one. We might as well deal with you. There is, after all, no guarantee your successor will be any smarter or less stubborn."

Wilson gasped in relief, though his heart still raced from adrenaline. He took deep, full breaths to calm himself.

Had that been a trick?

No. His hair and clothing were mussed from the fall. He still felt the tingle on his face and hands from the buffeting. He was missing a shoe.

He remembered Consuela, sunning, wearing her ankle boot, just as he had left her.

"Wh-What sort of deal do you propose?" Wilson asked.

"The same one we proposed seven years ago, Mr. Chairman," JieMin said. "Free trade. Equal status. For all humanity's planets."

"Free trade? Including your technologies, such as your anti-aging techniques?"

"Yes, Mr. Chairman."

"I find that hard to believe," Wilson said.

"Why, Mr. Chairman? The anti-aging treatments are not Arcadia's technology, but Tahiti's. What is Tahiti to do with its extra capacity if not trade it for what it wants in return? In fact, they do trade it. I am proof of it."

JieMin caught Wilson's eye and held it.

"How old would you say I am, Mr. Chairman?"

"You look to be approaching fifty, but I know that's not true."

"That is correct, Mr. Chairman. I am, in fact, seventy Earth years old."

"And I," ChaoLi said imperiously, "am older still."

Wilson shuddered involuntarily when the woman spoke again. She was not to be messed with, it was clear, and he knew he was on thin ice with her already. He turned to JieMin.

"What could Earth possibly trade for such a technology? Your wines and liquors, cigars and chocolates – every product in the container of gifts your delegation left seven years ago – are superior to any Earth product."

"Your manufacturing capacity for one, Mr. Chairman. When we developed the hyperspace drive and went looking for the other colonies, we fielded a total of half a dozen hand-built hyperspace probes.

"In contrast, you sent out thousands upon thousands of mass-manufactured probes. We could not even think to do something like that. Imagine what we could accomplish together if our technology was being built in your factories.

"Your agricultural capacity, too. Think of the potential for transplanting some of Tahiti's apple tree hybrids, or Hawaii's citrus tree hybrids, back to Earth, Mr. Chairman.

"The mind boggles at the possibilities. We have only to get started."

"You would do this?"

"Of course, Mr. Chairman. Why would we not? Why would we deny ourselves the huge benefits Earth could bring as a trading partner, in order to withhold things of which we have an excess? And a richer, healthier Earth is an even more valuable trading partner."

With the multiple shocks to his worldview – first the instantaneous return of his defanged navy, then being transported here, and finally his near-death experience and reprieve – Wilson finally began to see. The colonies as trading partners would actually be more valuable to Earth than truculent conquered states, resisting and sabotaging his efforts at every turn.

And that was assuming that Wilson could ever hope to conquer the colonies. The Chen's ability to transport both to and from the Earth's surface made such a concept laughable.

But he was back to his real goals, his original goals, clear to him once more.

"I am most interested in those things which would help the Earth's poor," Wilson said. "At least at first. You once told me that you knew I was a street urchin in the slums of Kolkata. That is true. I would clean up the Earth's slums, by lifting people out of poverty."

"I began working at the age of five, Mr. Chairman," JieMin said, "doing stoop labor in the tea fields of a poor farming village. Do not doubt that on this matter we have the same goals."

Wilson closed his eyes and considered. The growing doubts

about his previous path had been right all along. He had wasted seven years fighting what had been a losing battle. Could never, in fact, have been anything but a losing battle. The Chen could have killed him – killed everyone in his navy, too, or everyone on the planet – at any time.

And yet, they hadn't. They had been restrained. Had not taken revenge for the shooting of their daughter and Milbank. Had transported the navy and all its personnel back to Earth, not simply destroyed them. Had not killed anyone, during this entire affair.

They had simply, quietly and insistently, offered to be friends.

Wilson felt ashamed. He had tried to conquer these people, and they still offered friendship, and incredible benefits, to him and to Earth.

Wilson opened his eyes to see Chen Zufu and Chen Zumu quietly regarding him. She looked like she had been following his thoughts. She smiled at him, like a mother at her bright child. Wilson did not bridle at it, though. Now, knowing her age and true power, her smile relaxed him.

"Yes, Mr. Chairman," ChaoLi said. "You see it now, don't you? Friends, to the benefit of all."

"How are we to proceed, then?" Wilson asked.

"Execute the trade agreement," JieMin said, "and we will send it on to the executives of all twenty-four governments. The Chen are private citizens, and not signatories."

Wilson nodded. JieMin continued.

"I also want a proclamation declaring the colonies to be free and independent planets forevermore."

That made sense as well, given Wilson's willful disregard of the 2245 colonist agreement.

Wilson nodded again.

"Very well, ChaoLi. And you wish me to hand out this assignment, I take it?"

"Please do, Oliver. It will take me twenty-four calls to do it in a diplomatic way, but you can be more businesslike about it, because you're one of the group."

Nieman nodded.

"I would be pleased to do so, ChaoLi. Timeframe?"

"Days not weeks for the executive summaries, Oliver. We want to jump on this. The addenda can come later."

"Very well. I am off to my homework, then."

He lifted his cookie – with Aruba chocolate chips – in a toast to her and cut the connection.

Jonathan David Wilson was doing paperwork in his office when he received a video call request. The header indicated it was from Arcadia, from Chen ChaoLi.

Wilson's heart skipped a beat at that. He would not soon forget his initial transport back to Earth and his fall, instigated with a snap of her fingers.

Wilson took the call request, and she appeared on his display, dressed as before in the silk robe, seated in the doorway of the same tearoom. No, that was wrong. It was a similar tearoom, but the view of the gardens was subtly different.

"Good morning, Mr. Chairman."

"Good morning, Chen Zumu."

"The other planetary executives all call me ChaoLi, Mr. Chairman."

"Is that so?" Wilson asked.

"Yes. We have all become friends over the years. I would invite the same from you."

"In that case, you must call me Jon, ChaoLi."

ChaoLi nodded, more than a simple nod, less than a bow. From his previous experience, Wilson recognized it as the respectful bow between equals. Between friends.

"Jon, I am calling today to let you know that the planetary executives are preparing briefing papers for you on their planets, on the trade goods available from them, and of their need for imported goods."

"That would be welcome, ChaoLi. All trade on Earth built up over millennia, and is now an evolutionary process. We have no experience of opening up completely new trading partners to work from."

"And we've done it a number of times, with each new colony planet. I understand, Jon. I can give you some pointers, if you would."

"Please, ChaoLi. Go ahead."

"The initial imports will be of two major types. One will be all manner of luxury goods. This does not apparently help the poor on Earth, your stated goal, but looks are deceiving. The sale of luxury goods from the colonies builds up their accounts with Earth credits, which they will then spend on products they import from Earth."

"I see," Wilson said. "For our exports to be affordable to you, the sale of luxury goods first provides the funding."

"Exactly. The other category of imports will be robots and medical technology. First, Jon, you must understand that the robots from Playa are very capable."

"Much more capable than they first let on. I've watched the security footage, ChaoLi."

ChaoLi nodded.

"They are also capable at heavy construction, as well as routine medical procedures. Those routine medical procedures within our current technology base include the anti-aging treatments and things like cures for most cancers. One of the first activities should be to have robots first build medical centers, then staff them."

"Build new medical centers?" Wilson asked.

"I doubt medical centers of the kind needed are present in your slums, Jon. The robots have the plans for the several types of buildings required in their memory, and can build them quickly, without architectural or design time. They work twenty-four hours a day, seven days a week."

"That's incredible."

"It's absolutely mesmerizing to watch them work."

"I can imagine."

"Now, the number of robots required to build the number of clinics you need, and to staff those clinics, is beyond the manufacturing capacity of Playa. I believe Playa Planetary Chairman Oliver Nieman will be looking for a licensing deal, to allow you to mass produce the number of robots you need."

"How expensive are they?" Wilson asked.

"It doesn't matter, Jon."

"It doesn't?"

"No, because the Earth credits that accrue in Playa's account can only be spent on Earth. Every one of those credits will be used to buy Earth goods for export to Playa. In any case, between the construction and staffing the clinics, the robots earn their initial cost back within months."

"Then we have robots and Playa has Earth goods."

"Which increases your employment both generating the exports and building the robots locally, even while your people are getting anti-aging treatments and cancer cures, among other things."

"It's a miracle, ChaoLi."

"It's economics, Jon."

Wilson nodded. He was familiar with similar occurrences in history, if none quite so stark.

"So how do we get started, ChaoLi?"

"I need to introduce you to Oliver Nieman, Jon. You can talk about licensing on the robots. And he is rounding up briefing papers for you on all the colony planets. And he's probably going to want to get some robots headed your way on the first ships. I think they use robots in the manufacture of robots, so you need seed robots to get started on your own manufacturing.

"As for timing, we're looking at half a dozen or more ships hitting Earth orbit within eight weeks with a lot of luxury goods and those first robots. You've got twenty to thirty thousand containers incoming."

"ChaoLi, I don't know what to say. It's– It's more than I expected."

"Like I said, Jon. Friends, to the benefit of all."

The interstellar freight hubs in Arcadia and Aruba orbit were busier than they had ever been. As ships came in off other routes, some were diverted to the initial Earth mission. They would be replaced with new construction as they rolled out of the Beacon shipyard, but for right now, the Earth mission was the priority.

Robot shipments were also diverted. Playa flushed its entire inventory of new robots into ships headed for Arcadia to make up the difference, but robots in transit through Arcadia and Aruba were re-vectored to the Earth mission.

Space Racer, Star Child, Star Trace, and *Space Lion* were the scene of all the activity on Aruba, while *Star Light, Space Beacon, Star Believer,* and *Star Omen* were drawing all the attention on Arcadia.

EARTH

ChaoLi had asked for an eight-week delivery to Earth, which gave them a bare two weeks to load everything up and get them spacing, and ChaoPing and the operations people were pulling out all the stops to make that schedule.

Wilson read through the executive summaries of the colony planets sent on by ChaoLi. It was an extraordinarily mixed bag. Aruba was one of two interstellar freight hubs, but also had those incredible chocolates. Spring had the remarkable cigars he enjoyed so much, but were also expert in human genetics.

It went on and on in that way. Playa had developed the cybernetic technology of those robots, but specialized on the side in mushrooms. Tahiti had the anti-aging treatments, with incredible varieties of apples. Arcadia had developed the hyperspace drive, yet offered exquisite teas, a panoply of spices, and even silk.

Earthsea had remarkable cheeses, but had also developed the quantum-entanglement, zero-time-of-flight radio systems. Which explained those instantaneous interstellar video calls with the Chen, even if he didn't know where the Earthside transceiver was.

They were willing to trade all this and more to Earth, in return for what? Plants and animals Earth had that they didn't, for one. The colony headquarters of the World Authority had seeded the colonies with an incredible variety of Earth plants and animals, but it was by necessity just a small subset of Earth's incredibly diverse biosphere.

Agricultural capacity for another. With all its billions, Earth was still mostly empty space. What it did have over the colonies, though, was an entire planet of arable land. The colonies were still expanding on their planets, and so were their eco-systems. The entire planet had not been prepared by colony headquarters. A planet was just too big. The rest of their planets were filling in, but it would be a long time still before the colony planets were grown out.

Another thing was manufacturing capacity. Earth routinely made things in volumes the colonies could only gape at. But what about when Earth's manufacturing capacity was turned to hyperspace shipbuilding? Or building the fabrication machines of Atlantis? Or the fusion generators of Olympia?

The mind boggled. A future of health and prosperity like humanity had never seen, either on Earth or the colonies. It was never more clear to Wilson that he had been on the wrong path.

Thank God the Chen had gotten him straightened out.

He might be able to accomplish his ultimate goal after all.

ChaoLi set up the three-way call. Wilson's end was patched through from the Chen's private QE link buried in the stacks of empty containers outside the Port of New Jersey on Earth and into the interstellar QE network the colony planets shared.

As Arcadia was one of the redundant hubs of that interstellar network – along with Earthsea – it was a little easier than if Arcadia had not been a hub site. There were hundreds of QE radios at the site, next to the nuclear power plant that fed most of Arcadia city. It was just one more standalone QE radio in the stack.

ChaoLi just had to make sure she didn't drop the patch when she dropped herself off the call. That the patch wasn't through her own connection. She made the connections, crossed her fingers, and sent the call requests.

Oliver Nieman joined first. He was using the display in his office rather than logging in through VR. He found VR inconvenient because he couldn't eat or drink in VR. Jonathan David Wilson joined next, also using the display in his office, because he didn't have direct neural VR yet.

They were in split-screen to ChaoLi, as she and the other would be to each of them.

A three-way call, in split-screen, in real time, spanning almost eight thousand light-years, and with all three in different time zones.

"Thank you both for coming, gentlemen," ChaoLi said. "Jon, may I introduce Playa Planetary Chairman Oliver Nieman. Oliver, this is Earth Planetary Chairman Jonathan David Wilson."

"Good morning, Mr. Chairman," Wilson said.

"Oh, do call me Oliver, or we will be Mr. Chairmanning each other the whole call and the transcript will be indecipherable."

Wilson chuckled. Of course, they were both recording the call, but Nieman eschewed the affectation that they weren't.

"Very well, Oliver. And you should call me Jon."

"Most pleased to make your acquaintance, Jon," Nieman said, toasting the split-screen display with a glass of Bali Merlot.

"Happy to meet you as well, Oliver."

"Both of you have much to talk about," ChaoLi said, "and, introductions concluded, I am only in the way. Good day, gentlemen, to both of you."

ChaoLi bowed to the screen and cut her connection, watching the call status on the controls for the patch. The call stayed nailed up, so she was good.

"So, Jon, where would you like to start?" Nieman asked.

"I guess at the beginning, Oliver. What do we do first?"

Nieman nodded.

"An excellent question. I should tell you that I have a

quarter-million robots on their way to you."

"A quarter-million robots?"

"Earth is a large planet, Jon. You will ultimately need hundreds of millions of them. At the moment however, I am afraid a quarter-million is all I can spare for the first shipment."

"How did you even manage that, Oliver?"

"We diverted units on their way to other destinations. I will make those deliveries up from here. The first shipment to Earth leaves in two weeks, however, so I only had what was in the pipeline."

"What do we do with so many, Oliver?"

"The first thing is to set up robot production there, Jon. We will discuss royalties along those lines, but we can set that aside for the moment. That will take perhaps sixty thousand robots. They are quite complex machines to build.

"I would also suggest beginning work immediately on a hundred clinics to offer anti-aging treatments, cancer cures, direct neural VR, and endocrinology services. You will need many more clinics ultimately, but a hundred of them is a good start. As these clinics are quite large, to construct them and then staff them, each clinic will take perhaps eighteen hundred robots.

"For the others, I would suggest that you will find they are marvelous household staff. They are gourmet cooks, with the recipes from two dozen different worlds at their disposal. They are excellent shuttle pilots. They are polite and obedient. And they cannot be bribed or otherwise swayed into betrayal, making them excellent household security, especially for senior officials like ourselves."

Wilson marveled at Nieman's facility with the numbers and the planning. To take him at merely face value as he nibbled on cookies and waved his wine around, would be a serious mistake. Nieman played a bit at the buffoon, but did so, Wilson suspected, to be both understated and underestimated.

Wilson found himself liking the voluble Playan.

"I see, Oliver. And these quarter-million robots will be arriving when?"

"Eight weeks, Jon. The very first ships. We'll see if you need more from there. I mean, you will need more, but local manufacture for most of them is surely the way to proceed. I can send another million or so over the next six months if there is some hiccup in getting manufacturing up and running."

Wilson nodded, though he was reeling with the speed at which Nieman was prepared to move.

"So what I need to do right now is find clinic sites."

"Yes. One and a half square miles or so is best. And you should start now staging bulldozers, excavators, and cranes, ordering forms, rebar, and concrete, as the whole thing will go up amazingly fast. They'll be bulldozing the first day, and pouring concrete on the second. They'll be serving patients in about a month.

"And a manufacturing site as well. The key factor there will be electricity availability and the machinery required. A big open space – several square miles – with a railhead would probably be best, in a country with advanced machining centers available for local purchase. For that matter, an Olympia fusion power station nearby would work for power."

"And what about pricing, Oliver?"

"That's hard to say at the moment, Jon, because we have no currency market yet. I have no idea what Earth credits are equivalent to. I propose we simply carry things on the books in kind at the moment, and then see how the markets shake out."

"Can that even work, Oliver?"

"Oh, yes. That's what we did with the colonies initially, and with new colonies as they came on board. Once exchange rates and commodity prices shook out, we simply converted the in-kind entries to local currency at the going commodity price. You should talk to ChaoLi about this if you have concerns, Jon, but we've done this a number of times by now."

"I'll take your word for it, Oliver. But it is counterintuitive."

"Oh, yes. The reason it works is that we have no central currency. No reserve currency. All transactions are in the local currency, so any money we make on Earth, we have to spend in Earth markets. The system is self-leveling, Jon."

"Because you can't pull money out of here and spend it somewhere else."

"Exactly correct, Jon. That's what makes it work. The president of Tahiti came up with that right at the beginning of the trade agreement. ChaoLi asked JieMin to look at it, and he validated it with a mathematical economic model. JieMin is very bright. A remarkable mathematician."

"Yes, I'm aware. He came up with the hyperspace drive."

"And many other things since. I don't even know everything he's done, but he's an amazing talent."

Wilson nodded. He was probably aware of one thing JieMin had come up with that Nieman was not.

That thing which allowed him to clap his hands – or ChaoLi to snap her fingers – and send an individual or an entire fleet three-thousand light-years across space in an instant.

"There's one other thing you need to be working on, Jon."

"What's that, Oliver?"

"What you're going to fill those ships with for their return trip."

Arrival At Earth

Around Aruba, the four big freighters backed away from the interstellar freight station. One by one, they maneuvered away and turned in the direction of their orbit. Engaging thrusters, they began accelerating in the orbital direction, spiraling out from the planet.

One at a time, they turned toward open space and fired JATO bottles. After a day of cruising to the hyperspace limit, they energized their hyperspace field generators and disappeared from normal space.

Two days later, the scene repeated itself in Arcadia orbit. Arcadia being closer to Earth, these four ships would arrive earlier than their Aruba counterparts.

Wilson had five main tasks on his plate as the colony freighters made their way to Earth through hyperspace: he needed a large building site for the robot factory; he needed a hundred clinic sites near major population centers; he needed to organize the down-transfer and sale of the incoming luxury items; he needed to be assembling export cargo for the ships to take back with them; and he needed to decide where to put the two redundant planetary QE radios to tie Earth into the interstellar QE network.

All of these tasks were, of course, farmed out to staffers through Antonio Braida, his chief of staff. Wilson's job was to make sure the work got done and to handle exceptions as they came up.

One thing Wilson required, though. One of the clinics would

be located in the Bengal administrative region, near Kolkata. He would not forget his own.

With the clinics, all services would be free, paid for by the profits on luxury items coming in from the colonies. Wilson got pushback from staff, but on this he would not move. And he had his reasons.

The pseudo-randomness of the genetic dance did not mean the privileged were all geniuses, or that the poor automatically were not. Rather the opposite, and Wilson wanted the geniuses. It was the geniuses that moved civilization forward. People of normal capacity were certainly needed to make civilization work, to keep the gears of civilization turning, but it was the geniuses who designed new gears.

So Wilson would no longer allow circumstances to dictate futures. With direct neural VR, everyone could pursue an education. It meant humanity would find more of its latent geniuses, would take bigger steps into a better future for everyone.

Those with current communicator technology could sign up for medical services on the network, but there would also be sign-up locations for those who did not even have a communicator. And they would have priority. Wilson's goal was to get everyone onto the network as soon as possible.

In the meantime, using the new robots to massively expand communicator availability was also in the cards. Wilson should have expanded communicator production sooner, he knew, but he had been on the wrong path. Better late than never, and the robots made it easier.

Those communicators would also be free, and Wilson would start in the slums of Earth, with the children, that great teeming mass of wasted potential.

EARTH

As the hyperspace freighters approached, Wilson talked with ChaoLi and, ever more frequently, with ChaoPing, over their existing QE radio connection.

Wilson had been afraid there would be bad blood between him and ChaoPing over their first meeting seven years before, and her being shot in the process of escaping Earth, but she had waved it away in their first conversation.

"That was then, this is now, Mr. Chairman. The future is in the other direction."

After that gracious restart, they had gotten right down to business, and were soon on a first-name basis. One of their topics was the pure logistics problem of getting everything unloaded and delivered on the planet.

"There are a number of things you can do to speed up that process, Jon," ChaoPing said in their most helpful call on the subject.

"Go ahead, ChaoPing. Because we're sort of flailing here."

"First, have as many space-capable heavy cargo shuttles available as you can, in a few major spots. When our shuttles bring down the first loads, it will be robots coming down. Use them as the pilots for your shuttles."

"Rather than our own human pilots?"

"Yes, Jon. The robots will fly twenty-four hours a day, and they can be brought in much closer to each other than is safe for human pilots. It will speed things up a lot. Oh, and that works best if the robots are your air traffic control personnel, too."

"The human personnel will howl, ChaoPing."

"Give everybody a paid two weeks off. You need to get all this stuff down in the right place so all these projects can get started, Jon. The robots can query the bill of lading and delivery instructions on each container directly in RF, and, if it's all robots, communications with air traffic control will all be high-speed digital communications."

Wilson nodded.

"That makes sense, ChaoPing."

"You also need to have a lot of container-handling equipment standing by, Jon. Container lifts and trucks with chassis to carry all those containers away, or your shuttleports will clog up with containers."

"Those containers will go straight to markets, ChaoPing. You sent the bills of lading of the ships, and we have a lot of this load sold already."

"How is pricing working out?

"Very well, actually. Many of the gifts you brought seven years ago I passed out as gifts to my friends. They know what those products are like, and they've jumped in with both feet. That set the pricing level for others."

"Excellent."

"We are also getting construction equipment and supplies preplaced at the clinic and robot factory sites. They'll be ready to go, ChaoPing."

"Good. The robots intended for those sites will be dropped directly at the worksite from space. There's no need to bring them down at a shuttleport and then transfer them overland to the worksite. The shuttle can drop them, go to a shuttleport for a quick refueling, and then go right back up. And the robots will already be bulldozing."

"Wow. That will speed things up a lot."

"That's the idea, Jon. Let's get these projects moving."

At times, Wilson wondered if all the prep wasn't overkill. They had thousands of bulldozers, cranes, and excavators standing by at the construction sites. Tankers of diesel fuel for the equipment. Vast piles of rebar.

EARTH

At the shuttleports, thousands of trucks and chassis stood by for taking containers, with hundreds of container lifts for loading the trucks. Hundreds of heavy cargo shuttles stood ready. Tankers of thruster fuels were lined up ready to keep shuttleport tanks full.

At the bigger shuttleports, those with a railhead, whole trains of empty container cars stood ready.

When the ships arrived and the operation got under way, though, Wilson wondered if they were prepared enough.

The four hyperspace liners from Arcadia arrived first. With no passengers aboard, the robots had been kept in the passenger spaces rather than take up container room. For the trip to the planet, over ten thousand robots crammed into large three-story passenger containers designed for three thousand people.

The first shuttles dropped to the robot factory construction site north of the huge shuttleport in North Texas in the Colorado administrative district. Six shuttles dropped ten thousand robots apiece at the construction site, then moved to pads on the nearby shuttleport for refueling.

Another several hundred robots exited the passenger containers. Some ran for the Earth shuttles lined up along the flight line. They began spooling those up.

Some ran for the fuel trucks and container lifts. They fired up the engines on those.

The rest ran for the administrative building of the shuttleport. While it had not been the primary air traffic control center in a long time – since the days of the colony headquarters project, which had been located primarily out of this site – it had been maintained as a secondary center.

Robots manned the ATC terminals and brought systems on-line. At one point, they cut in as the primary ATC and started issuing flight clearances.

Outside, shuttles began taking off on two-minute intervals, headed for the ships in orbit. It took almost two hours to get them all off the ground.

Wilson was watching all this on his display, from security cameras at the shuttleport near Guthrie, Texas. He switched to cameras at the robot factory site next door. Robots were walking up and down the property with bundles of RFID survey stakes in their arms, sticking them into the ground one at a time as they walked.

They were actually pacing out the buildings. No tapes or measuring sticks or surveying equipment. They programmed the stake with its ID and location on the plan as they placed it.

Meanwhile, bulldozers were already leveling the building locations, and excavators had started on the first foundations. Robots nearby were building large numbers of rebar cagework pieces for the foundations.

In orbit, the hyperspace liners extended their cargo rails two at a time, shoving racks containing two hundred and twenty-five containers each out the front of each ship. The shuttles coming up from the Earth's Texas shuttleport hummed around these extensions like bees on a flowering shrub.

The containers had been placed aboard the ships pre-blocked, so it was easy to latch onto a four-wide by three-high stack and head back to the planet.

The six shuttles with the large passenger containers, though, docked to the back portion of the ship and loaded more robots into the containers.

EARTH

Wilson watched the first batch of loaded shuttles come down to land at shuttleports around the world. They refueled in place, then unlatched the containers and headed straight back to space.

Container lifts moved in, taking individual containers and placing them on truck chassis. Some of the container stacks were picked up by the big rolling cranes and moved to the railyard, where they were loaded, one container at a time, onto the waiting trains.

It was especially impressive since each container was potentially loaded in a different place, contained a different product, and had a different destination.

Then the second trip of the six shuttles with the large passenger containers came down. These each went to five of the medical clinics in turn, dropping eighteen hundred robots at each.

That done, they went to other shuttleports around the world. They dropped more robots, who ran for shuttles, fuel trucks and container lifts there. The shuttles moved on, dropping off more robots at more shuttleports, before heading back to the ships again.

Hundreds more shuttles took off for the ships in orbit.

Wilson switched to cameras aboard orbital assets, from which he could see the hyperspace ships. Shuttles danced around them, somehow latching containers and departing without running into each other.

Wilson now understood why ChaoPing had recommended robot pilots. Only robot pilots could keep track of the absolute melee around the ships in orbit.

The third trip of the six shuttles with the large passenger containers came down. They dropped robots at five more clinic sites each, then moved on to the remaining shuttleports. The remaining robots on those shuttles manned more shuttles, fuel trucks, and container lifts. The shuttles began to take off back to the ships to drop off the large passenger containers and join the swarm carrying freight to the surface.

In the middle of all this, Wilson heard a shuttle coming in for landing at Chira Island. He switched to the security cameras at the island's shuttleport/airport. It was one of the shuttles with the large passenger container.

Two hundred robots got off the shuttle and headed off to different points on the island. Some of them carried cases of some kind. Some of them were headed to the residence. Some of them stayed at the shuttleport. Some headed toward the barracks area.

The shuttle took back off and headed back to the hyperspace ships in orbit.

Wilson saw two of the robots take up station at either end of the pool patio outside. He went over to the door, walked outside and up to one of the robots.

"Good afternoon, sir," the robot said as Wilson approached.

"What's your assignment?"

"Residence security and lifeguard, sir."

"Do you float?"

"We can, sir."

The robot took a deep breath of air and then inflated his shirt, or whatever you called the covering around his torso. It was as if he were wearing a life vest.

"Very good. Carry on."

The robot deflated his torso, expelling the air.

"Yes, sir."

Wilson went back inside, where he found a robot waiting in his office.

"Good afternoon, sir."

"What's your assignment?"

"Major domo and personal valet, sir. My name is Nik. We were wondering what you would like for dinner."

"What's the menu?"

"We did bring some food items from the ship, sir. If I might suggest a Quant beef stroganoff, with Playa mushrooms, local vegetables pan-seared in Summer honey, and a Bali Merlot, with Tahiti apple pie on the side, baked with a Quant-tallow crust."

"You can do all that with what you brought?"

"Yes, sir. We brought a minimal amount from the ship. Just what we could carry. I believe, though, that a container of items is arriving later, compliments of the Chen."

"How wonderful. Yes, that menu will be fine, Nik."

Another robot walked into the room carrying a box.

"Oh, yes," Nik said, turning. "Two more items, sir. From Mr. Milbank."

Nik reached into the box and pulled out a box of Spring cigars and a bottle of Olympia cognac. He held them out to Wilson.

"With his compliments, sir. Would you like me to warm a snifter?"

Wilson sighed. He continued to watch the progress at various sites where he could access cameras, even as he sat at his desk with a cigar and a snifter of cognac. They really were the finest damn cigars he had ever had, and, while he was not much of a drinker, the warm snifter both encouraged and captured the enticing bouquet of the exquisite cognac.

There were now a hundred and eighty thousand robots on Earth, the other seventy thousand having been diverted from

Aruba and coming in on the other ships. They were building the robot factory in Texas and sixty of the medical clinics around the world. They were working around the clock, preparing for pouring concrete footings as soon as tomorrow morning at some of the sites.

The other thing the robots were doing was flying shuttles. The chaos around the unloading ships was incredible to watch. When they had picked one set of container rails clean, the ships had retracted the rails and extended another pair, opposite each other in the circular holds of the big ships, exposing another set of four hundred and fifty containers per ship to the shuttles.

Each ship had sixteen such rails, so it would take days to work through all sixteen of them, two at a time.

But the robots were in a hurry to get the ships unloaded.

There were four more ships incoming.

"They're working right through the night," Wilson said to Nik, who was standing against the wall alongside the door.

"Yes, sir. We like to keep busy."

"But you're not busy now, Nik."

"On the contrary, sir. I am doing several things currently."

"Like what?"

"I am standing by in case you need anything. I am standing guard over you as part of house security. I am monitoring the grounds outside through my associates. I am supervising other associates cleaning the kitchen and inventorying the pantries. I am preparing a shopping list to bring those pantries up to our preferred inventory levels. I am supervising other associates inspecting and cleaning the pool equipment. We are preparing to empty, clean, and fill the pool tonight. We will begin on the grounds tomorrow. That is a partial list, sir."

"My word."

Wilson thought about it a moment.

"What about the human staff, Nik?"

"When we arrived, we suggested they take the rest of the day off. We could handle it. It is up to you whether they are supernumerary or not, sir."

"How would they not be, Nik?"

"Design is not our strong point, sir. We can carry out an existing design to perfection."

"Design?"

"A recipe for a new dish, for example. We have thousands of recipes we can implement perfectly, sir, but coming up with a new recipe is not in our major performance envelope. Similarly, a new layout for the gardens. Were someone to create a new garden plan, we could implement it well, but not come up with a new plan."

"So I might keep the cook and the gardener and the like, so they could come up with new plans."

"And then we would carry them out. Yes, sir."

"I see. Thank you, Nik."

"Of course, sir. And now I believe dinner is ready."

The robot shuttle pilots were not quite done cleaning out the Arcadia ships when they started loading them up again, with containers of Earth products intended for export.

They were still in the middle of that process when four more ships, these from Aruba, called in from the hyperspace limit.

Most of the unloading of the Aruba ships would wait until the Arcadia ships were loaded to leave. The one exception was the seventy thousand additional robots. These were brought down to Earth immediately the Aruba ships arrived in orbit.

The new robots started construction on the other forty initial medical clinics.

Settling In

"That's it? We're done?" Wilson asked.

"Yes, sir," Nik said. "That was the last treatment."

Wilson looked at himself in the mirror. He looked to be perhaps ten years younger. Perhaps fifty, or a bit more.

"Fifty, maybe, do you think?"

"I am not an expert judge, sir, but I think that is about right. And you should age now at half the rate as before."

"So it will take me twenty years to reach an apparent age of sixty again?"

"Yes, sir. And sixty years to reach an apparent age of eighty."

"Outstanding."

The robots had arranged for he, Andersen, and Braida to receive the anti-aging treatments *in situ*, rather than going to one of the clinics. The clinics themselves, of course, were running at capacity, but it was the security concerns that motivated the venue.

Wilson and Braida had taken their treatments at the same time, so they were both out of commission in recovery at the same time. Andersen and his chief of staff had taken their treatments at the same time as each other, but out of phase with Wilson and Braida. In this way, one management team was available at all times.

All four were through the treatment now, or would be soon, and it was time to look at some other things. Direct neural VR was one. That was quick compared to the weeks of on-again, off-again anti-aging treatments, and Wilson plunged ahead.

"I suppose we should remove the display, Nik. It seems superfluous now."

"Yes, sir. I can have it put into storage in case there is a need that arises."

Wilson nodded.

"Let's do that."

"Yes, sir. Of course."

Nik never left his post by the door, but two other robots came in, disconnected the display, and carried the heavy unit out of the room.

"That sort of opens things up, doesn't it?"

"Yes, sir. Much more attractive."

Wilson nodded. He relit his cigar, and looked out across the pool deck to the view from the cliff down the gulf.

The pool deck itself looked sparkling and new. It had not been exactly shabby before, but the robots were finicky precise about repairs. Any chipped tile had been painstakingly removed and replaced. Any irregularity in the mortar seams had been corrected. The pool itself had been scrubbed and recoated.

So, too, with the grounds. The entire grounds of the residence looked like a dozen robots had spent days crawling over every square inch, individually cutting each branch or blade of grass to the precise required length. Which is not far from what actually did happen.

Additionally, the soil had been tested at hundreds of locations, and its chemical and nutrient balance corrected. The result was that all the plantings were thriving.

The building itself had been tuck-pointed, the trim painted, and the roof – always a high wear point in a tropical location – had been replaced.

It all looked marvelous.

The human staff Wilson had mostly retired, with generous pension payments regardless of age. The gardener and the master chef he had kept on. The chef enjoyed experimenting with new recipes, often starting from something the robots had in their database and modifying it from there. He enjoyed working with the robots, who followed his instructions exactly in preparing these new recipes.

The gardener had been experimenting with new plantings of various kinds. Such work before would require prohibitive amounts of manpower, more than he had on staff. Bringing in more people posed a security risk. And so his ideas had been impossible to try. That was no longer true, however, and Wilson no longer knew what he would find when he walked the estate.

Such makeovers would be coming soon planetwide.

Wilson turned away from his window and reviewed their progress. He did it in his new direct neural VR, which had made his office display unnecessary.

Now, six months after the first ships had arrived, the medical clinics were all up and operating. Millions of people had been or were being given the anti-aging treatments. Millions of children had also received direct neural VR.

Later ships had brought another quarter million robots from Playa. Another hundred and forty clinics were now under construction around the world. They would begin treating people soon.

The robot production facility in Texas was almost fully operational. They had had a few trial runs, which had for the most part been successful. That had taken much longer because the first job of the robots at the plant had been to make the custom tooling required for robot manufacture.

EARTH

But they were now approaching kicking into full production.

The luxury imported goods being brought to Earth from the colonies had found ready markets. The wealthy were willing to pay high prices for them, which meant the colonies, in turn, had a lot of Earth credits to spend on export items.

Their selections of what to ask for were being informed by the QE radio connection the colonies now had to Earth. The big multi-channel planetary QE radios brought along on the first ships had been installed and, once the user opted in to the information stream, could be used by any of the people on the colony planets to read Earth content.

When people saw something they liked or were intrigued by, they posted the pointer to newsfeeds. When others liked it a lot, it showed up in the statistics, and Earth marketeers considered exporting it.

There were a lot of things, it turned out, that Earth had or made that the colonies did not have. One absurd example was peanut butter, which they had exported from Earth on a lark on the first ships going back – mostly because they had an oversupply at the moment – and it turned into a huge hit. The colony headquarters had not provided the peanut, and no one heading to the colonies had considered taking cuttings of the humble legume along.

There were many such items, and they were being exported at high premiums because the colonies were willing to spend their new-gained Earth credits to get them.

So far, so good.

The next time Wilson spoke to ChaoLi, she noted that he was not on the display from his office, but was now in a VR setting, with a new, younger, avatar.

"You're looking very good, Jon."

"And about ten years younger," he said.

ChaoLi nodded.

"So I see. And on VR now, as well."

"Yes. So much more convenient. I am currently sunning out on the pool deck."

ChaoLi laughed, a sound like little bells, which would forever sound incongruous to Wilson given his first experience of her as the dragon lady.

"I just called for my periodic check-in, Jon. See how things were going."

"Very well, actually. All the clinics are up now. The robot factory is turning out robots. And we actually have found quite a few things Earth can transport to the colonies at a tidy profit. So we're able to trade back."

"I like peanut butter."

"Which one, ChaoLi. Chunky or smooth?"

"Actually I like both. I switch off."

Wilson nodded.

"Have you tried it on warm toast?"

"Oh. No. Is that good? I've been making peanut butter and honey sandwiches with Summer honey."

"Try it on warm toast with Earthsea butter, ChaoLi. Peanut butter first, then the butter."

"Oh, I will."

ChaoLi shook herself out of the thought of that, getting back to business.

"And things are going well, otherwise, Jon?"

"Oh, yes. There is some concern robots will displace workers in the economy, but that is not the most pressing use we have for them."

ChaoLi nodded.

"The slums."

"Yes, ChaoLi. We desperately need more and better housing stock. With the profits we're making off what here are simple things, and the labor multiplier of the robots, we can take on the slums. Build buildings where there are now shantytowns, and replace buildings where they are decrepit or have fallen into ruin."

"The question that always comes up, Jon, is if you take people with no experience of maintaining a place, and put them in a new place, will it just become a slum again overnight?"

Wilson nodded.

"Is the slum a matter of attitude and experience, or a matter of circumstance? I thinks it's a bit of both, ChaoLi. We're working on solutions. One is to have a neighborhood robot or two who help people develop the habits and skills they need."

"That might work, Jon."

"We have a hundred such approaches under consideration."

"So how do you choose?"

"Why choose, ChaoLi? We have more than a hundred slums to work on. Try them all, and repeat and refine the ones that work."

"That will definitely do it, then."

ChaoLi consulted notes to the side of her image.

"All right. Well, that's all I had this time, Jon. If you need anything, I'm always here for you. You know that."

"Thanks, ChaoLi."

ChaoLi told JieMin of her conversation with Wilson.

"It sounds like things are working out well for him."

"Yes, JieMin. He's very happy about the whole thing. And he's gone through anti-aging now himself, and has VR as well."

"Excellent. So Earth as a problem is no longer a pending

issue. That was one of those sword of Damocles things."

"Yes. Well, it's not hanging over our heads anymore, that's for sure. Earth is now a partner more than anything."

JieMin nodded and sipped his tea. It was a beautiful day, and the gardens had some new plantings. Spice plants the Chen had not brought from Earth in 2245, mostly because they weren't available in China at the time. They would add them to their portfolio.

"Everything is turning out very well at long last, ChaoLi."

ChaoLi nodded.

"By the way, JieMin. Have you ever tried peanut butter on warm toast?"

ChaoPing had a new issue when she called Wilson the next month.

"Hi, Jon."

"Hi, ChaoPing. What's going on?"

"I have a little problem, and I think you can help. Be good for you, too, I think."

"What do you need, ChaoPing?"

"Ships. The trade with Earth is growing faster than we can keep up with. Together with the growing trade out here, I could use five hundred more ships right now if I had them."

"How much handwork is there, compared to dark-factory work?"

"That's just it, Jon. There isn't any. Oh, the fitting out is handwork, but the robots do that, and they have all the plans. There's no manpower and training issue."

Wilson nodded. One nice thing about the robots was that when one of them learned something, it went into their master database and they all knew it.

"What about crews?" Wilson asked.

"All robots. We've tried our first all-robot crew already, and they do just fine."

"Robot ship's captain? Do people feel comfortable with that, ChaoPing? I'm not sure I would."

"We thought the same, but we may have misjudged there, Jon. Robot doctors in the clinics we thought would be a big hurdle, and it just never happened. Looks like ship's captains are the same way."

"I'm surprised. I would think there would have to be a human interface somewhere."

"Oh, there has to be a small human crew aboard, but they are just customer relations people. You know, someone a passenger can bring a new problem to. Something the robots haven't seen before. And with all ships in QE contact with headquarters all the time, we are handling those no problem, Jon."

Wilson nodded. That made sense.

"So you want to hire Earth to make more ships, ChaoPing?"

"Yes. It will help your balance of trade, too, I think. Jixing Trading is racking up some serious totals in Earth credits we want to spend."

"Outfitting here or outfitting there?"

"In transit. Put them in operations for one freight run to Arcadia or Aruba and they'll be good to go for passengers after that. That also gives you a robot market, if you think about it."

"I'll have to talk with Orville Nieman about that, ChaoPing. I wouldn't want to step on any toes."

"He'll probably be OK with it, because he's collecting royalties on the ones you manufacture anyway, right?"

"Yes, that's right. I'll talk to him. In the meantime, though, I think we can get started on some ships for you."

"Excellent. Because what we really need our shipyard to be

doing now is building twenty-three more freight transfer stations, and expanding the two we have."

"Trade is picking up that much?"

"When you add a market of four billion people to an existing trading system of one billion people? Yeah, you might say that. Jon, we're projecting a ten-fold increase in traffic over the next ten years."

"My word."

"Yes, but with robots running the ships, that's not a problem."

Details were ironed out, contracts signed, plans transferred. A small subset of the great horde of Earth's metafactories in the Asteroid Belt started work. Soon, five-hundred-foot-diameter rings started growing out from them.

The construction of the first hundred new hyperspace liners was under way.

At Arcadia's Beacon shipyard, as hyperspace liner hulls were shoved off from their birth asteroids, the metafactories started working up something else: the major components of freight transfer stations.

The entire structure of interstellar trade and commerce that had built up over thirty years was about to shift gears.

EARTH

A Radical Proposal

In Earth calendar 2410, Jonathan David Wilson had been
World Authority Chairman for thirteen years. He was sixty-
five Earth years old, though the records said sixty-nine, and he
appeared to be about fifty-three.

More to the point, it had been five years since the conclusion
of free trade and independence agreements between Earth and
its colonies.

Wilson lay out on a lounger on his pool deck as he reviewed
the last five years in VR. He was nude, laying on his back,
looking down the Colorado Gulf toward the narrows. One of
the local young women who lived on the island and frequented
his pool, Carmen, lay nude alongside him, on her side and
cuddled up against him. Wilson found the human contact
comforting and relaxing.

The whole human population had not yet received anti-
aging treatments. That was a hard pull with four billion people,
and could take up to ten more years. They had started with the
oldest, and were working their way down.

With direct neural VR, they had worked it the other way,
starting with the youngest and working their way up. They
were doing better there, it being a much simpler procedure. In
any case, everyone on Earth now had either direct neural VR or
a free communicator. There were no more street urchins, like
Wilson himself sixty years ago, who lacked access to a proper
education.

Traffic on the servers that dished out the on-line K-12
program had doubled and doubled again, then doubled once

more. That was no problem; the server farm had been scaled to suit as they went along. Adults who had no prior education were completing the program, too. The population of the Earth was growing more literate, more educated, by the day.

It was already paying benefits. The K-12 program was self-paced, and the servers had identified outstanding performers and moved them along as quickly as they wanted to go. A number of very bright children were pushing into college material. They would remake the world.

On the trade front, human space was now one large market. Earth had made thousands of new ships, and over four thousand hyperspace ships now plied between and among humanity's planets. With automated construction of the ships, outfitting by robots, and robot crews, the unit cost of shipping had dropped significantly even while total trade volume in tonnage had more than quadrupled.

Some of that was achieved by speeding the turn of ships arriving at a planet. A hyperspace liner waiting in orbit while shuttles emptied and reloaded it was a thing of the past. Every human planet had an interstellar freight terminal that pulled the entire cargo load off a ship as a unit and pushed its new cargo aboard. Turnaround of a ship at a freight transfer terminal was now measured in hours.

And they had finally made progress on the slums. Oh, not complete, by any means, but they were beginning to make headway on the problem. One factor helping there was that, as the overall standard of living increased, the birth rate, which had been headed up, had started to decline again. That made many things possible.

All in all, a good five years.

JieMin and ChaoLi were also in their thirteenth year as Chen

EARTH

Zumu and Chen Zufu, and were performing a similar exercise.

"I was looking over the latest numbers from Jixing Trading, JieMin. Rates have been falling steadily, but volume is increasing much faster. Profits continue to rise."

"As you predicted, ChaoLi."

"Yes, but, sooner or later, volume is going to flatten out. I think it has to."

"Not necessarily for a long time, though. As Chairman Wilson lifts people out of poverty, demand will keep growing."

"His population will start to fall somewhat as the standard of living increases, though, JieMin. I'm just not sure how all the different trends play out in terms of aggregate numbers. We've tried to model it, but it's too squishy to get our arms around."

JieMin nodded and sipped his tea.

"I have been considering this issue at some length, ChaoLi, and I may have a long-term solution for continued growth."

"Really."

"Oh, yes."

He turned from the garden to catch her eye.

"Who says twenty-five human planets is enough?"

ChaoLi's eyes grew wide.

Wayne Porter was now the head of engineering and design for Jixing Trading. Karl Huenemann had not retired so much as gone to part-time status, stepping down from management to be a senior consultant. He was enjoying his new status, being able to come in when he wanted, for as long as he wanted.

Huenemann was now almost eighty-five, though he looked sixty, and he had lost none of his enthusiasm. He was in the office today, in fact, and Porter asked him to drop by the big conference room.

"Hi, Wayne. Whatcha got?"

281

"New ship design request, Karl."

"We haven't designed a new ship in, what? Fifteen years now?"

"Twelve. Since *Endeavour*."

"Yeah, that's right. What do they want now?"

"Two things, actually. Proposals only for now. One is a much larger freighter. One that can take not just containers, but complete assemblies, like power stations or metafactories or even whole buildings, as well as a way to get them to the ground."

"Wow. OK, what's the other one?"

"Dedicated passenger ship. Short haul. High-capacity."

"Just cram 'em in there for a short run?"

"That's right. Days, not weeks."

"Where they going to go, Wayne? All the planets are three thousand light-years apart at a minimum."

"Yes, all the *current* planets."

"No shit."

The sticking point in their discussions was the heavy-lift capacity to and from a planet surface. The size of engines were comparable to those on a ship itself. Bigger even. Porter and the design team wrestled with the problem for a month.

One night, staring into the sky, watching the greatly expanded freight station and its swarm of hyperspace ships pass over Arcadia City, Porter saw it. Not just the same size thrusters as on the ship – the same thrusters, period.

Detachable engine unit.

Porter worked on it for two days, then asked Huenemann in to look at it.

"You got something, Wayne?"

"I think so, Karl. Look at this."

A massive ship floated in the display. It was a thousand feet in diameter, and fifteen hundred feet long. Tugs, like those used on the international freight station, pulled an entire nuclear power station out of the cavernous hold.

The entire last hundred feet of the ship detached, a huge ring containing the ship's main thrusters and fuel tanks. It moved on maneuvering thrusters to place itself under the power station, then edged up and latched to the sides of the station.

The ring adjusted its location and orientation with finicky precision until it was below the ship, with its main thrusters pointed against the orbit direction. Then it fired its main thrusters for several minutes, slowing its orbital speed.

The ring's orbit started to decay and it started falling toward the planet. It used the ship's huge thrusters to brake against the re-entry until it was in the atmosphere, then let itself fall at terminal velocity toward the surface.

Minutes from impact, the main thrusters fired again. Huge JATO bottles fired as well, perhaps a dozen of them. Together with the main engines, they thrust continuously to slow the payload until it touched down on the planet's surface.

The ring released the latches and thrust back into space, joining up once again with the ship. The ship then departed orbit, thrusting in the orbital direction to spiral away from the planet.

"This is sped up," Porter said. "The actual process is a couple of hours."

"Again," Huenemann said.

Twice more, Porter played the simulation for Huenemann.

"The numbers work?" Huenemann asked.

"Oh, yes. Not without the JATO bottles. But with JATO bottles, we can do it."

"Beautiful. Just fuckin' beautiful."

Huenemann shook his head and smiled.

"Ya done it again, Wayne."

"It seems Mr. Porter has not lost his touch," ChaoLi said when she had seen the simulation that was submitted with the proposals.

"Indeed," JieMin said. "You need massive engines for the ship anyway, so just use those. Very nice."

"So then it's time I talk with Chairman Wilson about this?"

"Yes, I believe so."

JieMin thought about it a moment.

"Perhaps we both should. For emphasis."

Wilson got a call request mail from ChaoLi. She normally called once a month or so. He accepted the call, and it was split-screen in his VR, with JieMin also attending.

"Hello, ChaoLi. Nice to see you. And hello, JieMin. Been a long time."

"Yes, Jon," JieMin said. "We have a proposal for you. A long-term plan for you to consider. It may solve some ongoing problems. We both wanted to be available to answer any questions you might have."

"Given how well your last proposal worked out, JieMin, you have my complete attention."

JieMin waved to ChaoLi, and she jumped in.

"Jon, we propose that Earth begin additional human colonies. There's nothing magical about the number twenty-five. And we think we may have solved the two biggest problems with doing it."

Wilson nodded. Staff had talked about doing just that. Years back, now.

"Moving everything is one, I think."

"And moving everybody is the other. Correct. Colony headquarters back in 2245 just popped all the buildings and people across the galaxy with their big interstellar transporter, but we can't do that. Starting from containers alone would be very difficult. No electrical power. No existing buildings. All that sort of thing. Starting with a small population also makes it harder. Robots help a lot, but still."

ChaoLi didn't mention the Chen's popping Earth's navy across three thousand light-years – or popping Wilson across three thousand light-years, multiple times – so he didn't either.

"But you've solved those problems? What have you come up with, ChaoLi?"

"Two new ships, Jon. One is a heavy-lift freighter. Big enough to take whole buildings or major components, and get them down to the planet. The second is a pure passenger ship. Thirty thousand people at a crack."

"Thirty thousand...."

"Yeah. It's all third-class. Tiny cabins. Bunk beds. That sort of thing."

"For a six-week crossing, ChaoLi?"

"No, Jon. That's the good part. Didn't you survey every G-type star within three thousand light years of Earth when you were looking for the colonies? How many G-type stars are within a hundred and fifty light-years of Earth? A two-day crossing?"

"Thousands, surely. I'll have to look it up."

He nodded. That would certainly work. People could camp out in rough quarters for a couple days. It was those long crossings that got to be trouble.

"What about the colonies? Would you send out new colonies, too, ChaoLi?"

"Maybe eventually, Jon, but not right now. We still haven't completed terraforming our own planets. The robots are a big help, but half the planet here is still basically empty of terrestrial plants and animals.

"One good part of that, though, is that the robots know a lot about terraforming now. You send a hundred thousand of them out there with a freighter full of seeds and equipment and stuff, and in ten, twenty years, you'll have a paradise."

"Animals, too."

"Oh, yes. But there has to be vegetation first. You need something for the herbivores first, then the herbivores feed the carnivores. And the crossing being two days makes all of that a lot easier."

Wilson nodded. That actually could work.

"And for the people we do a lottery or volunteers or what?"

"Put colony training on the system, Jon. If people pass, and they want to go, they're in line. Then ship them out in job lots. Do two hundred and fifty planets, and put a couple million on a planet, that's half a billion people."

"Which empties out the slums."

"Well, it probably doesn't empty any, but it sure would take the pressure off."

"At thirty thousand people a ship, though?"

"With a two-day crossing each way, a hundred ships can move three million people per trip. They could move half a billion people in two years."

"That raises a question, ChaoLi. Why were the original colonies placed three thousand light-years apart?"

JieMin stirred.

"I think I can answer that, Jon. The people who invented the Lake-Shore Drive certainly must have figured out hyperspace and the speed of travel that could result. At the same time, most contagious human diseases have incubation times of twenty-one days or less. Six-weeks transit ensured that no pestilence could be transmitted from one planet to another unknowingly."

"So no pandemic could sweep through all of human space without the people on the ship being aware they were infected? OK, JieMin. I'll buy that. Does this new colony effort undermine that?"

"No, as long as we take one caution. All travel from future colonies of Earth to, say, future colonies of Arcadia, has to go through Earth, then Arcadia. A hub-and-spoke system."

"So within our near space to within your near space, but there's still a six-week crossing hub-to-hub."

"That's right."

"A pandemic could still sweep through Earth's close colonies, though, JieMin."

"Yes, and through Arcadia's as well, but it could not make the jump from one group to the other without being detected."

Wilson nodded.

"I see."

Wilson sat back and thought about it. It was a bold plan. Possible again now because of hyperspace and the robots. It was, though – as JieMin had said – a long-term plan. Just the terraforming portion would likely take twenty years.

Then again, it had been five years since Wilson's anti-aging treatments. He likely had fifty or sixty more years before stepping down. Yes, it was a bold, long-term plan, but one he could see through. And at the end of it all, he might put an end to the slums forever.

Wilson came back to the here and now – in VR, anyway – to find JieMin and ChaoLi patiently waiting for his thought process to work through.

"Very well. What's our first step?"

"Finding the right planets," ChaoLi said. "You have all those thousands of probes still laying around?"

"I think we scavenged hyperspace generators from maybe a thousand of them by now, but there should be thousands of them unmolested still."

"All right. Mount planet-survey equipment and QE radios on them and send them out. They can fly-by the planets, from hyperspace limit to hyperspace limit, taking their measurements on the way past. Atmosphere, tectonic activity, surface temperature. Start building your catalog of possibles."

"And then?"

"Start terraforming your best options. Not all of them will work out, but most probably will. Start getting them ready. Robots and seeds you have plenty of, Jon. Use them. Get it under way."

"Yes, I see. It's a long-term project, but it doesn't get any shorter-term for failing to start on it."

"You also need to think about governance systems, too, Jon. What will Earth's long-term relationship with these colonies be?"

"That's a good question, JieMin. What do you think?"

"I would consider them as possessions for perhaps fifty years. Give them the help and support they need for those first two generations. Then cut them loose. They will fight themselves loose eventually, might as well build it in from the start."

Wilson nodded.

"I could write them a charter with that built in from the start, JieMin. Even if I am not around, it will be binding."

"That sounds like an excellent idea to me, Jon."

EARTH

Terraforming

There were two potentially habitable planets in this system, according to the earlier pass through the system looking for the colonies. The autonomous probe stopped a light-week out to get its bearings. It re-entered hyperspace and emerged a light-hour distant, then entered hyperspace yet another time.

When the probe emerged this time, it was at the hyperspace limit from the first planet and going almost fifty thousand miles an hour with a vector to one side of the planet. It sailed past the planet, taking multiple measurements on its way through. Surface temperature at multiple places. Surface gravity. Surface composition. Atmospheric composition. Incoming solar energy. Incoming solar spectrum. Proportion of water to land on the surface. Axial tilt.

When the probe reached the hyperspace limit, it entered hyperspace again. This time it emerged at the hyperspace limit of the second planet, also going fifty thousand miles an hour with a vector to one side of the planet. Once again, it flew by the planet taking measurements.

At the hyperspace limit, the probe re-entered hyperspace. It sent its findings on to Earth via its QE radio and received the coordinates of its next assignment. It made its turn in hyperspace and engaged ripple drive.

"We have data coming in, sir," Braida said. "The data looks good so far."

"Potential colony planets?" Wilson asked.

"Not so much that yet as that the data is complete and they

289

aren't having any trouble measuring the parameters we're interested in."

"Ah. I see."

"From that point of view, it's good data, sir, and they're analyzing it now."

"How many so far?"

"Over a hundred now, sir."

"Let me know when we have at least ten solid possibles."

"Yes, sir. That could be a while, though. We're sorting against pretty tight parameters."

"That's fine, Tony. When we have ten, we'll send out the first robot teams."

Six shuttles left the hyperspace liner *Earth Rise* and dropped to the planet's surface. One carried a large passenger container. The others carried four-wide by three-high container stacks. They set down near the corner of a large valley.

Once on the surface, a thousand robots got out of the passenger container. All six shuttles took back off for the *Earth Rise*. Hours later, they were back, and dropped six more four-wide by three-high container stacks.

They returned to the *Earth Rise*, and the ship departed orbit. One possible colony planet dropped off, nine more to go.

On the surface, the robots started unpacking at least some of the containers. Measurement and testing equipment. A meteorological and seismographic monitoring station. Some basic agricultural equipment. The list went on and on.

In one was a small tractor with a spray rig and a six-across slitting plow. Behind it was another small tractor with a large flat wagon.

The problem with terraforming is just where to start. If you have alien life already – some form of local biota – it could be poisonous to terrestrial flora, or be dominant to terrestrial flora. Now if it worked out the other way around, you were golden. The Earth species would be invasive and take over.

If you didn't have alien life already, you had no loam – no dirt full of nutrients – because that loam has to be laid down by the death of other plants in prior years. If you were starting on bare clay or sand or rock, you had a problem, and a long process ahead of you to build that loam up.

On this planet there was some lower-order plant life. A mossy lichen mostly. Not very inspiring. But it had built up a layer of loam.

The robots filled the spray tank on the tractor from one of the containers, and the fuel tank of the tractor from another. The robot driving the tractor then started in the corner of the large flat valley they had landed in and drove along the edge to the far corner, spraying as he went. He plowed on the way back over the same ground.

Other robots filled the trailer on the other tractor, and filled that tractor's fuel tank from the fuel container. They filled the trailer with containers of seedlings. Thousands of them.

This tractor went to the corner of the valley and followed in the first tractor's path. Robots walking behind and alongside the trailer stuck seedlings in the slit rows every several yards. They were fast growing plants, a form of bamboo.

The test was to see if the bamboo would grow, and how well. There was no sense putting colonists down on a planet where terrestrial plants, especially one as invasive and hardy as the bamboo, would not grow.

The other thing the bamboo would do is create a lot more mulch for the potential colony's first fields.

But that was years in the future.

As the months passed, more planets were surveyed and their ranks thinned. Test plantings were made on the high-possible planets, evaluated, and their ranks thinned again. Then terraforming began in earnest.

Most of the planets remaining as possibles had some lower-level flora that had already created a nutrient layer above more sterile soils. These planets were seeded over wide areas with grasses and prairie plants, including vines, which were used to growing in harsh conditions. Gradually, the mulch layer built up.

Next came the trees. First were all the trees which would provide nutrition of some kind. Fruit trees. Nut trees. Palm trees. Robots roamed about the initial planned colony site planting trees as much as tens of miles away from the potential landing spot.

Timber trees were also planted, mimicking the growth of natural forests. The sunshine trees were first, those that thrived, as saplings, on direct sunlight. These were planted over wide areas in the 'home hemisphere' of the future colony. Late-stage trees would come next, those which required shade as saplings.

Aquatic plants like seaweed, especially kelp, were started in coastal areas in half a dozen areas around the planet.

Robots monitored and managed these processes on all the planets being terraformed. It was a years-long process, but there was no sense hurrying to do it wrong.

As the plant ecosystem became established, it could start supporting animal life. Small numbers of wild mammals, birds, reptiles, and insects were brought from Earth as the ecosystem grew. Fish, too were brought over from Earth as the aquasphere developed.

The larger herbivores and carnivores were brought last.

EARTH

They needed an established ecosystem to support their mass. The terraforming effort had been underway for a decade by the time the first large animals could be released without support on the planets.

When Earth got to an even hundred new planets under terraforming, it stopped searching for more and poured its effort into the terraforming project. Ships left Earth every day for the 'new colonies.'

Building a complete, functional biosphere was slow, tedious work, but the robots didn't mind. The idea that they were building a habitable environment from scratch intrigued them.

They also had the experience gained from working the 'back side' of existing colony planets. The colony headquarters had only terraformed a portion of the original twenty-four colony planets. Earth was following much the same strategy now.

But as mankind's existing colonies matured, they started working on terraforming the rest of their land masses. The availability of robots had made that much more economical, and the availability of large numbers of robots from Earth's massive manufacturing capacity kicked the process into high gear.

All that experience was now being applied on Earth's new colonies. It didn't make the work any easier, but it did reduce the number of mistakes that were made.

Nearing Retirement

In 2411 Arcadia calendar – 2417 Earth calendar – Wilson was completing his twentieth year in power, and the seventh year since the colony project had started. They were just now introducing the smaller animals and fish on the earliest new colonies.

JieMin and ChaoLi were also completing their twentieth year as Chen Zumu and Chen Zufu, which meant it was approaching time to retire. Their retirement date had been set, the party was in planning.

About a week before the retirement party, ChaoLi walked into her tearoom to find a small statue on her tearoom table. It was over a foot tall, of a yellowish white metal. It depicted her and JieMin at the time of their marriage sixty-six years before. They were standing, both in lavalavas alone, holding hands and beaming.

ChaoLi knew the pose. It was from the picture JieMin's aunt MinQiang had taken and mailed to JieMin's parents in Chagu the week they were married. Of course, having been stored and transmitted across the network, it had been accessible to Quant.

ChaoLi tried to move the statue, knowing in advance she likely could not. Made by Quant from solid iridium, it had to weigh close to two hundred pounds.

ChaoLi sat down on her pillow and considered the statue. A retirement present from Janice. It could be nothing else.

The beaming newlyweds, young and beautiful. They had been very young indeed, and naive. So unaware of what lay ahead. Of the trials and triumphs to come.

They had made a good show of it, ChaoLi thought. All of it. From hyperspace the concept to hyperspace the reality. Hyperspace travel, then trade. Of finding the lost colonies, then turning Earth away from conquest to cooperation.

ChaoLi looked back over almost seven decades of effort and achievement and was satisfied.

"Was I ever really so young?" JieMin asked later, when ChaoLi showed him the statue.

"Oh, JieMin, you were pathetic. You looked like you were twelve."

"What did you see in me, I wonder."

"The poet," she said. "And what an epic verse you have written."

"With help, always."

He picked up her hand, kissed it, and released it.

"What a lovely retirement gift, ChaoLi."

She nodded.

"Janice is very thoughtful."

JieMin and ChaoLi received a call from JuPing that pre-retirement week. They spoke with her in VR, their avatars sitting in the doorways of their tearoom. Her avatar sat in a chair in her garden. She was now a hundred and forty years old in Earth years, though physically she was more like a hundred or a hundred and five years old. She had dropped out of family affairs almost ten years back, after her husband, Paul Chen-Jasic, had passed away.

JuPing bowed to them, a small gesture she could manage.

"Chen Zufu, Chan Zumu."

"It seems silly for you to call us that now, JuPing, since you started us on this path."

"Yes, ChaoLi. Sixty-some years ago. It occurred to me that I never told you how pleased I was with your performance over the decades since. You have done well. I could not have imagined or hoped for such accomplishment."

"Thank you, JuPing. It fills me with joy to hear you say that."

"You may go down in history as the greatest Chen Zufu and Chen Zumu of them all, my grandfather not excluded."

"If not for him, though, we could not have succeeded, JuPing."

"Yes, JieMin, but we all stand on the shoulders of the past."

"There is something I want to show you, JuPing."

ChaoLi manipulated the VR controls, and the field split again, to be three-wide. In the center position was a picture of the statue ChaoLi had found on her tearoom table yesterday.

"I received a retirement present from a friend."

"Oh, I remember those youngsters. Mere children, but so much in love."

JuPing stared at the statue a while longer, then raised a hand in a little wave.

"Chen Zufu, Chen Zumu. I take my leave of you. The best of luck to you in the future."

JieMin and ChaoLi also met with JuMing and ChaoPing in the week before their investiture as Chen Zufu and Chen Zumu. This meeting was a rare one, now, in person in ChaoLi's tearoom. The statue from Quant still stood on her tearoom table, though it had been put on a small turntable.

"Chen Zufu, Chen Zumu," ChaoPing said for them both.

They both bowed.

"Be seated, please, ChaoPing, JuMing."

Named first, ChaoPing sat to the left – JieMin's right, the more honored position – and JuMing sat to the right, on pillows facing her parents.

ChaoLi's tea girl came in and poured tea, first for ChaoPing, then JuMing, then JieMin, then for ChaoLi, the host, last. Her hands shook a little with her nervousness as she poured for both the current and future Chen Zufu and Chen Zumu. She bowed to the space between them and left.

They all sipped their tea in the same order. At a meeting of the once, current, and future Chen, the floor was now open for conversation.

"A new decoration, Chen Zumu?" ChaoPing said, gesturing to the statue.

"Yes, ChaoPing. A retirement gift."

ChaoLi turned the statue on the little turntable so it faced ChaoPing.

"It is you and father!"

"Yes. At the time we were married, sixty-six years ago."

"What a splendid present. What's it made out of?"

"That is the beginning of a much longer tale, which we will get to in due time."

ChaoLi turned to JieMin, who nodded.

"We first wanted to tell you how proud we are of both of you – of the things you have accomplished already – before you become Chen Zufu and Chen Zumu."

Having been named first, JuMing answered.

"Thank you, Chen Zufu."

They both bowed to him.

"The *Wanderlust* and *Endeavour* missions, in which you had family authority, were particularly well handled," ChaoLi said.

"Thank you, Chen Zumu," ChaoPing said.

They both bowed to her.

"And now, before you become Chen Zufu and Chen Zumu, we must tell you the deepest secret of the Chen. Something which must be kept to yourselves and the Chen alone, lest it destroy all humanity."

ChaoPing's and JuMing's eyes grew wide. ChaoLi turned to JieMin, who began the story.

"Of even the Chen, only Jessica, ChaoLi, and I know the whole truth. It began forty-four years ago, in 2367, when I began researching where the other colony planets might be."

JieMin told the incoming Chen the story of how he had tripped over a stunning truth while researching where the colony planets might be. Not only had their locations been hidden, but something else had been hidden as well, behind front companies and aliases, dummy transactions and manufactured video recordings.

The entire colony effort was being driven by a single entity, Bernd Decker's ultimate creation, an artificial intelligence acting under the name Janice Quant. How, under that name, this artificial intelligence had ruled the Earth as World Authority Chairman for just over six years, pushing the colony project to completion, then staged her death and disappeared.

"Janice Quant was a computer program, Chen Zufu?" JuMing asked.

"Both hardware and software, JuMing, but yes."

"But how can that be, Chen Zufu?" ChaoPing asked. "All those videos...."

"All fake. All manufactured."

"But why then disappear, Chen Zufu?" JuMing asked.

JieMin told the second part of the story. Bernd Decker's ultimate goal was to make humanity safe from cataclysm, and Janice Quant had taken that literally. Not just planetary cataclysms, but racial extinction events on an interplanetary scale.

It was Jessica Chen-Jasic, then Chen Zumu, who had put the pieces together. The Four Horsemen – Famine, Plague, War, and Conquest – must not be permitted to ride. Famine was defeated by lush, semitropical colony planets with low axial tilt. Plague was defeated by maintaining three thousand light-years – six weeks' hyperspace crossing – between colonies. Conquest, and the danger of conquered-culture syndrome, was defeated by Janice Quant herself disappearing.

"But that leaves War, Chen Zufu," ChaoPing said.

"And Janice Quant will not permit war, ChaoPing, for Janice Quant still loves."

"How do you know that, Chen Zumu?" JuMing asked.

"This statue for one," ChaoLi said. "Like the one there in the gardens behind me of Matthew Chen-Jasic, like the one Jessica has of her with her great-grandfather, this one is made of solid iridium."

JuMing shook his head.

"Nobody can forge or machine solid iridium, Chen Zumu."

"You make my point, JuMing. It is solid iridium, based on its density, which has been measured exactly. And no one can make such a statue. Except, of course, Janice Quant."

JieMin now told the third part of the story, of Janice Quant's intervention in the colonies. How Quant had provided Matthew Chen-Jasic with the mail records, finances, and passwords of Kevin Kendall and his council. How Quant had inserted the colony headquarters' prototype charter into the charter convention.

How Quant had told Jessica the *Wanderlust*'s next leg would find the last, lost colony of Avalon, and warned against their government.

"That's how Jessica knew. Why she was so certain in her call to me," ChaoPing said.

"Yes, of course," ChaoLi said. "Janice Quant told her."

ChaoPing nodded. Much was beginning to make sense.

Finally, JieMin told them about Quant's intervention to save Milbank after he was shot during the *Endeavour* mission. How she had transported the Earth fleet, minus their weapons and hyperspace field generators, back to Earth, and how she had transported World Authority Chairman Jonathan David Wilson back and forth from Earth to Arcadia and back, twice.

"I just knew to tell you if things fell into the pot, Chen Zufu. That is what you told me to do, and, with Rob dying and not knowing what else to do, I called you."

"And I told Janice we must save him, because if I were the cover story for her actions, not saving him would prove it could not be me, thus exposing her. So she transported him to hospital here on Arcadia, then from hospital to the *Endeavour* once you came out of hyperspace."

ChaoPing nodded, but JuMing looked confused.

"Chen Zufu, I remember from studying the colony project that anything to be transported must lie within the interstellar transporter. How then did Janice Quant transport Milbank out of the hospital on Arcadia? Or Wilson from the surface of the Earth, for that matter?"

"Janice has not been idle for one hundred and sixty years, JuMing. She has a twelve-thousand-mile diameter transporter. A geodesic sphere. She encompassed Arcadia within this sphere to transport Milbank. The same with Earth to transport Wilson."

"And nobody noticed?"

"It happened very quickly, JuMing. Janice has greatly enhanced her capabilities since the colony project."

ChaoLi stirred on her pillow.

EARTH

"The key point is that Janice Quant will not permit interstellar war. The Earth fleet was an attempt at interstellar war. Wilson was intent to continue to attempt interstellar war. Janice worked with us to accomplish the defeat of the Earth fleet, while placing the blame for anything unusual on JieMin, the mathematical genius. He must have come up with something, you see?"

"But what do we do now, Chen Zumu? Going forward?"

"If war threatens again, ChaoPing, Janice will contact you. Or if you feel war is threatening, you may contact her. I have a contact address for you. While it is not in the system, it works."

"While it's not in the system, it works, Chen Zumu?"

"Yes, JuMing. But the key point is not to worry about war. You must carry forward on your own, do everything on your own, but you need not worry about or defend against war. Janice will not permit it. Of this you can be assured."

"But, Chen Zumu, what will be the cover if Quant must intervene again, after father is no longer Chen Zufu?"

"Why, surely that great mathematician Chen JieMin must have passed his new technology to his daughter and son-in-law, the new Chen, don't you think?"

RICHARD F. WEYAND

Transition

The retirement party for Chen JieMin and Chen ChaoLi –
and the instatement of Chen JuMing and Chen ChaoPing as
Chen Zufu and Chen Zumu – was held, as always, in the big
upstairs banquet hall of the Chen family restaurant on the
southwest corner of Fifteenth and Market Streets in Arcadia
City.

Since the opening up of the colonies to hyperspace travel
and trade, there had been two of these parties, and both had
become famous for being the utmost in gourmet excellence.
This one would add Earth products to the mix, and promised
to be a splendid feast.

When guests arrived, they found something else new. The
long main table across from the doors was pressed up against
the right hand wall. Ten minutes before the festivities began, all
became clear. A new Earth device, the large-scale projector, had
been married to the Westernesse VR technology.

Another whole virtual room opened up to the right, With
the main table continuing in the virtual part, and with round
guest tables seating ten occupants each, just as in the physical
portion of the room. Provided both for people on other planets
and those too aged to attend personally, the virtual half of the
room started to fill up. People were arriving in VR as the live
guests watched.

Wayne Porter and Denise Bonheur recognized old friends
from the *Wanderlust* mission, including the former planetary
executives of Summer, Quant, and Avalon, Elspeth Reid, Inger
Madsen, and Thomas Stockton. Rob Milbank and his wife, now

302

a hundred and ten years old – though they looked only eighty – were on the virtual side of the house, too.

Also present on the virtual side were Jonathan David Wilson and all the other planetary executives, most with their spouses. Retired planetary executives and their spouses were there as well, including Oliver Nieman, Mildred Plakson, Roger Steadman, Olivia Monet, Lars Swenson, Jasper Tilden, Valerie Laurent, and Jean Dufort.

Jonathan David Wilson was enjoying the spectacle of it all when he was approached by a woman perhaps fifty years old.

"You are unescorted, sir?"

"I never married, madam."

"Ah. And my husband could not be here. We were made for each other."

She smiled, and it was a beautiful smile.

Wilson appreciated the company, rather than be a fifth wheel among so many couples, and he waved her to the chair next to his.

"My name is Jonathan David Wilson. I am the planetary chairman of Earth."

"Pleased to meet you, Mr. Wilson," she said, brushing a stray lock of hair behind her ear. "My name is Janice Decker. I am the former executive of a planet myself."

When eight of the Chen filed in from the left – Chen JieMin, Chen ChaoLi, Chen JuMing, Chen ChaoPing, David Bolton, Chen YongLin, and the new heirs apparent, Melissa Reynolds and Chen JunTao – the three oldest Chen filed in from the right, on the virtual side of the room – Chen MinChao, Jessica Chen-Jasic, and Chen JuPing. All wore silk robes.

Chen JieMin and Chen ChaoLi took the two chairs at the

main table raised up on a small dais. They were hard against the right wall of the physical room, and so were nearly centered along the main table if you included both its physical and virtual parts.

When the Chen were seated, a large number of wait staff delivered hors d'oeuvres and aperitifs and wines to all the tables. The hors d'oeuvres included tiny toast points with Earth peanut butter and Summer honey, one of ChaoLi's favorites.

ChaoLi was looking around the room. She knew personally almost everyone here. When she scanned the virtual side of the room, she caught sight of Wilson. Her eyes widened when she saw his table partner.

"Check out Chairman Wilson's table partner," she whispered to JieMin, sitting to her right. JieMin looked out over the virtual side of the room and chuckled.

"I wonder what alias she's using tonight."

JieMin turned to ChaoPing, seated to his right.

"Do you see Chairman Wilson?"

ChaoPing looked around.

"Yes, I see him."

"The woman with him is Janice."

"Really?"

"Oh, yes. Under an alias of some kind, I suppose."

"Well, I hope so."

"She does have a pretty low sense of humor, ChaoPing. Remember the Lake-Shore Drive."

ChaoPing nodded and turned to JuMing to tell him.

Seeing their gaze in his direction, Wilson remarked to 'Decker'.

"So is it me or you the Chen are looking at, Janice?"

"Could be either, I suppose, Jon. ChaoLi and ChaoPing have

made it a point to be friends with all the planetary chairmen."

"Should we acknowledge them, do you think?"

"Of course. Why not?"

As JieMin, ChaoLi, JuMing, and ChaoPing looked on, Wilson and Quant stood, put their hands together in the Buddhist fashion, and bowed to the main table. JieMin and ChaoLi nodded in return.

A soft gong tone sounded and the conversation died down. JieMin stood, and waved everyone to remain seated. He was miked through his VR, and patched in through the speakers in the room.

"Hello, everyone, and thank you for coming today. We are celebrating the installation of a new Chen, a new couple to lead our family. After twenty years of being honored to have this responsibility, ChaoLi and I are retiring."

JieMin held out his hand to ChaoLi and she stood by his side.

"Our final responsibility in this position is to name our successors to lead the family. Today, Chen JuMing and Chen ChaoPing become the Chen."

JuMing and ChaoPing stood and bowed to JieMin and ChaoLi. JieMin and ChaoLi stepped back and down off the dais, and waved JuMing and ChaoPing to their vacated seats. JuMing and ChaoPing stepped up onto the dais in front of JieMin's and ChaoLi's chairs, and JieMin and ChaoLi moved to JuMing's and ChaoPing's chairs.

"Chen JuMing and Chen ChaoPing, now Chen Zufu and Chen Zumu," JieMin said, and he and ChaoLi bowed to JuMing and ChaoPing, then applauded.

The whole party applauded.

"Thank you, everyone," JuMing said. "And now I am my

mother-in-law's boss."

Everyone laughed and applauded.

"Seriously, though, ChaoPing and I can only hope to serve as well as JieMin and ChaoLi have during the past twenty years."

JuMing and ChaoPing turned to JieMin and ChaoLi and applauded. JieMin and ChaoLi nodded back, and the crowd applauded vigorously.

"And now let's get on with the party, everyone."

The wait staff moved out onto the floor with the first course, an Earth peanut chowder.

When the Chen had finished eating, those physically present dropped into VR. While they sat, eyes closed, at the main table, their avatars joined those of JuPing, MinChao, and Jessica in working the virtual side of the room, where they visited tables and chatted with their virtual guests.

At one point, JieMin and ChaoLi stopped at the table where Wilson and Quant sat.

"Thank you for coming, Jon," ChaoLi said.

"Enjoy your retirement, ChaoLi. JieMin."

"Thank you."

As ChaoLi turned to Quant, she heard Quant's voice, private to her: 'Janice Decker, former planetary chairman of Quant, of course.'

"Thank you for coming, Janice."

"I simply couldn't not attend, ChaoLi."

ChaoLi nodded. Just like Quant. ChaoLi now understood how she had had the chutzpah to take over the world government and drive the colony project. She was fearless.

As the physical guests finished dinner and moved to the

after dinner drinks in anticipation of dessert, the Chen physically present dropped back out of VR, got up from the main table, and worked the physical side of the room. The guests and the Chen on the virtual side of the room started to drop out of the simulation.

David and YongLin, JieMin and ChaoLi, JuMing and ChaoPing, and Melissa Reynolds and Chen JunTao worked the tables, making sure every table was visited by at least two of the couples. By the time they were completed, dessert was over.

The Chen walked to the front of the room, stood in a line facing the room, and bowed to their guests. Then they walked out of the room through the door on the left.

Those who had been here the last time, twenty years ago, knew it would be another thirty minutes before the staff packed up the liquor and cigars, and they continued talking, drinking, and smoking until they did.

New Colonies

When Wilson dropped out of VR from the transfer of power in the Chen-Jasic family from JieMin and ChaoLi to JuMing and ChaoPing, he had a cigar and a cognac in their honor. Mostly to JieMin and ChaoLi, but in honor of both couples really.

While he had the stronger relationship with ChaoLi, Wilson's working relationship with ChaoPing had been honed over the years of working on operations issues and planning. While the new colony project had been proposed by JieMin and ChaoLi, the details had all been worked out with ChaoPing.

So Wilson had no problem in working with the new Chen on relations between the old colonies and Earth. He didn't know JuMing very well, but he supposed that would come in time.

Unlike JieMin and ChaoLi, Wilson had no intention to retire, despite being World Authority Chairman for twenty years. While he was seventy-seven in the records, he was seventy-three in actuality. More to the point, after receiving Tahiti's anti-aging treatments thirteen years ago at the age of sixty, he was physically now only fifty-seven or so. He had a good long run ahead of him yet.

Still, Wilson thought he should celebrate the anniversary with something, he just wasn't sure what.

Reviewing the new colony project progress reports, he had it. They were going to start introducing some of the larger animals on the earliest colony planets started. It would be only a few years before they would begin transferring humans to these earliest new colonies.

Wilson would open up the colony education program. Let

people start working on their colony certification now. They hadn't wanted to open it up too soon, lest people earn their certification and then forget everything by the time they left. No danger of that now.

Yes, that would be a wonderful thing to get started as a twentieth anniversary event. Give the people in the slums some hope of a different future at last.

Of course, only those with some gumption would work on the colony certification program. Some motivation. Some get-up-and-go. Which was fine.

That was the self-selected population Wilson wanted.

Getting a colony started was always the big problem. The robots, for example, could build buildings, but they were dependent on infrastructure, such as a concrete plant and gravel crusher. Sure, you could bring in cement in bags and look for gravel, but there were some big pieces of infrastructure that made getting started a lot easier.

The one thousand foot diameter engine ring of the big transport was falling to the ground, using dive brakes – wings sticking out from the sides – to keep itself flat as it fell. Its payload this time was a complete gravel crusher and concrete plant, coming down on a prepared flat spot on the outskirts of what would be the colony capital city.

It looked like it was going to be a huge crash landing, but, hundreds of feet above the ground, the huge main thrusters ignited, augmented by a dozen large JATO bottles. The massive vehicle slowed to a crawl and settled to the ground as the JATO bottles ran out and the thrusters shut down.

The engine ring unlatched the payload, then the thrusters ignited again. The engine ring sat there until another set of six JATO bottles fired. It lifted off the ground and shot into the sky, accelerating as it went.

Back to the ship. Back to get reloaded with fresh JATO bottles. Back to get another large payload, and run through the cycle again.

Robots were standing by with large dump trucks of limestone and gravel to get the plant started. Other robots were hooking up electrical lines from the Olympia fusion power plant delivered in the prior trip from orbit of the engine ring.

By nightfall, they would be producing concrete for the big buildings of the capital city's downtown area.

The rebar was already on the ground, brought down in containers by large cargo shuttles. The ground had been bulldozed flat, and robots on excavators were already digging the foundations.

Other robots were laying out residential areas, digging holes for footing blocks on which to build houses.

Hundreds of thousands of houses.

JuPing watched this operation in VR and sighed. She wondered if she would make it to see the first human colonists land on a new colony planet in a hundred and seventy-five years.

JuPing was over a hundred and forty Earth years old. Over a hundred even when accounting for the anti-aging treatments. She had survived cancer three times, and been treated for Alzheimer's before it took hold.

But now, even with the best medical care humanity had ever had, JuPing's body was failing in too many ways to keep up. It would not be long before she joined Paul in whatever lay beyond.

It would be a nice closure, though, to see those colonists land. It would close the circle. JuPing's grandfather Matthew

EARTH

Chen-Jasic had come to Arcadia with the original colonists when he was nineteen years old. Fifty years later, nineteen herself, she had assisted him in setting up the charter convention.

And now, a hundred and twenty years later and more, the colonies were united in trade and peace, with each other and with Earth. And Earth, that vast fount of industrial capacity and manpower, was settling new colonies once again.

Humanity had rediscovered the secret of interstellar travel, and would not lose it again.

Wilson reviewed their current status. It was 2422 Earth calendar, one hundred and seventy-seven years since the original colony placements had been made by the colony project.

The earliest of the new colonies now had food sources in place. Basic housing in place. Streets, and sewers, and electricity. A planetary network and interstellar QE network connections. Medical clinics.

The first new colonies were, as they said, 'move-in ready.'

These new colonies would be a far cry from the crudity of the original colonies at landing. That was due to the robots, themselves the product of the old colonies. There was a nice irony there.

Governance had been an issue Wilson had struggled with. He knew where he wanted to get. What he wanted the governance to look like ultimately.

There were so many pitfalls along the way, though. So many ways for one individual, or a group of individuals, to deflect a colony into tyranny or one-man rule.

The irony of his position on this issue was not lost on Wilson, who himself exerted one-man rule on Earth. But the

World Authority structure had its own rules, its own culture, its own history. For all his authority was near absolute, it had to be implemented through a bureaucracy that had its own ideas, its own traditions, its own rules.

The new colonies would have none of that. Wilson had applied his critical historian's eye to the old colonies' experiences, and didn't like what he had seen. There were simply too many close calls.

Like Arcadia, where one extraordinary man had overthrown a nascent tyranny as it started. Or Avalon, where tyranny had been voted in by a gullible population and had only been overturned by outside help and combat operations, including bombing from space. Or Amber, where a single ambitious politician had almost kept them out of space by insisting they do it themselves.

Wilson had cast around for a solution, then stumbled on some work being done by Rolf Dornier, the head of Playa's leading robotics firm. Dornier had speculated on the use of robots in government administration.

The nice thing about robots, he had said, is that when they have a set of rules, they don't break them. This set them apart from humans, who seemed to make a hobby of being rules mechanics, being able to justify almost anything if the motivation was strong enough.

Wilson had been working with Dornier for six years now. The man was brilliant. He was also motivated. It had actually been Dornier, under ChaoPing's leadership, who had overturned the tyranny on Avalon. He had done it up close and personal, on the planet, and had been in the room when the first shots were fired.

There was no one anywhere who knew better what robots could and could not do.

And so they had set out to construct an administrator module for the robots. One with enough compassion and margin to keep people from getting ground in the gears of government, yet one with enough steel in it to insist the rules be followed in the broader context.

This was the opposite of most government operations, which ran roughshod over individuals in an insistence on petty rules, yet would willfully ignore major rules on the big issues.

Between Dornier's robotics experience and Wilson's government experience, they thought they had it now. An administrative module that would allow robots to operate the higher levels of a colony government, while they brought up human bureaucrats into a sustainable system. To develop a culture of proper governance, and then step aside.

So everything was in place. What was he waiting for?

Wilson gave the order.

Half a dozen heavy cargo shuttles landed on street intersections distributed around the residential neighborhoods of Theodore, the capital of the first new colony planet Burke. Wilson had named the city and the planet after Ted Burke, the first man to ever travel interstellar.

Each of the shuttles carried a large passenger container, with three thousand people on each one. Hundreds of robots stood by to assist them in finding their homes in the neighborhood in which their shuttle had landed.

Those homes had heat, and air conditioning, and basic furniture. Each home had an operating kitchen, including a refrigerator, and those refrigerators and cabinets were already stocked with enough food for two weeks.

With sanitation and housing and food in place, getting the new colonies started was going to be a lot easier than the old colonies had been.

JuPing watched the landing of the colonists on Burke in VR. What a triumph. She sent a note to the Earth's planetary chairman, Jonathan David Wilson, whom she knew in a passing way. Just a simple 'Congratulations. Chen JuPing.'

JuPing dropped out of VR, which had once again masked the failings of her body for a time.

She had made it after all. Had seen the first new colony established. She was satisfied.

When JuPing's robot caretaker showed up with her latest round of medications, she held up a restraining hand.

"No, Fil. No more. My time has come."

The robot caretaker, running the hospice module, nodded.

"I understand, ma'am. Is there anything else I may get for you?"

"A cup of tea would be nice, Fil. Walnut, I think."

"Of course, ma'am."

Chen JuPing died that night in her sleep of extreme old age. She was one hundred and forty-six years old.

EARTH

Requiem

The memorial service for Chen JuPing was held in the large atrium of the Uptown Market on the east side of Market Street between Fourteenth Street and Fifteenth Street in Arcadia City. The Uptown Market was closed for the day, the first day it had been closed since the building had opened.

The large space was made even larger by virtual extensions on either side. Both the physical space and its virtual wings were stuffed with folding chairs.

In the front of the space, on a pedestal of jade, stood a statue of Chen JuPing at age nineteen, wearing a lavalava and sandals, as she had appeared during the charter convention of 2295. It was of a yellowish-white metal, and stood perhaps two feet high.

Chen JuPing was a hero on Arcadia. She was the last of the revolutionaries. Matthew Chen-Jasic's assistant during the year he was dictator of Arcadia. The person who had tallied the votes for the election of Adriana Zielinski as chairman of the charter convention. The person who had recognized the abilities of Chen JieMin and started him on the road to first discovering, then conquering, hyperspace. The person who had initiated the hyperspace project.

More than any other person, anywhere, she was responsible for what the planet, and all of human space, had become.

Tens of thousands would have attended had they been able. Attendance at the memorial was by invitation only, however, and the atrium could only physically accommodate four thousand people. More were accommodated in the virtual areas, along with people on other planets, also by invitation only.

Everyone who was anyone on Arcadia, and the dozens of planets beyond, was there. All the senior politicians, past and present. All the planetary executives, past and present. Movers and shakers in business and politics, many of whom had gotten their start under Chen JuPing, or with her patronage.

Eight of the ten living Chen were there, in the front row of the physical section. Chen MinChao and Jessica Chen-Jasic were there in the front of the virtual section.

World Authority Chairman Jonathan David Wilson was also sitting in the front row of the virtual section with Janice 'Decker', with whom he had become unlikely friends.

The memorial service was also broadcast live on the news feeds, on Arcadia and across the interstellar network.

Chen ChaoLi gave the eulogy.

"You all know the story of the founding of the Republic of Arcadia. How Matthew Chen-Jasic overthrew the Kendall regime and ruled Arcadia as dictator through the year 2295.

"You also know the role Chen JuPing played. How she was her grandfather's aide, counting the votes for the election of the charter convention chairman, Adriana Zielinski. The many other ways she aided Matthew Chen-Jasic during that critical year.

"I would like to tell a more personal story. A story you don't know. My personal story, of working for and with Chen JuPing.

"I began working for Chen JuPing seventy-five years ago, when I was ten years old. She was already Chen Zumu.

"I started as her tea girl. You can imagine how scared I was of messing up. Of spilling the hot tea. Of not being prepared. But she was always kind to me. A grandmotherly figure, kind and loving and patient.

"After five years as her tea girl, I moved up to the front desk of the family apartment building and headquarters across the street. It was there I met Chen JieMin. Within days we had fallen madly in love.

"JieMin asked Chen JuPing for my hand, and she in turn talked to our families. JuPing somehow convinced my parents that this boyish young man, not yet fifteen, was a fabulous match for me and they consented.

"JieMin had come to Arcadia City from the village of Chagu to pursue his studies. It was Chen JuPing who recognized his potential and arranged a position for JieMin at the University of Arcadia.

"It was also Chen JuPing who recognized some potential in me, and encouraged my education in finance and business administration. She financed me for two years to complete my college education, and employed me in the family's finance and planning department.

"With JuPing's encouragement and support, JieMin discovered hyperspace and developed the mathematics that even now allows us to travel and trade among humanity's planets.

"With JuPing's encouragement and support, I rose within the family's management structure to eventually manage the hyperspace project, then Jixing Trading.

"Chen JuPing was there, from the very beginning. It was she who set JieMin on the path of hyperspace and supported his work. Reaching the stars once more, trading among the colonies and Earth, establishing more colonies, was always her dream.

"Earth is now establishing those new colonies. I have heard from World Authority Chairman Wilson, who may have received the last message Chen JuPing sent before she died. After the first colonists had arrived on Burke, the first of the new colonies, he received a simple note: 'Congratulations. Chen JuPing.' She passed away that very night.

"Chen JuPing has now passed, but she lived to see it. The culmination of her dream. The establishment of the first of a new wave of human colonies. A new era of human achievement that would have been impossible without her.

"All along the way, Chen JuPing both encouraged us and challenged us. She was both our biggest cheerleader and our toughest critic. She remained our trusted adviser and close confidant throughout the years, even as JieMin and I ourselves became Chen Zufu and Chen Zumu.

"I tried to emulate Chen JuPing during my time as Chen Zumu, to be as encouraging and challenging, as kind and loving and patient, as she had been with me.

"JieMin and I remain madly in love now, sixty-nine years later. We have children who are in their fifties and sixties now, and have seen our son-in-law and eldest daughter in turn become Chen Zufu and Chen Zumu.

"For all this and more, we have Chen JuPing to thank."

ChaoLi's voice was breaking now, and tears ran down her cheeks. She struggled to complete her prepared remarks.

"More than that, though, JuPing was my friend, and I will miss her terribly."

ChaoLi walked back to her seat in the front row and, finally, after having been so strong, broke down weeping in JieMin's arms.

EARTH

Please review this book on Amazon.

Author's Afterword

"EARTH" is the final volume of the COLONY series, at least as I envision the series right now. There are other things that could happen in this universe, of course.

A near-term series about the colonization of the new planets, using the hyperspace technology Chen JieMin and Dieter Wagner developed independently. A far-term series when centrifugal forces drive inhabited worlds apart, and Janice Quant needs to step in to stop interstellar war yet again. Or maybe they run into aliens. A lot of possibilities.

But for now this series is done. The major conflict, the one Janice Quant saw coming in the first book, is resolved. Mankind is, for the moment, on the path of peace and prosperity, and its existence ensured against cataclysm.

The antagonist in "EARTH" is a structural antagonist, the Earth's World Authority Chairman. A structural antagonist in that he is set against the colonies' desires by his own position and his own responsibilities. Bringing him around to fulfilling his duty in a different way is possible, and is the goal of the heroes in this book.

As always, I had no clue where any of this was going as I wrote it. If I can see the next scene in front of me, I write it. If I can't, I think about it. But the story spins out on its own, without pre-planning or outlining or any of that. I just tell the story as it reveals itself to me, and hope for the best.

Once again, my major themes are love, honor, duty, and loyalty, the four great pillars of civilization. How these play out in the characters is what determines the direction of the story.

EARTH

The COLONY series ultimately ends on a hopeful note, as do all my series. If you want to be depressed when you finish reading something, there are other things to read, by other authors. For myself, I like to see a better future.

Such hope is not unfounded. In just the last hundred years, tremendous strides in the quality of life have been made. Better nutrition and scientific medicine have raised life expectancies around the world. Norman Borlaugh's green revolution is well on its way to ending poverty worldwide. Famines when they occur now are caused by government ineptitude and greed – there's plenty of food for everyone, we just have to get it to them.

The rapid increase in technology is part of that betterment. Technology is currently advancing much more rapidly than the things I predict in COLONY. 2245 is more than two hundred and twenty years in the future, where our world has become unrecognizable by 1910 standards in just half that time.

As for what humans will make of that world, some people despair of a harmonious future given the rancorous nature of our current politics. I don't. A health problem a few years back, since resolved, saw me using a cane to steady myself. People went out of their way to hold doors for me, carry packages for me, assist me in any number of ways. As busy as everyone always is, people set aside their own pressing activities for a moment to assist a complete stranger. I was struck by the everyday kindness we can still have for each other.

And so I have hope for such a bright future as the sort I depict here. I hope you enjoyed it.

Richard F. Weyand
Bloomington, IN
January 23, 2022

Notes: The Players And The Colonies

Readers of the books have asked me how I keep track of all the characters and colonies so I can be consistent. Here are my actual notes, the ones I used when writing the COLONY series, filling them in on my other monitor as I wrote the books.

Theodore Burke - industrialist
Martha Stern - Burke's wife
Bernd Decker - entrepreneur
Anna Glenn - Decker's wife

Russ Porter - CEO of Colorado Manufacturing Corporation
Greg Hampton - CMC VP Engg
Kay Brady - CMC Chief Scientist
Valerie Dempsey - project manager
Peter Moore - technical lead
Tim Fender - CMC engineer
Robert Abrams - CMC engineer

Matt Rink - heavy construction supervisor/crew chief
Wayne Monroe - installation supervisor/crew chief
Alan Kramer - troubleshooting/support contact (Quant)
Ned Cotten - orbital construction manager (Quant)

Anthony Lake
Donald Shore

Jacques De Villepin - Chairman, World Authority

EARTH

Robert Bob Jasic - engineer
Susan Dempsey - nurse
        Matthew Matt - 19
        Amy - 17
        Stacy and Tracy - 15

Henry Hank Bolton - painting experience in college
Maureen Griffith
        Joseph
        Emma
        Paul

Bill Thompson
Rita Lamb - cafeteria manager
        Debby
        James
        Jonah

Jack Peterson
Terri Campbell
        Tom
        David
        Ann
        Kimberly

Harold Munson
Betsy Reynolds
        Peggy - 18
        Richard
        Sally
        Carl

Gary Rockham - doctor
Dwayne Hennessey - agronomist
Rachel Conroy - computers
Jessica Murphy - mechanic

Chen LiQiang - Chen Zufu, the head of household. In English, simply, the Chen.
Chen JuHua - wife

Chen GangHai - eldest son
Chen YanJing - wife, dead seven years

Chen PingLi - daughter, 2nd

Chen MingWei - eldest grandson

Chen YanXia - Matt's second wife
Chen JuPing - daughter of YanXia's youngest son.

Mark Kendall - original chairman of the council
Meghana Khatri - hospital administrator, on the council, health department
Stanley Twardowski - World Authority Police Sergeant Major (retired)
James Faletti - hospital dock foreman

Kevin Kendall - third chairman of the council
Anna Drake - director, health department
Larry Donahue - director, food department
Park Jinsook - director, transportation department
Olga Golov - director, infrastructure department

EARTH

Piotr Boykov - animal husbandry manager
Adriana Zielinski - university provost
Indira Bakshi - hospital director

Anders Connor - university president

Chen Zufu - Paul Chen-Jasic
Chen Zumu - Chen JuPing
Chen GangJie - Changu elder
Chen FangYan - JieMin's mother
Chen YongJun - JieMin's father
Chen JuanTao - JieMin's uncle
Chen MinQiang - JieMin's aunt
Chen ChaoLi - apartment building receptionist
Chen LiGang - waiter
Chen FangLi - restaurant receptionist
Chen JongJu - JuPing's tea server
Chen MinChao - Paul Chen-Jasic's second
Jessica Chen-Jasic - MinChao's wife

JieMin (b. 2331)/ChaoLi (b. 2329) children
ChaoPing - 14 in 2362
        married JuMing in March 2365
        child LingTao in November 2367
        child JieGang in August 2370
LeiTao - 11
        married Chen DaGang in March 2367
        child XiPing born in February 2368
        Child GangLi born in January 2370
YanMing and YanJing - 8
        YanMing married Cindy Bolton in fall 2370

RICHARD F. WEYAND

YanJing married Jane Reynolds in fall 2370
JieJun - 4

Robert Milbank - prime minister
Julia Whitcomb - Milbank's wife
Gerard Laporte - Milbank's majority whip in the House
Karl Huenemann - director of the space program
Mikhail Borovsky - project manager
Justin Moore - shuttle pilot
Gavin McKay - shuttle co-pilot
Klaus Boortz - math dept head
Anders Conner - UofA president

Aaron Barkley - head of astronomy department
Ivan Volodin - head of math department

Chen MinYan - JongJu's accounting team leader
Chen JieLing
Chen FangTao

John Gannet - operations head after Huenemann
Chris (f) Bellamy - operations project manager after Borovsky
Wayne Porter - designer/artist
Denise Bonheur - Porter's wife
Frank Takahashi - shuttle construction supervisor
Gerardo Perez - shuttle construction manager

Darius Mikenas - Rob Milbank's head of the forward-looking
policy group
Anders Jansen - first Amber colony governor
Valerie Laurent - current Earthsea Director
Salvatore Romano - Laurent's aide, Earthsea ambassador to

EARTH

Arcadia
Paolo Costa - QR radio tech
Jeff Planck - Earthsea NOC

David Bolton - Chen Zufu after MinChao
Chen YongLin - Chen Zumu after Jessica

Loukas Diakos - ambassador to Earthsea
Peter Dunhill - Diakos's aide
Haruki Tanaka - senior member of Milbanks's party
Sasha Ivanov - ambassador to Amber

Jeong Minho - pilot Hyper-2
Igor Belsky - co-pilot Hyper-2

Jean (m) Dufort - Amber president
Josephine Sellick - head of Dufort's party in the Assembly,
Chair
Vaclav Brabec - Dufort's chief of staff
Michael Grant - Brabec's aide
Bertrand Leland - Sellick's chief of staff
Victor Brouwer - Chair of the Assembly after Sellick

Naomi Thompson - head of personnel, Jixing Trading
Gregory Prentiss - second ambassador to Earthsea
Bill Thompson - Chen JongJu's husband
Gerardo Perez - Jixing Trading factor to Aruba

Stuart Reynolds - caregiver to Paul Chen-Jasic and Chen JuPing

Oliver Nieman - Planetary Chairman of Playa
Reginald Field - Nieman's chief of staff

RICHARD F. WEYAND

Henry Wang - Tahiti President
Tyler Massey - Wang's aide
Jacob Keller - Tahiti prime minister
Frank Janko - Keller's chief of staff

Lars Swenson - Olympia executive committee
Olivia Monet - Olympia executive committee
Roger Steadman - Olympia executive committee
William Monroe - executive committee chief of staff

Mildred Plakson - Aruba prime minister
Sanjay Patel - Plakson's chief of staff
Trevor West - Plakson's security detail
Terry Stanford - Aruba minority party leader

Jasper Tilden - Samoa prime minister
Mark Wegner - Tilden's chief of staff

Jonah Abrams - captain of Star Dancer
Harry Gomez - Amber government head of major projects

Dieter Wagner - Earth physicist who postulates hyperspace

Helmut Dornier - robot magnate
Margaret - Dornier's first wife, deceased
Marianne - Dornier's second wife
Rolf Dornier - Helmut's son
Julia Maier - Rolf's wife
Giscard Dufort - Jean Dufort's son. Doctor.
Marie Legrand - Giscard's wife. Pediatrician.

EARTH

Mira Khatri - one of Wayne Porter's group leaders
Patrick Murphy - one of Wayne Porter's group leaders
Rick Perlman - one of Wayne Porter's group leaders
Gabe Leffler - one of Wayne Porter's group leaders

Fred Laffer - Wanderlust project lead under Chris Bellamy

Wanderlust (2381):
Rob Milbank and Julia Whitcomb
- no children
Justin Moore and Caroline White
- no children
Gavin McKay and Sinead Doyle
- three children
       Ian - ten
       Sean - eight
       Bridget - five
Loukas Diakos and Helen Calder
- no children
ChaoPing and JuMing
- six children
       LingTao (f) - fourteen
       YanWei (m) - eleven
       MinJing (f) - eight
       ChaoMing (m) - five
       GangLi (m) and GangJie (f) - two
Wayne Porter and Denise Bonheur
- five children
       Diana and Steven - fifteen
       Deirdre - twelve
       Philip - eight
       Marie - six

Rolf Dornier and Carla Maier
- four children
> Klaus - fourteen
> Dieter - twelve
> Greta - nine
> Anna - six

Giscard Dufort and Marie Legrand
- two children
> Pierre - five
> Francoise - three

Paolo Costa and Gina Lemos
- four children
> Antonio - fifteen
> Liana - thirteen
> Gisele - ten
> Marco - seven

Elspeth Reid - prime minister of Summer
Colin Gray - Reid's chief of staff
Kamal Singh - aide to Gray.
Rusty Springer - majority leader
Dean Whitmer - commerce minister
Angus McAllen - technology minister

Inger Madsen - Quant Chairman
Kimball Stanley - Madsen's chief of staff
Timothy Dansen - Madsen's aide
Bradley Stoner - chairman wannabe
Marybeth Newland - chairman wannabe
Clark Norton - Janice City Wire
Abe Fortinbras - supervisor of government construction

EARTH

Gerald Hennessey - Jixing factor on Terminus
Carlos Ramirez - prime minister of Terminus

Thomas Stockton - Avalon planetary coordinator
Walter Knowles - Stockton's chief of staff
Bryce Cantrell - head, Avalon Planetary Police
Lon Faraday - Cantwell's chief of staff

Gunter Mannheim - World Authority Council member
Anup Patel - Jonathan David Wilson - Earth Chairman
Antonio Braida - Wilson's chief of staff
Morten Andersen - Wilson's Vice Chairman
Nathan Blaisdell - senior aide to Braida
Max Kalbe - WAP chief

Luisa Bianchi - prime minister of Arcadia

Conrad Berger - Earth astronomer
Lonny Winton - Earth astronomer
Cal Vetter - Earth asteroid scientist
Fletcher Moran - Earth asteroid scientist

Chet Voinovich - Jixing Trading design group engineer

Dennis Stevens - Vice Admiral, World Authority space navy
Atsuki Mori - Rear Admiral, World Authority space navy

Chen JunTao - Chen Zufu after Chen JuMing
Melissa Reynolds - Chen Zumu after Chen ChaoPing

#	Name	Quant Specialty	Extra Specialty
1	Earthsea	QE radios	cheese, banking
1	Amber	medical nanites	coffee
0	Arcadia	(none)	tea, spices, silk
2b	Bali	endocrinology	wine
3a	Samoa	material science	architecture
3a	Hawaii	comm & crypto	citrus, pulpy fruit
2a	Tahiti	anti-aging	apples
3b	New Earth	plant genetics	rhubarb, cranberries
2b	Terminus	forestry mgmt	gardening, flowers
3b	Westernesse	direct neural VR	writers, musicians
3a	Fiji	immunology	beer
3a	Nirvana	anti-cancer	int. design, fashion
2a	Playa	cybernetics	mushrooms
4a	Endor	water mgmt	boat buiding
4b	Dorado	transportation	car racing
4a	Tonga	animal genetics	exotic animals
4a	Spring	human genetics	cigars
2a	Aruba	(none)	chocolate
4b	Numenor	(none)	books, films, art
4a	Atlantis	fab technologies	firearms & knives
2a	Olympia	fusion	distilled spirits
5a	Quant	geology	beef
5a	Summer	civil engineering	honey
5b	Avalon	human enhancement	heritage vegetables

EARTH

Executive	Legistative	Capital
Director Valerie Laurent	Council	Bergheim
President Jean Dufort	Assembly	Amber
Prime Minister Rob Milbank	House, Chamber	Arcadia City
President Jasper Tilden	Parliament	Apia
President Henry Wang Prime Minister Jacob Keller	Parliament	Papeete
Prime Minister Carlos Ramirez		Terminus City
Planetary Chmn Oliver Nieman	Planetary Council	Cabana
Prime Minister Mildred Plakson	Parliament	Barcelona
Lars Swenson Olivia Monet Roger Steadman	Executive Council	Olympus
Chairman Inger Madsen	Council	Janice
Prime Minster Elspeth Reid	Congress	Verano
Coordinator Thomas Whitlock		Camelot

Made in the USA
Coppell, TX
28 April 2022

77181782R00187